Edgar Wallace was born illegitimately in 1875 in Greenwich and adopted by George Freeman, a porter at Billingsgate fish market. At eleven, Wallace sold newspapers at Ludgate Circus and on leaving school took a job with a printer. He enlisted in the Royal West Kent Regiment, later transferring to the Medical Staff Corps and was sent to South Africa. In 1898 he published a collection of poems called *The Mission that Failed*, left the army and became a correspondent for Reuters.

Wallace became the South African war correspondent for *The Daily Mail*. His articles were later published as *Unofficial Dispatches* and his outspokenness infuriated Kitchener, who banned him as a war correspondent until the First World War. He edited the *Rand Daily Mail*, but gambled disastrously on the South African Stock Market, returning to England to report on crimes and hanging trials. He became editor of *The Evening News*, then in 1905 founded the Tallis Press, publishing *Smith*, a collection of soldier stories, and *Four Just Men*. At various times he worked on *The Standard, The Star, The Week-End Racing Supplement* and *The Story Journal*.

In 1917 he became a Special Constable at Lincoln's Inn and also a special interrogator for the War Office. His first marriage to Ivy Caldecott, daughter of a missionary, had ended in divorce and he married his much younger secretary, Violet King.

The Daily Mail sent Wallace to investigate atrocities in the Belgian Congo, a trip that provided material for his *Sanders of the River* books. In 1923 he became Chairman of the Press Club and in 1931 stood as a Liberal candidate at Blackpool. On being offered a scriptwriting contract at RKO, Wallace went to Hollywood. He died in 1932, on his way to work on the screenplay for *King Kong*.

BY THE SAME AUTHOR
ALL PUBLISHED BY HOUSE OF STRATUS

THE BLACK ABBOT
BONES IN LONDON
BONES OF THE RIVER
THE CLUE OF THE TWISTED CANDLE
THE DAFFODIL MYSTERY
THE FRIGHTENED LADY
THE JOKER
THE LONE HOUSE MYSTERY
SANDERS
THE SQUARE EMERALD
THE THREE JUST MEN
THE THREE OAK MYSTERY

Big Foot

HOUSE OF
STRATUS

This edition published in 2001 by House of Stratus, an imprint of Stratus Holdings plc, 24c Old Burlington Street, London, W1X 1RL, UK.

www.houseofstratus.com

Typeset, printed and bound by House of Stratus.

A catalogue record for this book is available from the British Library.

ISBN 1-84232-661-9

CONTENTS

1	SOOPER	1
2	THE UNEXPECTED HANNAH	6
3	A LAWYER LOSES A CASE	11
4	DINNER AT BARLEY STACK	19
5	THE SNIPER	26
6	THE STORY OF THE $100 BILLS	37
7	A JOURNEY SOUTHWARD	45
8	THE KITCHEN	52
9	THE VISITOR	61
10	ELFA'S STORY	67
11	THE SEALED ENVELOPE	74
12	LATTIMER'S UNCLE	80
13	SOOPER INQUIRES	88
14	THEORIES AND DEDUCTIONS	94
15	ELFA LEIGH'S HOME	101
16	A LITTLE DINNER	108
17	SOOPER'S SENSATION	116
18	THE PASTRY	135
19	SMOKE FROM HILL BROW	141
20	THE WARNING	148
21	TEA IN THE PARK	153
22	CHLOROFORM	161
23	THE WARRANT	167
24	AMBUSHED	171
25	THE NOOSE	185
26	MR WELLS	192
27	THE FAREWELL FEAST	197

SOOPER

It was a coincidence that Sooper made a call at Barley Stack this bright spring morning, for at that moment he knew nothing of the attempt to burgle Mr Stephen Elson's house, was ignorant that such a person as Sullivan the tramp existed, or that his crazy companion in crime was wandering loose around the fair countryside, singing foolish little songs about love – and those in a foreign and unintelligible language.

But Barley Stack had for Sooper the fascination which the flame has for the moth, or, a better illustration, the battle for the veteran war-horse. Though he must have known that at this hour Mr Cardew had long since departed to the City, for Gordon Cardew, though retired from his profession, had the nine o'clock habit ineradicably implanted in his system.

Nevertheless Sooper called. Failing a more poignant thrill of crossing swords with this man Cardew, there was generally a certain amount of satisfaction to be had from an encounter with Hannah Shaw. Mr Cardew's attitude of mind towards him was one of resentment, for Sooper had hurt him. Hannah, on the other hand, was incapable of feeling or expressing the fine nuances of personal regard, and hated this ancient superintendent of police with a loathing which she never attempted to conceal.

Hannah stood squarely in the porch of Barley Stack, and the malignant light in her brown eyes might have spoken for her. She was a woman below middle height and rather plump, and her black alpaca dress did not enhance her comeliness. Comely she was, in a way. Her

1

heavy face was unlined, the thick black fringe over her forehead untinged with grey, though she was well past forty. If her features were big they were regular, and in spite of her proportions it would have been unfair to describe her as dumpy.

"Nice weather we're havin'," murmured Sooper. He leant languidly against his dilapidated motor-bicycle, his eyes half-closed as though, in the warmth of the morning and the beauty of the surroundings, he was predisposed to take his siesta. "And the garden's looking lovely too. Never seen so many daffydils as you've got in the park, and carnations too! Got a good gardener, I'll bet. Mr Cardew in?"

"No, he isn't!"

"Out followin' the trail of the Boscombe Bank hold-up, I'll bet!" said Sooper, shaking his head in simulated admiration. "Soon as I saw that hold-up in the papers, I said to my sergeant, 'It wants a man like Mister Cardew to trail that gang – ord'nary police couldn't do it. They'd never find a clue – they'd be baffled from the start.'"

"Mr Cardew has gone to his office, as you very well know, Minter," she snapped, her eyes blazing. "He has something better to do than waste his time on police work. We pay rates and taxes for the police, and a precious lot of use they are! An incompetent, ignorant lot of men who haven't even an education!"

"Can't have everything," said Sooper sadly. "Stands to reason, Mrs Shaw – "

"Miss Shaw!" Hannah almost shouted the correction.

"Always think of you that way," said Sooper apologetically. "I was only sayin' to my sergeant the other day, 'Why that young lady doesn't get married beats me: she's young – '"

"I've no time to waste on you, Minter – "

"Mister Minter," suggested Sooper gently.

"If you've any message for Mr Cardew I'll take it – otherwise, I've a lot of work to do and I can't waste my time with you."

"Any burglaries?" asked Sooper as she half-turned to go.

"No, there aren't any burglaries," she answered shortly. "And if there were, we shouldn't send for you."

"I'll bet you wouldn't," said Sooper fervently. "I'll bet Mr Cardew would just take the size of the burglar's footprint an' look him up in his book on anthro – whatever the word is, an' the poor nut would be pinched before night."

Miss Hannah Shaw turned round on him in a fury.

"If you think you're being clever, let me tell you that there are people in London who can make you look small, Minter. If Mr Cardew went to the Secretary of State and told him half of the things you do and say, he'd have your coat off your back before the end of the week!"

Sooper examined his sleeve critically.

"What's the matter with it?" he asked, as she slammed the door viciously in his face.

Sooper did not smile, nor was he annoyed. Instead he filled his foul pipe with great deliberation, gazed admiringly at the glorious colouring of the spring flowers that filled every bed in sight, and, stopping only long enough to fix a stolen pimpernel in the lapel of his worn jacket, went noisily down the drive to the main road.

Half an hour later:

"When a man's got to my age 'n' exalted position," said Sooper, blinking rapidly at the sober-faced young officer who sat on the other side of the table, "he's entitled to be temp'ramental. I'm temp'ramental today. There's a touch of spring in the air, an' I'll bet I didn't hear a cuckoo last Sunday? And when there's cuckoos around and the bluebells are growing in the woods, I'm temp'ramental. Besides, I've just had a talk with the Belle of Barley Stack, and my head's full of sentimental ideas. You ask me to give a good look at this here tramp an' I reply that I'd sooner go chasing primroses on the river's brink."

Sooper was tall and angular and very untidy. His suit had been an old one in pre-war days, and now, cleaned and turned, was a mockery of clothes. His lank, brown face and awkward grey eyebrows gave him a distinction which his garb did much to dissipate. Hannah Shaw's contempt for his wardrobe was one of his dearest joys.

3

There were many superintendents of police, but when you spoke in Metropolitan Police circles of Sooper, you meant Superintendent Patrick J Minter and nobody else.

"Go you and interview the vagrant, my good sergeant." He waved his big hand with a lordly gesture. "The serious business of criminal detection belongs to my past – it was too simple! Got me going senile – that's why I took this job, where I can live in the country an' keep chickens an' rabbits an' study nature in all its majesty an' splendour."

"I" division of the Metropolitan Police covers that part of rural London which comes up against the Sussex border. It is notoriously a sleepy division, a backwater into which men drift gratefully from the turbulent waters of Limehouse and Greenwich and Notting Dale. "I" division dealt mainly with such surprising crimes as vagrancy, poaching and rick-firing. The men of "I" division, to the envy of their city fellows, impound straying horses and cattle and take active steps to deal with foot-and-mouth disease. They are known as "the yokels", "the hayseeders" and "the lost legion". But the men cultivate gardens (many raising their own garden truck), and can afford to smile tolerantly when jealous comrades make sneering references to their bucolic pursuits.

Sooper was transferred from Scotland Yard to this pleasant haven, not as a mark of his superiors' appreciation of his excellent services – he was one of the Big Five that smashed the Russian gang in Whitechapel – but (the truth had best be told) because he was a thorn in the side of certain police officials. Sooper was a source of constant irritation to headquarters. He respected nobody, from the Chief Commissioner downwards; he was polite to nobody; he agreed with nobody. He wrangled, he argued, and occasionally he defied. Most irritating of his qualities was the fact that he was generally right. And when he was proved right and his chiefs were wrong, he mentioned the fact some twenty or thirty times in the course of a working day.

"What's more," he went on, "talking to this low tramp's goin' to interrupt my studies. I'm takin' an intensive course of criminology. Never heard of Lombroso, I'll bet? Ah! Then you don't know anything about criminals' brains! Ord'nary brains weigh... I've forgotten what, but criminals' brains are lighter. Go bring me this man's brain and I'll tell you whether he was trying to break into Barley Stack. And prehensile feet: d'ye know that five per cent of crim'nals can pick up things with their toes? An' d'you know that oxycyphalic heads are all the fashion in crim'nal circles? You've missed sump'n'. Go take a tape measure and get that hobo's statistics and watch out for his assymetrical face! It was always simple, catchin' 'em. It's childish easy now!"

Sergeant Lattimer was too wise a man to interrupt his superior until his garrulity showed signs of running dry. This seemed a favourite moment to interject a remark.

"But, Super, this isn't an ordinary burglary. According to Sullivan – that is the tramp's name – "

"Tramps haven't got any names," said Sooper wearily. "You started wrong. They're 'Mike' and 'Weary' and 'Box Car Billy', but they haven't any family names."

"According to Sullivan, the other tramp who was with him would not allow him to get into Mr Elson's house and take money. He wanted something else – "

"Deeds of the family estate, maybe," interrupted Sooper thoughtfully. "Or the birth certificat' of the rightful heir? Or maybe Mr Elson, bein' a low-down American, stole the sacred ruby from the right eye of the great god Hokum, an' s'nister Injuns have followed him waitin' their opportunity? This is a case for Cardew – maybe you can tackle it. Go to it, Sergeant. You'll get your pitcher in the papers: and you're a good-looker too. P'raps you'll marry the girl that's supposed to be a housemaid but turns out to be the daughter of the duke, having been pinched by gipsies in her youth. Go on!"

THE UNEXPECTED HANNAH

The young officer listened with admirable patience.

"I took Sullivan because he was sleeping in the neighbourhood last night – and he has now practically admitted that he 'felt' the house for an entry."

"Go get his ear marks," murmured Sooper, taking up his pen. "Ever notice how crim'nals an' paranoiacs have windscreen ears? It's in the book. And the book can't lie. Detectivizin' is not what it was, Sergeant. We want more physiognomists an' more chemists. My idea of a real detective is a feller who sits in a high-class fam'ly mansion with a microscope an' a blood stain an' a bit of London mud, an' putting the three together can tell you that the jewels were pinched by a left-handed man who drove a Patchard coupé ('21 model) painted green. Ever meet a man called Ferraby?"

"Mr Ferraby from the Public Prosecutor's office?" asked the sergeant, momentarily interested. "Yes, sir: I saw him the day he called here."

Sooper nodded; his jaws closed like a rat-trap and he showed two rows of teeth. He was smiling.

"*He's* not a detective," he said emphatically; "he only understands fac's. If that feller was called in to unravel the myst'ry of the Rajah of Bong's lost wrist-watch an' he found that the Grand Vizzer or Visher or whatever they call him, had pawned a wrist-watch at Veltheim's Day an' Night Loan Office, he'd go and pinch the Grand – whatever he is. A real detective wouldn't be that foolish. He'd just deduce at once that the clock was torn off in a struggle with the young and beautiful st'nographer who's hidden behind a secret panel gagged 'n' bound an' ready to be freighted to the loathsome Injun palace built of lapsus laz – whatever it is. Now, old man Cardew *is* a detective! There's a man you might model yourself on, Sergeant."

Sooper pointed the end of his pen impressively at his subordinate.

"That man's studied crime from all angles; he's got the psycho – whatever the word may be – psychology, is it? Well, he's got that. And he's strong for ears an' prognathic jaws and as-sym-metrical faces an' the weight of brains an' all that. Got a library up at Barley Stack full of stuff about crime."

When Sooper started on the subject of that excellent amateur, Mr Gordon Cardew, he was a difficult man to turn, and the sergeant sighed lightly and respectfully.

"The point is, sir, would you care to see this man Sullivan? He has practically confessed that he went to Hill Brow to commit a burglary."

Sooper stared menacingly, and then, to Lattimer's surprise, nodded.

"I'll see this Sullivan – shoot him in."

The sergeant rose with alacrity and disappeared into the small charge-room. He returned in a few minutes accompanied by a very big, a very unprepossessing, and an altogether embarrassed tramp.

"This is Sullivan, sir," reported the officer, and Sooper put down his pen, wrenched off his pince-nez and glared up at the prisoner.

"What's this stuff you've been giving us about the hobo who wouldn't let you go into Hill Brow?" he asked unexpectedly. "And if you're lyin', tramp, lie plausibly!"

"It's true, Sooper," said the tramp huskily. "If I die this minute, this crazy fellow nearly killed me when I tried to open the window. And we had it all fixed – he told me about the place an' where this American kept his 'stuff'. If I die this very second – "

"You won't: hobos never die," snapped Sooper. "Sullivan? Got you! You went down for three at the London Sessions for robbery – Luke Mark Sullivan, I remember your holy names!"

Mr Luke Mark Sullivan shuffled uneasily, but before he could protest himself an injured and innocent convict, Sooper went on:

"What do you know about this crazy tramp?"

Sullivan knew very little. He had met the man in Devonshire, and had heard something about him from other knights of the road.

"He's plumb nutty, Sooper: all the fellers say so. Goes about the country singing to himself. Doesn't run with any gang, and talks queer – swell stuff and foreign languages."

Sooper leaned back in his chair.

"You *couldn't* invent that. You haven't the weight of brain. Where's his pitch?"

"Everywhere, but I got an idea he's got a real pitch near the sea. He used to ask me – I've been on the road with him for a week – if I liked ships. He said he looked at 'em for days passin' on the sea, and got to wonderin' what kind of ships couldn't sink. He's crazy! An' after we'd fixed to go into this house, what do you think he said? He turned on me like a dog and said, 'Away!' – just like that, Sooper – 'Away! Your hands are not clean enough to be the…' well, sump'n about 'Justice'…he's mad!"

The superintendent stared at the uncomfortable man for a long time without speaking.

"You lie in your throat, Sullivan," he said at last. "You couldn't tell the truth: you've got odd eyes! Put him in the cooler, Sergeant – we'll get him hung!"

Mr Sullivan was back in his cell, and the sergeant was halfway through his lunch, before Sooper moved from his chair. He sat glowering at the office inkpot, motionless, his dry pen still in his hand. At last he moved with a grimace, as though the effort pained him, kicked off the slippers he invariably wore in office hours and pulled on his worn boots with a grunt.

Lattimer had reached the apple pie stage of his feast when the old man shuffled into the officers' mess-room.

"Know anything about this American feller Elson?" asked Sooper. "Don't stand up, man – eat your pie."

"No, sir – except that he's a bit of a rough diamond. They say he's very rich."

"That's my deduction too," said Sooper. "When a man lives in a big house an' has three cars an' twenty servants I put two an' two together and deduce that he's well off. I'm goin' up to see him."

Sooper had a motor-cycle that was frankly disreputable. It bore the same relationship to an ordinary motor-cycle that a slum bears to Buckingham Palace. Every spring, Sooper took his machine to pieces, and, under the dazed eye of Sergeant Lattimer, put it together again in such a manner as to give it an entirely different appearance. This illusion may have had its cause in his passion for changing the colour of the weird contrivance. One year it was a vivid green, another year it was a flaming scarlet. Once he painted it white and picked out the spokes in sky-blue. Sooper was so constituted that he could not pass a hardware shop that displayed bicycle enamel without falling. In the little hut behind his cottage were shelves covered with tiny paint pots, and the year when, yielding to the influence of the war, he employed a dozen sample cans in camouflaging his machine, is one remembered by the whole of the Metropolitan Police force.

Yet it was a good motor-bicycle. By some miracle its two cylinders were capable of developing tremendous energies. Its once silvery handlebar had long since been painted over; its saddle seat was held in position by string, and its tyres were so patched that even the least observant village child could tell, from an examination of the dustprints, not only that Sooper had passed, but in what direction he was moving; but it "went".

He chug-chugged his way up Dewlap Hill, skirted the high red wall of Hill Brow, and, dismounting, pushed open the gate and passed between the elms that bordered Mr Elson's drive. Leaning his bicycle against a tree, he walked slowly towards the big house, up the broad steps, and halted in the open doorway.

The hall was empty, but he heard voices, a woman's and a man's. The sound came from a room that opened from the hall. The door was ajar, he saw four plump fingers at the edge as though somebody had paused in the act of pulling it open. Sooper looked round for a bell-push and then saw that it was in the centre of the front door. He was stepping into the hall to reach the push when…

"Marriage or nothing, Steve! I've been kept fooling around too long. Promises, promises, promises!… I'm sick of 'em!… Money? What's the use of money to me?… I'm as rich as you…"

At that moment the door opened and the speaker came into view, and though her back was towards him, Sooper recognized her. It was Hannah Shaw, the ungenial housekeeper of Barley Stack.

For a second he stood looking at the figure, and then noiselessly stepped back to the angle of the wall, dropped lightly over the balustrade of the steps and melted out of sight. Hannah did not even see the shadow of him as he passed. To make doubly sure that his presence should escape notice, Sooper wheeled his bicycle a mile before he mounted.

A LAWYER LOSES A CASE

The Temple, on a day in early summer, with a blue sky overhead, is a very pleasant and drowsily restful place. For there are rooks in Temple Gardens, and the green leaves of the trees that wave their branches over the worn flagstones are translucent in the sunlight, and the fountain splashes musically. The grim fronts of ancient buildings, so menacing in the thin fogs of February, take on a bland beauty of their own, so that hurrying lawyers in their grey wigs and long black gowns hesitate on the threshold of their own offices in momentary doubt as to whether or not they have, in a moment of aberration, wandered into some strange and more charming locality than that to which use has accustomed them.

Jim Ferraby, strolling at leisure from Fleet Street to his rooms in King's Bench Walk, paused by the fountain to rescue a small girl's hat from destruction, and passed on, whistling softly, his hands deep in his pockets, his brow unruffled, a good-looking and contented young man on the indiscreet side of thirty.

He reached the walk, paused again on the stone steps of his chambers, and surveyed, with evidence of approval, the silvery stretch of river visible from this point. Then he slowly mounted the gloomy stairs, and, stopping before a heavy black door, pulled a massive key from his pocket and inserted it in the huge lock.

He was twisting the key when he heard the door open on the opposite side of the landing, and, looking round, flashed a smile at the girl who stood in the open doorway.

" 'Morning, Miss Leigh," he said cheerfully. The girl nodded.

11

"Good morning, Mr Ferraby."

Her voice was very soft and curiously sweet. It was Elfa Leigh's voice which had first attracted him to old Cardew's secretary. He agreed with himself that this too was the principal attraction; and the fact that she had the kind of face that artists draw but men seldom see, and a straight figure which was lovely in spite of its slimness; that she had grey eyes set wide apart and almost Oriental in the slant and depth of them had nothing to do with his interest in the sole member of Mr Gordon Cardew's office staff.

Their acquaintance, extending over a year, had begun on that dusty landing, and had progressed with a certain primness. There was really no reason why old Mr Cardew (he was really fifty-eight, but fifty-eight is very old to the twenties) should have an office in King's Bench Walk, for he was a non-practising member of his profession. Once upon a time the firm of Cardew and Cardew had enjoyed a clientele unequalled in quality and wealth in the whole of London. They had been agents for great estates, trustees of vast properties, legal representatives of powerful corporations, but during the war the last of the Cardews had grown weary of his responsibilities and had transferred his clients to a younger and, as he said, more robust firm of solicitors. He might have followed the traditions of the profession and taken a partner, preserving the name of a house that had existed for one hundred and fifty years. He preferred to wash his hands of his practice, and the large gloomy office on King's Bench Walk was now exclusively devoted to the conduct of his own prosperous affairs – for Mr Gordon Cardew was a man of some substance.

"I suppose you won your case and the poor man has gone to prison?"

They stood now in opposite doorways, and their voices echoed across the hollow hallway.

"I lost my case," said Jim calmly, "and the 'poor man' is now, in all probability, drinking beer and sneering at the law he cheated."

She stared at him.

"Oh… I'm sorry!… I mean, I'm not sorry that the man is free, but that you lost. Mr Cardew said he was certain to be convicted. Did the other side bring fresh evidence? What a shame!"

She talked cold-bloodedly of "the other side", as lawyer's clerk to lawyer.

"The other side brought fresh evidence," said Jim deliberately. "Sullivan was acquitted because I prosecuted him. The truth is, Miss Leigh, I have a criminal mind, and all the time I was talking against him, I was thinking for him. It is the first case in which I have ever appeared for the State, and it will be the last. The judge said in his summing up that my speech for the prosecution was the only reasonable defence that the prisoner had made. Sullivan should have gone to jail for a year, instead of which he is going about the country stealing ducks."

"Ducks?… I thought it was a case of attempted burglary?" She was puzzled.

"I quoted an ancient *non sequitur*. I'm a ruined man, Miss Leigh – I have the brain of a master criminal combined with the high moral outlook of a Welsh revivalist. From now on I'm just a nameless official at the office of the Public Prosecutor."

She laughed softly at his solemn declaration, and at that moment came a firm step on the stair and, looking down, Jim saw the shining top of Mr Cardew's immaculate hat.

A grave, aesthetic face, eyes that gleamed good-humouredly from under shaggy brows, a punctilious neatness of attire, and a pedantic exactness of speech – that was Mr Gordon Cardew.

His furled umbrella was under his arm, his hands were clasped behind him as he came up the stairs, and momentarily his face was clouded. Looking up, he saw the young man.

"Hullo, Ferraby, your man got off, they tell me?"

"Bad news travels fast," growled Jim. "Yes, sir: my chief is furious!"

"And so he should be," said Cardew, with the ghost of a smile in his fine eyes. "I met Jebbings, the Treasury counsel. He said…well, never mind what he said. It isn't my business to make bad feeling

13

between members of the Bar. Good morning, Miss Leigh. Is there any urgent business? No? Come in, Ferraby."

Jim followed the lawyer into his cosily furnished room. Mr Cardew closed the door behind him, opened a cigar-box and pushed it towards the young lawyer.

"You're unfitted for the job of prosecuting the guilty," he said with a quizzical smile. "Socially and financially, there is no reason why you should follow a profession at all. So I don't think, if I were you, that I should worry very much about what happened at the Central Criminal Court today. I am naturally interested in the case, because Mr Stephen Elson is a neighbour of mine – a somewhat overbearing American gentleman, a little lacking in polish but a good fellow, they tell me. He will be annoyed."

Jim shook his head helplessly.

"I've a kink somewhere," he said, in despair. "My sympathies are on the side of law and order, and in the office I gloat over every hanging I've brought about. In court my intellect was working double shifts to discover excuses for this brute – excuses that I myself would have advanced if I was in his position."

Mr Cardew smiled reprovingly.

"When a prosecuting lawyer gets up and casts doubt upon the infallibility of the fingerprint system – "

"Did I?" asked Jim, flushing guiltily. "Lord! I seem to have made a hash of it!"

"I think you have," was the dry response. "You don't drink port so early in the morning?" And, as Jim declined, Cardew opened a cupboard, took out a black and dusty bottle, carefully wiped a glass and filled it with ruby-coloured liquid.

"I have yet another interest in Sullivan," he said. "As you probably know, I am – er – something of a student of anthropology. In fact, I rather flatter myself that there is a good detective wasted in me. And really, when one sees the type of man who occupies important positions in the police force, one wishes that the system was reorganized so that persons of ripe experience and – er – erudition could find an opportunity for exercising their talents. We have a man in charge of my division who is simply..."

Words failed him. He could only shrug helplessly, and Jim, who knew Superintendent Minter, concealed his amusement. It was common knowledge that Sooper had a most profound contempt for all amateurs and theorists: it was the attitude of the good workman towards the indifferent artist. And on one occasion he had been offensive (Mr Cardew described it as "boorish") over a matter of anthropology.

"Man, ye're childish!" snarled Sooper, when Mr Cardew had mildly suggested that a cracked voice and a bright, hard eye were inseparable from a certain type of criminal.

Mr Cardew often said that such an unpardonable act of rudeness was difficult to forgive.

Jim was wondering what was the reason for this unexpected invitation into Cardew's private office – it was his first visit, though he had known the lawyer off and on for five years – and that the invitation had a special meaning was obvious from the older man's behaviour. He was obviously worried and nervous, pacing the room with irresolute steps, and stopping now and again to adjust some paper on his desk or to move a chair to a different position.

"All the way up to town you have been in my mind," he said suddenly, "and I have been wondering whether or not I should consult you. You know my housekeeper, Hannah Shaw?"

Jim remembered very well the sulky-faced woman, who spoke in monosyllables, and who, ever since he had spoken well of Sooper, had never made any attempt to hide her dislike for him.

Mr Cardew was eyeing him keenly.

"You don't like her," he stated, rather than asked. "She was rather annoying to you the last time you came, eh? My chauffeur, who is something of a gossip, told me that she had snapped at you. Undoubtedly she is snappy and dour, and a most disagreeable person. But she suits me in many ways, and is, moreover, a legacy from my dear wife – she took her out of an orphan asylum when she was a child, and Hannah has been practically brought up in my home. With all respect

I might liken her to one of those Aberdeen terriers that snaps at everybody except his master."

He put his hand in his pocket, took out a leather case, opened it and showed some papers, and finally spread one on the table.

"I am taking you into my confidence," he said, and looked up again at the door to see if it was closed. "Read this."

It was a sheet of common paper. It bore no address or date of any kind. There were three hand-printed lines of writing, which ran:

I HAVE WARNED YOU TWICE. THIS IS THE LAST
TIME. YOU HAVE DRIVEN ME TO DESPERATION.

The note was signed "Big Foot".

"Big Foot? Who is Big Foot?" asked Jim, as he read the note again. "Your housekeeper has been threatened – she showed you this?"

Mr Cardew shook his head.

"No, it came into my possession in a curious way. On the first of every month Hannah brings me the household bills, places them on the desk in my study, and I write out cheques for the tradesmen. She has a habit of carrying bills around in her pocket and her bag, and scrambling them together at the last moment – she is the reverse of methodical. This letter was in the folds of a grocer's bill: she must have taken it hurriedly from her bag without realizing that she was giving me a private letter."

"Have you spoken to her?"

Mr Cardew frowned and shook his head.

"No," he hesitated, "I haven't. In a clumsy way I have hinted to her that, if she is ever in any kind of trouble, she must come to me, but Hannah just snarled at me – there is no other word, she snarled! It was – well, not to put too fine a point upon it, impertinent." He sighed heavily. "I hate new faces," he said, "and I should be very sorry to lose Hannah. If she had adopted another attitude, I should, of course, have told her of my discovery. And now, to be perfectly honest, I am scared to tell her that one of her letters is in my possession. We have had one

16

serious disagreement over a stupid joke of hers. The next will end our association. What do you make of the letter?"

"From a blackmailer of some kind," suggested Jim. "The letter is written with the left hand with the object of disguising the writing. I think you ought to ask her for an explanation."

"Ask Hannah?" repeated Mr Cardew in tones of alarm. "Great heavens, I dare not! No, the only thing I can do is to keep my eyes open, and at the first opportunity, when I get her in an amiable mood – and she is amiable at least twice a year – broach the subject – "

"Why not consult the police?" asked Jim.

Mr Cardew stiffened.

"Minter?" he suggested icily. "That uncouth, unimaginative policeman? Really, my dear fellow. No, if there is any mystery in the matter, I think – I rather *think* – that I am capable of probing the thing to its depths. And there is a mystery outside of, or consequent upon, this letter."

He looked at the door, behind which his innocent secretary was working, and lowered his voice.

"As you know, I have a little bungalow on the foreshore of Pawsey Bay. It used to be an old coastguard station, and I bought it for a song during the war, and have spent some very pleasant hours there. I go there very seldom nowadays, and usually I give my servants the use of the place. In fact, my secretary, Miss Leigh, had it for a week last year, and went down with some girl friends. Most unexpectedly, Hannah came to me this morning and asked if she could have the bungalow from Saturday to Monday. She has not been there in years; she hates the place, and told me as much only a week ago. Now I'm wondering whether that sudden trip to the coast has not something to do with the letter."

"Have her watched," suggested Jim, "by private detectives," he made haste to amend his suggestion.

"I have considered that," replied Cardew thoughtfully, "but I am loath to spy on her. Remember she has been in my service for nearly twenty years. Of course, I've given her permission, though I am a little worried in view of these facts. Usually Hannah spends her spare time driving about the country in an old Ford – my chauffeur taught her to drive some years ago – so that it isn't a change of air she wants. I pay her well; she could afford to stay at a good hotel, and there is no reason whatever why she should go to Pawsey, unless, of course, it is to meet this mysterious Big Foot. Do you know, I sometimes think that she is a little…" he tapped his forehead.

Jim was still wondering why he had been consulted: he now learnt.

"I am giving a little dinner-party on Friday at Barley Stack, and I want you to come down and – er – use your eyes. Two heads are better than one. You may see something which escaped me."

Jim's mind was busy hunting up excuses when Cardew went on: "You won't mind meeting Miss Leigh socially? My secretary I mean – she is coming down to index a new library I bought the other day at Sotheby's. A complete set of Mantagazza's works…"

"I'll be delighted," said Mr James Ferraby with great heartiness.

DINNER AT BARLEY STACK

"You know Mr Elson?"

Jim Ferraby knew Mr Stephen Elson well enough to be satisfied in his mind that he did not wish to know him better. He had been the principal (if reluctant) witness in the case of the State against Luke Mark Sullivan, and Elson had taken that light-fingered tramp's acquittal as a personal affront.

Jim was prejudiced against Elson for many reasons, not least of which was that gentleman's insolent admiration of Elfa Leigh. It was insolent from Jim's point of view, and, he hoped, from Elfa's. Not that she meant anything in his life. She was merely the girl on the other side of the landing; she had a beautiful soft voice and grey eyes set wide apart, and the colouring that is only seen in the advertisements of complexion soaps. But Jim Ferraby took a detached interest in her (as he told himself). She was just a very charming, very cultured, and, to tell the truth, rather beautiful young woman, and he admired her in an aloof, perfectly friendly and philosophical way.

But she was a lady, and therefore socially the equal of anybody in Mr Cardew's drawing-room. And Jim Ferraby didn't like the easy familiarity of Stephen Elson. That he was invited at all was a surprise, almost a cause for indignation, to Jim Ferraby. His host might not be a great detective, but he was sensitive to certain impressions, and he took the first opportunity of drawing the young man aside.

"I had quite forgotten that you had met Elson," he said. "It is very embarrassing, but the truth is, it was Hannah's suggestion that he should be invited. In fact, every time the man has been to this house it has been Hannah's suggestion. She pointed out to me that we had not asked him to dine in a year, and I thought this would be an excellent opportunity. I don't think I could endure him *tête-à-tête!*"

Jim laughed.

"I am not at all embarrassed," he said, "though he was infernally rude to me after the case. What was he, and how did he come to settle in England?"

Cardew shook his head.

"That is one of the little matters for investigation which I shall take up some day," he said. "I know nothing about him except that he's very rich." He looked across the drawing-room to where the broad-shouldered American was engaged in a frolicsome conversation with the girl. "They get on well together," he said irritatingly; "I suppose because they're both from the same country – "

"Miss Leigh is not an American?" said Jim in surprise.

Cardew nodded.

"Yes, she is an American girl: I thought you knew. Her father, who was unfortunately killed during the war, was an official of the American Treasury, and I believe spent a great deal of his time in this country, where Miss Leigh was educated. I never met him – the father, I mean – but he occupied quite a good position. In fact, she was recommended to me by the American Ambassador."

Jim was watching her all the time Cardew was speaking. He did not know that one of her colouring could look so exquisite in black, or that so plain a gown could enhance her beauty.

"I never dreamt she was American," was all he could say.

If he had been so ignorant, his *bête noir* could lay claim to having detected Elfa's nationality.

"New England, I guess?" said Mr Elson. "Queer thing I didn't know you were good Yankee the first time we got together."

"Vermont," said Elfa, by no means overjoyed at meeting a fellow countryman.

He was red-faced, coarse-featured, and about him was the perpetual aroma of whisky and stale cigar smoke. His cheeks were puffed and his nose bulbous.

"I'm from the Middle West myself," he said complacently. "Do you know St Paul? It's a pretty good little burg. Say, Miss Leigh, what's that lawyer doing here?" He nodded over towards Jim, and his voice was loud enough for that young man to overhear the question. He would have given a great deal to have heard the rejoinder.

"Mr Ferraby is supposed to be one of the cleverest lawyers in the Public Prosecutor's office," she said quietly.

She explained the mysteries of this department, which combines the functions of Federal, State and District Attorney.

"Is that so?" said the other thoughtfully. "Well, he may be a cracka-jack prosecutor out of court, but when he gets before a judge, I can tell you that fellow is just nothing!"

"Are you an old friend of Mr Cardew's?" asked Elfa, anxious to turn the talk to more agreeable channels.

Elson scratched his none-too-well-shaven chin.

"Why, he's a neighbour of mine. Pretty good lawyer, eh?" He was watching her through half-closed lids.

"Mr Cardew isn't in practice now," she answered, and he laughed noisily.

"He's strong for that sleuth stuff, eh?" he chuckled. "I've never known a grown man to get that way."

His admiring eyes did not leave her face, and in her discomfort she looked appealingly across the room to where Jim stood, and, recognizing the signal of distress, he came across and rescued her.

It was obvious both to the girl and to Jim Ferraby that Mr Cardew was ill at ease. So much so that he seemed to have forgotten the excuse of Jim's visit, and never once referred to Hannah. From time to time he looked at his watch and glanced anxiously, almost fearfully, towards the door; and when at last Hannah Shaw appeared, more stiff, more black, more forbidding than ever, and stated brusquely that dinner was ready, the lawyer almost dropped his glasses in his apprehension.

"Will you hold dinner," he begged, "for a few minutes? The fact is, Hannah, I've invited a friend of ours – the superintendent – to come along."

She bridled, but said nothing.

"I met him today: he was very civil," Mr Cardew hastened to excuse himself for his daring, "and really I don't see why we should be bad friends. I don't know why I'm telling you all this…"

He floundered into a morass of unintelligibility. It would have been pathetic if it were not amusing, this spectacle of the tyranny wielded over the master of Barley Stack. To Jim it was no new experience, for he had seen something of the sort on his previous visit. But Elfa could only stare in amazement as the woman stalked out of the room, disapproval in every line of her figure.

Cardew rubbed his chin uneasily.

"I'm afraid Hannah doesn't like our friend…and really, it's very disturbing, *most* disturbing."

He looked pleadingly at Ferraby as though imploring some moral support.

"Few housekeepers like to see their plans changed," said Jim soothingly.

Five uncomfortable minutes passed, and then Hannah reappeared.

"How long are we to wait, Mr Cardew?" she rasped.

"We'll go in immediately, Hannah," said Cardew, with a quick glance at his watch, and something of relief in his face. "I don't think our friend can be coming."

The girl sat next to Ferraby at the round table, with a vacant chair at her side, which should have been occupied by Superintendent Minter.

"Poor Mr Cardew!" she murmured under her breath.

Jim grinned, but a glance at the face of the woman, seated immediately opposite him, arrested his amusement. She was glaring at the girl with a malignity which for the moment took his breath. And then, as the soup plates were being removed, came the tardy guest.

Sooper was never strong for clothes. Jim had the impression that the ill-fitting dress-suit he wore must have been bequeathed to him by a long-dead relative, or possibly purchased from a waiter when it was long past restaurant use.

"Sorry, ladies and gentlemen," murmured the guest, looking round the company through his half-closed eyes. "Never take dinner at night as a rule, and only remembered your kind invite just as I was going to bed. Good evening, Miss Shaw."

Hannah's eyes slowly rose and met his.

"Good evening, Superintendent," she said icily.

"Nice weather we've been having – the warmest weather I can remember for this time of the year."

It was the first time Elfa had seen the redoubtable Sooper, and she felt a quick instinct of friendliness towards the grim old man in his worn and shabby dress-suit. The shirt he wore was frayed at the opening. There were two large iron-mould stains in the most conspicuous part of the breast; the tie about his collar had worked round halfway to his ear, but he carried himself like an aristocrat.

"I think he is splendid…is that the superintendent?" she said under her breath, when, later, Sooper's attention was diverted to his host.

"Yes: the King Pippin of all sleuths – in Europe, anyway. Listen… he's kidding."

"Not often I go out to parties," Sooper was drawling. "Seems I'm too unsociable to invite. Never can tell one knife from another, an' mostly use the wrong beer glass. That's where we poor policemen get wrong – no manners. Stands to reason, if I went after one of those swell mobs an' got myself dolled up for s'ciety, they'd know me first time. I was sayin' to my sergeant only this afternoon, 'there ain't enough swell amateurs in this game: what we want are fellers that can wear evenin' dress without lookin' as if they were in fancy dress'."

Mr Cardew looked at his guest suspiciously.

"The police have their proper functions," he said primly. "The only contentious point between us, Superintendent, is that certain cases require – er – a greater refinement of – er – intellect and a more intensive appreciation of psychology."

"Sure they do." Elson dropped his elbows on the table and leant forward, nodding mechanically. "That's what you fellers miss…"

Suddenly he stopped. He had caught Hannah's eyes, and in them Jim Ferraby read an urgent warning.

"That psychology's certainly good," agreed Sooper almost humbly, "an' that's just what we want. Every young officer ought to get soaked in it. Next to anthro – you know the word, Mr Cardew."

"Anthropology," said Mr Cardew graciously.

"That's him: next to that, psychology's the grandest ornament to a man's intelligence. Next comes good eyesight. I'm a bit short-sighted for readin', but I can see a million miles. Never have the blinds drawn, Mr Cardew?"

The bow windows of the dining-room were uncovered except for diaphanous casement curtains that draped the lower halves. The half-light dusk lay on the lawn outside, and the tall sycamores at the end of the garden showed black outlines against the deep blue of the sky. The rhododendron bushes nearer the house made a shadowy blot.

"No," said Cardew, in surprise. "Why? We're not under observation – the public road is nearly a quarter of a mile away."

"Just wondered," apologized Sooper. "I don't know much about swell houses: live in a cottage myself, an' always pull the blinds when I eat – keeps the meal private. How many gardeners might you have here?" he asked.

"Four or five – I forget," said Cardew, and Sooper was impressed.

"That's a lot to find sleepin' room for," he said.

"They don't sleep here: my head gardener has a cottage near the road. Going back to the subject of the police – "

But Sooper was not inclined to go back to the subject of the police. Rather was he anxious to add to his knowledge of Mr Cardew's domestic economy.

"Why, I thought you had to keep gardeners or odd men around at nights to water the flowers an' trap moles?"

Gordon Cardew was obviously bored.

"No; my gardeners leave at seven o'clock. I certainly would not allow them to prowl around – what is wrong, Superintendent?"

Sooper had risen and was walking to the door. Suddenly there was a click, and all the lights went out.

"Stand back from the table against the wall, all of you!" His harsh voice was vibrant with authority. "I turned the lights out – there's somebody in the shadow of those bushes and he's got a gun!"

THE SNIPER

Sooper came softly from the front door and stepped into the garden. The dining-room looked out from the side of the house, and he moved with incredible swiftness towards the bushes. The lawn was empty – there was no sound but the gentle rustle of leaves in the night wind. Keeping close to the cover of the shrubs, he covered the width of the lawn.

Beyond the flower-beds were the sycamores which marked the southern boundary of the property. To the right was a little pine wood, which could be the only avenue of retreat on the part of an intruder.

Sooper went forward from tree to tree. Beneath his feet was a thick covering of pine needles that would have made his movements noiseless in any circumstances. From time to time he stopped and listened, but there was no sound.

He was halfway through the wood when, right ahead of him and not fifty yards away, came the sound of singing.

> "The Moorish king rides up and down
> Through Granada's royal town…
> *Ay de mi Alhama…!*"

For a second, at the sound of the woeful Spanish air, Sooper's spine crept. There was something so plaintive in the music, something so desperately hopeless in the words of the centuries-old lament, that he stood stock still.

"From Eloira's gates to those
  Of Bivarramble on he goes,
  Ay de mi Alhama...!"

Sooper went forward at a run towards the voice. The wood was dark, and here the trees were set so closely together that it was almost impossible to see more than a few yards ahead. He came plunging out into the open without having seen a soul.

The wood separated the pleasure grounds of Barley Stack from a little farm. Nothing moved in the meadows, and Sooper turned back.

"Come out of that, tramp!" he shouted, but only the echo of his voice came back to him.

Then came the sound of feet rustling through undergrowth, and he guessed it was Jim before he saw the white shirt-front emerge from the dark.

"Who is it?" asked Ferraby.

"Tramp of sorts," said Sooper. "You were nearly as crazy to come out without a shotgun."

"I saw nobody."

"Nobody to see, I guess," replied Sooper gently. "Let's go back – I ought to have got my machine and patrolled the road."

They penetrated the plantations again, but heard nothing and saw nothing, and returned to the lawn to find the alarmed dinner party assembled.

"Did you see anybody?" asked Mr Cardew anxiously and somewhat incoherently. "Really, this is the most extraordinary... you've frightened these ladies... I must confess that I didn't see a man of any description."

"Maybe Minter's imagination's working," growled Elson. "You might see a man, but I'll be darned if you could see a gun in this light!"

"Saw it gleam," said Sooper, staring hard at the wood. "Just saw the light on it...must have been a gun. Got a lamp, anybody?"

Mr Cardew went into the house and returned with an electric lantern.

"Stood here," said Sooper, and flashed the lamp on the grass. "No marks – ground's too hard. Nothing…"

Swiftly he darted downward to the grass and picked up a black oblong something, and, holding it on the palm of his hand, whistled softly.

"What is it?" asked Cardew.

"Magazine of a .42 automatic – chock full of shells," said Sooper. ".42 automatic marked United States Naval Department – dropped out of his gun."

Mr Cardew's jaw had also dropped: it might have been his imagination, but Jim fancied that the face of the amateur detective had gone a shade paler. Possibly, he thought, this was the first occasion on which Mr Cardew had been brought face to face with the grim actualities of criminal detection.

"Well, I'll go to…!"

Stephen Elson was looking at the magazine open-mouthed.

"And he was there all the time…with a gun!" He shuddered. "Did you see him, Officer?"

Sooper looked round and dropped his hand on the other's shoulder.

"Nothing to worry about," he said kindly, almost brotherly. "No. If I'd seen him I'd have caught him. I'll use your telephone, Mr Cardew."

His host guided him to the study and left him.

"That you, Lattimer? Turn out divisional reserves and detain anybody that can't account for their movements – especially tramps. When you've done that, come up to Barley Stack; bring a gun and two hand lamps."

"What is wrong, Sooper?"

"Lost a collar stud," said Sooper calmly, and hung up.

He looked up into the troubled face of Cardew. And from the lawyer his eyes wandered to the packed bookshelves.

"Must be a lot there that'd help a feller to pull in a crazy tramp," he said. "I got to rely on common coppers and it's even odds they'll never find him."

The old twinkle was in his eyes: Cardew became conscious of the two stains on the shirt-front and the shabby dress-suit slightly redolent of mothball. He recovered his illusion of superiority.

"That is the sort of case where the very physical attributes of the police are so admirable," he said. "After all, there is nothing very subtle about the visitation of an armed tramp!"

"Nothing's subtle that matters," said Sooper, shaking his head sadly. "Not life nor death, nor stomach-ache nor money. Subtle timings don't count, not with me, anyway." He surveyed the packed book-shelves again and sighed. "That tramp feller was after Elson," he said, going off at a tangent.

Cardew was startled. "What makes you think that?" he asked.

"Elson expected him too," nodded Sooper, with a far-away look in his eyes. "Else why does he carry a gun?"

"Elson carries a gun – a pistol, you mean? How do you know?"

"Felt it in his pants," said Sooper, "when I was bein' affectionate. How was that for subtle? Just clapped him on the shoulder an' felt his pocket with my hip. I've got one of the most sensitive hips in the force. What's that a sign of from the anthrop'logical view?"

But Mr Cardew was not to be drawn.

"Why did you follow the superintendent, Mr Ferraby? Wasn't that rather foolhardy?"

Jim and the girl were alone on the lawn. Hannah had disappeared with the American, and though the young man had qualms about remaining outdoors in the growing darkness, his discretion was not proof against the lure of the night and the intimacy which their solitude brought.

"There wasn't any greater risk for me than for Sooper," he said; "besides which, I'll admit that I thought he had been deceived by a shadow – I had forgotten that the old devil has eyes that can see through a wall! Do you like that man Elson?" he blurted.

"Mr Elson? Why no…whatever made you think I did?"

"Well…he's American, and I suppose it's natural for people of the same country…" he ended lamely enough.

"If I were an English girl and I had met an English tough in New York, should I like him because he was English?" she asked with a smile.

"Tough? I didn't know he was anything unusual," he began, and she laughed softly.

"You don't know how rude you are being," she said. "Yes, Mr Elson is that: I can't think of a more elegant word than 'tough'; it isn't pretty, is it?"

"I didn't realize that you were American," he said, as they strolled slowly up and down the close-cropped lawn.

"I never dreamt that you realized I was anybody," she said dryly, "except one of the features of King's Bench Walk. You're not trying to flirt with me, are you?"

Jim went red at the amazing directness of the girl.

"Good lord, no!" he gasped.

"Then I'll take your arm. I *was* a little frightened," she confessed; "it was rather creepy – the lights going out and the horrible feeling that we were being watched."

Her arm rested on his. Jim Ferraby self-consciously kept his elbow rigid and she smiled at his propriety.

"You can let your arm drop – that's right; I shan't cling. Only I'm human enough to find comfort in a masculine arm – any masculine arm except perhaps Mr Elson's."

"I quite understand." He was inclined to be icy, but her soft laughter melted him.

"I don't like the country," she said. "Poor daddy loved it: he used to sleep out in the open even in stormy weather."

"Your father died in the war?"

"Yes." Her voice scarcely rose above a whisper. "Yes, he died in the war."

They paced to and fro in silence: the arm in Jim Ferraby's rested with greater confidence; once, by accident, the tips of her fingers brushed the back of his hand.

"How long are you staying here?" he asked.

"Until tomorrow afternoon. I have some indexing to do, and in any circumstances Mr Cardew would not let me stay after his housekeeper left. She is going away for the weekend."

"What do you think of her?" he asked.

She did not answer at once.

"She may be nice when one gets to know her," she said diplomatically, and then Sooper's long figure showed in the open doorway.

"Come in before the spooks get you, Mr Ferraby. Somethin' unusual has happened – my sergeant was awake. That feller reckons all the time he's not sleeping is time wasted. I think Mr Cardew was askin' about you, young miss."

Elfa passed into the house and Ferraby was following, but the old man detained him.

"Come for a stroll with me, Mr Ferraby, an' help me psychologize and anthropologize."

It was noticeable that, except when he was in the amateur scientist's presence, or (as Jim subsequently learnt) discussing such learned subjects with his sergeant, Sooper had no difficulty in pronunciation.

"Elson's got to go home tonight, and I'm deducin' that this miscreant with the gun will try to take a crack at him," he said. "The whole thing's subtle an' mysterious. One American tryin' to shoot another American! Angels have wept for less."

"You think the stranger on the lawn was an American?"

"He had an American gun; therefore he's American. I'm gettin' into this deduction business – it comes natural after a bit. My deduction is that he's a singer."

"What makes you think that?" asked Jim in surprise.

"Because I heard him singin'," said Sooper. "Ever play auction bridge, Mr Ferraby? If you do I'll give you a tip: a little peek's worth two finesses. Get that into your mind. Deduction's fine but seein' and hearin's better. That's official. Know anything against Elson up in Whitehall?"

"You mean at the Prosecutor's office? No, I don't remember hearing or reading anything, and I've charge of the alien section."

"Never call an American an alien: it makes him wild. Just the same as the English swell red when they get the alien tag in New York Harbour. It's a low word meanin' Peruvian and Slovak and Mongolian Hebrew. I was in Washington during the war, till our headquarters found I was efficient – then they shot me home. They can't stand efficiency."

Jim was considering whether he should, at the risk of displeasing his host, take Sooper into his confidence. He came to a decision.

"Sooper, you think that man in the garden was after Elson? You're mistaken."

"That sounds impossible," said Sooper, "but I'm open to conviction."

Briefly Ferraby told him of the letter which Gordon Cardew had shown him the day before, and the superintendent listened without interruption.

"Big Foot, eh? Sounds like one of those nancy Wild West Injun names. But what's Hannah done? That's pretty big news, Mr Ferraby, an' slightly alters things."

Cardew's voice called them from the house.

"Come along and finish your dinner."

"Wait." Sooper's sinewy hand gripped the young man by the sleeve. "Just wait whilst I get the logic an' psychology of this. She's going away for a weekend, you say... I know the house on Pawsey Beach. Cardew drove me down there once before we took the mat on the question of criminal science. A dog lonely place, miles from everywhere except the sea...big cliff with hundreds of smugglers' caves...house stands on an old post road that runs under a cliff but isn't used much since the new road was made over the cliff top. It's dangerous. Part of the cliff fell down the year I went there an' old Cardew made a fuss with the Pawsey Town Council because they didn't clear up the mess an' open the road. He knows a lot about that side of the law."

"Are you people coming in?"

Cardew was walking out towards them, and they turned in the direction of the house.

"Don't hint that you know anything," muttered Jim, and Sooper grunted his reluctant agreement.

Mr Cardew had quite recovered his poise, was boisterously cheerful as they resumed their seats at the table, and had a new theory.

"I've been looking up my de Carrilon," he said, "and curiously enough, I came upon an almost parallel case. De Carrilon has a chapter on what he calls 'The Crime of Embuchement'. He says that to a certain type of criminal mind the impulse to shoot from the darkness is irresistible..."

Sooper toyed with a quail on toast, and wondered why this clever lawyer had not associated the murderous visitor with the threatening letter to Hannah Shaw.

It was past one o'clock that night when Jim knocked at the door of Mr Cardew's study to bid him good night. By the light of a table lamp the lawyer was reading from a large and thick volume.

"Come in, Ferraby. Has the superintendent gone?"

"Just gone, sir."

Cardew closed the book with a sigh.

"A very practical man, but I doubt if he takes his work seriously. Police work largely develops into a mechanical routine. They will put guards on the roads and notify the country police, and I suppose arrest a few perfectly innocent citizens. They will do nothing which is worthy of praise and omit no precautions that would deserve censure. They will, in fact, play for safety. It is a very small and unimportant matter, but typical of the system. The more I study our old-fashioned methods, the more I regret that fate did not take me into a more exciting path of the law than that which meanders through the Court of Chancery. Well, what do you think of Hannah? Nothing very suspicious about her attitude, eh?"

"She is less distressed than I thought possible," said Jim quietly, and Mr Cardew's mouth opened in a gasp of consternation.

"Good heavens!... I never thought of connecting the letter with... I must have taken leave of my senses!"

He had gone suddenly white.

"I wondered why," said Ferraby.

Sooper had wondered too, and had privately expressed his surprise before leaving. It had required all Jim's powers of persuasion to prevent the old man from interviewing Cardew on the subject. But this Jim Ferraby did not reveal, though he knew that it was inevitable that Sooper would sooner or later discuss the matter with the master of Barley Stack.

"I never dreamt of connecting the man in the garden with Hannah," said the lawyer thoughtfully. "This is truly astounding! I almost wish that I had told Minter."

"Get him on the 'phone and tell him," suggested Jim, anxious to unburden his conscience.

Mr Cardew hesitated, took up the telephone and put it down again.

"I must sleep on it," he said. "If I tell him now, he'll come back and there will be a fearful scene with Hannah. Frankly, I'm scared of Hannah Shaw…terrified. It is absurd… I despise myself. And I'm a lawyer, supposedly without sentiment. No, leave it until the morning, or later. I'll ask the superintendent to come up to dinner. Hannah will be away."

It occurred to Jim as he was undressing that to leave the matter until Hannah had departed on her mysterious weekend trip had certain advantages. He almost regretted that he was taking an early departure and would not be present at the interview.

He prepared for bed leisurely, and a distant church clock was striking two when he finally put out the light. Whether the excitement of the evening or the ten minutes' nap he had snatched on his way from town was the cause, he could not sleep. He had never felt quite so wakeful in his life. For half an hour he lay, his mind working through the house from Elfa Leigh to Cardew, from Cardew to Hannah, and back again to Elfa. At last, with a sigh, he rose, walked to the little table where he had left his smoking materials and, lighting his pipe, walked to the window.

The moon was in its last phase, a thin rind of white in a clear sky, and its faint and ghostly reflection covered the world with pale radiance. From where he sat on the window seat, he could see one brilliantly lighted window in a wing running at right angles to the outer wall of his own room. Was it the girl's room, or Cardew's – or Hannah's? Whoever was in the room was busy – he saw an indistinct figure pass and repass the semi-transparent curtains, and presently his eyes accustomed themselves to the light and curtain veil, and he recognized the figure of Hannah. She was fully dressed and was engaged in packing a suitcase that she had placed on the bed. The gentle night breeze blew the curtain aside for a second and he saw into the room. By the side of the bed were two open trunks, and she was clearing out her wardrobe.

Jim Ferraby frowned. A weekend visit? She was packing like one preparing for a long absence. For an hour he watched, and then her light went out. By this time the grey of dawn was in the sky, and as the lamp was extinguished he felt a sudden overwhelming desire for sleep.

He had one knee on the bed when he heard a sound which filled him with wonder and made him doubt the evidence of his senses. It was somebody singing, and the voice came from the little wood.

> "The Moorish king rides up and down
> …Granada's royal town,
> *Ay de mi Alhama!*"

The singer! The man who had been on the lawn! In an instant he struggled into his overcoat and pelted down the dark stairs to the hall. It was some time before he could get the door open, but at last he was in the open. The world smelt sweet and cold, the grass beneath his slippered feet was wet with dew.

He stood motionless, listening, and then he espied a stealthy figure moving in the cover of the wood and darted towards it. As he came nearer, the man heard him and swung round.

"Steady…steady! Don't scare my song-bird," hissed a voice. "I want him for my anthr'p'logical av'ry!"

It was Sooper.

THE STORY OF THE $100 BILLS

"Go back an' rustle some clothes. I'll want your help, anyway. All my men are down in the Farnham area arrestin' the wrong people. If I'm not here, wait for me."

Jim was glad to obey the order, for the morning was chilly and he was shivering. In five minutes he was back to where he had left the superintendent, but that worthy man had disappeared, nor did he show himself for ten minutes.

"This time he's gone," he growled. "Must have heard you gettin' into the concert."

"Gone – how?"

"The wood runs down to the boundary wall. There's thick bush on the other side – that's where I heard him moving. I'll blow down to the main road, but he's as cunning as a monkey. Anything new?"

"Hannah Shaw is going away," said Jim, and told what he had seen during the night.

Sooper scratched his grey head.

"I'll bet Cardew doesn't know she's goin' for keeps," he said. "That'll be the best bit of news the poor fis – Mr Cardew's had in years. Wish I'd caught young Tetr'zini." He shook his head regretfully.

He was halfway down the gate road when he turned and came back.

"You got a motorcar, Mr Ferraby?"

"Yes – but not here. I came down by train."

Sooper nodded.

"Might bring it along to my station house tonight – somewhere round dusk. I'm thinking of goin' down to Pawsey. It's off my ground, and that skinny-gutted deputy at the Yard's certain to raise hell if anything comes out. But I despise him, an' when I despise a man, the grave's his only hope. I'd like to take you along with me to get the proper psychology of the position – I'm short on that."

Sooper did his best laughing with his eyes – he was laughing now.

Apparently nobody in the house had heard the singer, and Jim returned to his room unchallenged by anxious inquiry. Sleep was impossible now, and he shaved and dressed at leisure. He was down in the garden by the time the sun was on the lawn, and he strolled round the house to kill time.

From the rear of Barley Stack he had a clear view of Hill Brow, the lordly house of Mr Elson, a sprawl of red brick topped by a square and architecturally pleasing tower.

What freakish whim had induced this American to settle down in surroundings which had no pleasure for him? A man of the people, self-made, without culture or refinement.

When he came back to the lawn he saw a slim figure in grey walking away from him, and his heart raced for a second or two.

"Yes, I am early – I didn't sleep very well."

Elfa gave her hand with a smile that dazzled him. Never before had he seen her under the sunny skies and at an hour which few women choose to submit their charms to the critical eyes of men.

"Is it permissible to offer my arm?" he asked boldly.

"Permissible but unnecessary," she laughed quietly at his embarrassment. "I am full of courage this morning. Did you sleep well?"

"To be truthful, I didn't sleep at all," he admitted, and she nodded.

"My room is next Miss Shaw's, and she was moving about all night," she said.

He could have confirmed that information, but she went on: "I shall be glad to get back to my own little apartment. Barley Stack and Miss Shaw have a very bad effect on my nerves. I've only spent one night in the house – a year ago; and that was a most unpleasant experience. Do you mind my telling you this?"

Did he mind! He could have listened to her all morning. He suggested as much.

"Miss Shaw was in worse than her usual bad temper. She wouldn't speak to me or to poor Mr Cardew. She shut herself up in her room and refused to come to meals because, Mr Cardew told me, she thought he had slighted her. And then she did an extraordinary thing. Very early in the morning, when I woke up and looked out of the window on to the little side lawn, I saw the letter 'B' picked out on the grass with dark paper. There was something rather familiar about those little oblong slips, and I went downstairs to make sure. The pieces of paper were hundred-dollar bills – there must have been fifty of them, and they were fastened to the earth with long black pins!"

Jim could only look at her incredulously.

"Did Cardew know?"

"Yes, he'd seen them from his window, and he was furious."

"Was anybody else staying here at the time?"

She nodded and made a little face.

"Mr Elson. His house was in the hands of the repairers and Mr Cardew asked him to come and stay. I don't think he's been here since until last night. It was Miss Shaw's suggestion that he came at all – he told me that."

"But how do you know Hannah marked the lawn with bills – it may have been a freak of Elson's: I can well imagine his doing such a crazy thing."

She shook her head.

"It was Miss Shaw. She came and gathered up the money after Cardew sent for her. He pressed her for an explanation but she would give none – she wouldn't even tell him where she got the money."

And then Jim remembered what the lawyer had told him. This, then, was the "stupid joke" which had nearly led to a domestic breach.

"I think she is a little mad," said Elfa, "and that is why I hated the thought of coming to Barley Stack. It was only when I heard – "

She ended the sentence abruptly, but a warm glow came over the young man and his pulse beat a little faster.

There was nothing to betray her energetic night in Hannah's face when she appeared at the breakfast table. The dark eyes were as bird-like as ever; she was a model of composure and self-possession. Cardew, on the other hand, was irritable and snappy, though apparently he had slept well enough. He was one of those admirably-tempered individuals who bring the essence of their grievances to the breakfast table. The day dilutes them down to their normal strength and importance, but in the first hour of waking they overcloud the morning sun.

"Even now I'm not sure that this pestiferous fellow hasn't been playing a joke on me. I personally saw nothing, and I think my eyesight is as keen as anybody's. If there had been a man in the shadow of the hedge as he suggested, why is it that nobody else saw him?"

Jim was on the point of telling about the song that so startled him at dawn, but remembered that Sooper had asked him to say nothing about that strange occurrence.

"As to the – er – magazine, well, that might have been part of the stupid joke," said the suspicious Mr Cardew. "I may not have had a great deal of criminal practice, but I've come upon some very remarkable cases of deception even in the Chancery Court. You remember, Miss Leigh, the story I told you about a client of mine who concealed his assets in bankruptcy and nearly earned for me a reprimand from the judge!"

Miss Leigh had heard the story: she had heard it many times. It was the one purple patch in Mr Cardew's humdrum law practice.

"What time do you go, Hannah?" He looked over his glasses at the stolid woman.

"At eleven."

"You are taking your machine? Thompson tells me that the hood needs repair."

"It is good enough for me, and should be good enough for Thompson," she said shortly, and thereafter Mr Cardew's interest in her plans ceased.

He himself was going into town to get his letters, and offered to drop Jim at his flat in Cheyne Walk.

"As soon as breakfast is over," he said, and it appeared to Jim Ferraby that he had fixed the hour so as to be out of the house before his sour housekeeper.

There was only a brief opportunity for seeing Elfa before he left, and this Jim seized, to find her busy in Cardew's study, a dozen heaps of books on the library table and a look of tragic despair in her eyes.

"He wished me to get them finished before he returns," she said helplessly. "There are two days' work here – and I'm determined not to spend another night in this house! You are going, Mr Ferraby?" Her tone was one of disappointment, and Jim revelled in the unaccustomed prospect of being missed.

"Yes, I'm going, but I want you to give me your address, so that I can find out if you have reached home safely."

She laughed.

"That is one of your lamest excuses. But I will give you my address."

She scribbled it down on a piece of paper and he put it into his pocket.

"I'm not worrying about getting home safely, because Mr Cardew told me I could leave, even if I was not finished, at four, and he had not returned."

"I'll call – " he began.

She shook her head.

"You'll find my 'phone number on that piece of paper," she said, her lips twitching. "Perhaps I will let you call one day and take me to a theatre, if it will not jeopardize your position – they tell me you are something very special in the Prosecutor's Department."

"My position is so hopelessly compromised," said Jim firmly, "that my only chance of getting back is to be seen in respectable company."

He held her hand quite as long as was necessary, perhaps a little longer, and carried away with him the most fragrant memory, and at the same time the most extraordinarily exalted views of womanhood that his heart had ever held. Throughout the journey to the City, Jim had a confused idea that Mr Cardew was talking about Superintendent Minter, or it may have been Mr Elson; but all that he heard he instantly forgot. His heart was singing a wild and dangerous tune, his head swam in the amber clouds of romance. Which is not the most profitable environment for an official of the Public Prosecutor's Department.

It was when Cardew switched to the subject of Hannah that Jim came slowly to earth.

"I have been thinking the matter over very carefully and very thoughtfully," said the lawyer, "and I have decided that I cannot go on in the way I have been during the past few years. I have tolerated Hannah because she is at heart a good girl. But I've only just begun to realize how tremendously my whole life is determined by her whims and fancies. And then there is this infernal mystery, and I will not have mysteries – at least, not at Barley Stack. There is another thing: I cannot help thinking that there is something between Elson and Hannah. You may think that is a preposterous idea?"

In truth Jim Ferraby thought it extremely preposterous, for at that time Sooper had not taken him wholly into his confidence.

"I have intercepted glances between them. Once I came upon them talking at the end of the road. They saw me and scuttled like rabbits, and to this day they're under the impression that I did not see them. I don't know what this Elson is, whether he is a bachelor or whether he is married. He is a very disagreeable person, yet, if he has any liking or affection for Hannah – which is extremely doubtful, for such a man could not have any true affection for anybody but himself – well, I should be very glad. On one point, however, I am determined: Hannah – must – go." He struck the floor of the car with his umbrella to emphasize each word. "She is getting on my nerves," he went on. "I would willingly pay a thousand pounds if she decided to take another position."

"You know, of course, that she has packed all her boxes?" began Jim, when the older man jerked round at him.

"Packed her boxes?" he almost squeaked. "How do you know?"

"I saw her in the night through my window. She made no attempt to hide the operation. She cleared all her dresses out of the wardrobe, and, so far as I could see, packed them in her trunk."

Mr Cardew was silent for a long time. His ordinarily smooth brow was wrinkled in the scowl which accompanies concentrated thought.

"I don't think there's anything in that," he said at last. "She has packed her trunks before, when she has been annoyed with me, and like an everlasting fool I have invariably gone down on my knees to her, metaphorically speaking, and begged her to stay. But this time…" The wag of his head was ominous.

He dropped Jim in Whitehall, and for the next two hours Mr Ferraby was wholly occupied with an accumulation of correspondence. There were statements to be examined, prima facie cases for arrest to be digested, and, in the absence of his chief from town, he had his lunch brought in and cleared off all arrears by three o'clock in the afternoon, when he strolled up Pall Mall to his club.

His work might have been easier and more expeditiously concluded if there had not been, between the paper and his eyes all the time, the vision of a face that had no definite form or shape, but was stabilized by a pair of steadfast grey eyes, set widely apart. Once his typist brought back a document and asked him coldly who "Elfa" was, and he discovered that he had so christened a notorious car-stealer whose case was up for consideration.

He found that she lived in Bloomsbury. There was no real reason why he should take a cab to Cubitt Street to look at the house from the outside. It bore a striking resemblance to every other house in the street. But there was some satisfaction in deciding that the window with the little white curtains was her room, and he felt a strange friendliness towards a billboard advertisement of a corn cure which must meet her eyes every morning. Not till some days later did he learn that she slept in a room at the back of the house, which was visible from no angle of the street.

At four o'clock he telephoned her: she had not returned. Since she did not intend leaving Barley Stack until four o'clock, it was unlikely that she had. At five o'clock there was no news of her. At half-past five, when he had worked himself up into a condition of panic, and his big black car was quivering and rumbling at the door of his club, ready for a lightning spin to Barley Stack to rescue her from unimaginable dangers, her cool voice answered him,

"Yes, I'm back…no, Mr Cardew has not returned. He telephoned to say that he was staying in town for the night."

"Won't you come and have tea?"

He heard her laugh.

"No, I'm going to have a quiet evening, thank you very much, Mr Ferraby. It is lovely here."

"I should say it was," said Jim fervently. "I can't imagine any place where you are – "

Click! She had hung up on him. Nevertheless, he went home in a state of elation that bordered upon imbecility.

There was a visitor, he was told by his chauffeur, who was also his valet and his butler. It was Mr Cardew, very much at a loose end.

"Your man tells me you're going out tonight," he almost complained. "I came along to ask you if you would come to the Opera House: they are playing 'Faust' tonight, and I bought two seats in the hope that you'd be able to accompany me."

"I'm sorry," said Jim, "but I've an engagement."

"Could you come to dinner?"

Again Jim made his apologies.

"I'm unfortunate," said Cardew, running his fingers through his hair. "I can't do much else but go back to Barley Stack tonight." And then, miserably, "I wonder what the devil Hannah is doing at Beach Cottage tonight – I'd give a lot of money to know."

Jim might have promised to supply the information, but discreetly he refrained.

A JOURNEY SOUTHWARD

The street lamps had been lit and the last glow of light was fading from the west, when Ferraby's big Bentley shot down the main street of a countrified suburb and pulled up before the most rustic of all London police headquarters.

Sooper was in his tiny office, discussing a large and indigestible wedge of pie and a steaming mug of cocoa. He looked up and pointed to a chair.

"Sit down, won't you?" he said indistinctly. And when at last he had swallowed at a gulp the scalding contents of the mug, and wiped his lips on a handkerchief that had seen better days, he took a box of cigars from the drawer of his desk and offered the interior to Jim.

"No, thank you, Sooper," said Mr Ferraby hurriedly.

"What's the matter with 'em?" demanded Sooper, hurt. "Never seen anybody who didn't like these cigars."

"Take a good look at me," said Jim.

"The country's growin' decadent," said Sooper mournfully, as he applied a match to the end of a poisonous-looking cylinder. "People are gettin' cowardly. I believe in standin' up to a thing and conquerin' it. I've conquered these cigars, though I admit they've sent to the floor more people than I can count. I've always admired strength and punch."

He puffed the noxious fumes into the air with every evidence of enjoyment.

"You couldn't buy this cigar under ten cents in America – and that's where it's grown."

"I take leave to doubt it," said Jim.

"As a matter of fact," confessed Sooper, "they're made of home-grown tobacco. They're a sort of patriotic experiment. And they're not so bad, once you get used to 'em. Our divisional surgeon says that they're healthy. He says no bug could live in a radius of a mile. He says that coming here brings back the war very vivid – he was gassed in France."

He coughed, choked, looked dubiously at the cigar, and, shaking his head, threw it into the fireplace.

"That one's not so good as the others," he said, and filled his pipe. "We'll make a start soon," looking up at the clock. "I've sent Lattimer down in advance, because he's a useful kind of man, but if anything comes out, he's not in it."

"You mean, if there's any trouble about your going beyond your territory?"

Sooper nodded.

"I like Lattimer, though I never let him know it," he said. "A young fellow gets all puffed up if you hand him bouquets, and he's temp'ramental, the same as me. He doesn't like work."

As Sooper was shuffling about, finding coats and wraps, Jim thought it was an opportune moment to tell him Elfa's story of the banknotes in the shape of a "B". Sooper listened intently.

"Elson was there that night, was he?" he said softly. "That's rather a wonderful coincidence, for that woman is sweet on Elson, or my deductions are wrong. And she's got a pull, too. I seem to have an idea that we've got to be pretty clever sleuths tonight to understand all we see – I almost wish Mr Cardew was coming along."

And then, when Jim asked a question, he shook his head.

"No, we haven't picked up that tramp, and it's not so wonderful as you'd think. The ground's broken and woody round here, and, what's more, Cardew's place is just off the main southern road. Empty market trolleys are going past all day long, and it would be the easiest thing in the world to sneak under a waterproof cover and get away. And, talking of waterproof covers…"

He walked down to the street and examined the sky, came back and tapped an ancient barometer on his desk, and nodded.

"I've got a corn that'll beat this thing ten yards in twenty. Have you brought a mackintosh?"

"I've one in the car," said Jim.

"You'll want it," replied Sooper laconically.

The moon showed wanly through a fog of cloud as they struck Horsham Road, and they had not gone a dozen miles before the southern horizon flickered and glowed redly, and little swirls of dust showed in the light of the headlamps. Sooper sat huddled by Jim's side, and did not speak for a very long time. They were on the outskirts of Horsham when the rain began to fall, and Jim stopped to fix the hood. The roll and growl of thunder was audible now.

"Like thunderstorms," said Sooper cheerfully. "Nothing subtle about a thunderstorm. Thunderstorms are facts: there's no psychology to 'em. They're just like catching a man in the act."

And then, when the car had cleared Horsham and was thundering up the Worthing Road, he said: "When a woman's got her heart set on marriage, she's about as reasonable as a hungry wolf in a meat store – I wonder what 'B' stood for?"

"I suggest Big Foot," said Jim… "That's a beauty!"

Ahead of them the skies suddenly cracked whitely, blindingly. Sooper waited until the crash and roll of the thunder had made him audible.

"Big Foot? Yes, possibly." And then: "Why do you think I am risking my life this stormy night by the side of a speed fiend, dashing madly into the ragin' elements? To satisfy my curiosity about Hannah Shaw? No, sir. I'm going," he spoke slowly and deliberately – "to unravel a mystery – that's the expression, unravel a mystery."

"And what is the mystery, if it isn't Hannah's peculiar behaviour?" asked Jim good-humouredly.

"I've been on the track of this mystery," said Sooper, nodding solemnly, "for six and a half years. It's the mystery of an appointment that was never kept!"

Jim stared at him.

"I'll buy it, Sooper."

"There's nothing to buy," said Sooper complacently. "It's just a fact, like that there flash of lightning, and the artillery of the heavens, if one may use a high-class expression that I read in a book, the name of which I forget. Never could remember the names of books. Six and a half years," he ruminated. "It's a long time, but it's a short time for an old man. Flick! It comes and it goes, quicker than lightning – an' that doesn't exactly loiter. He asked me to go to his house in Chellamore Gardens. Sir Joseph Brixton was his name, and he was an alderman of the City of London. He's now dead and pop'larly supposed to be in heaven. But he asked me to go to his house, and I went, and he was not at home. At least, he said he wasn't at home, but sent me a letter by his butler, thanking me for all the trouble I'd taken, and two ten-pound notes. Which I gave to a charity." Sooper paused. "The charity that begins at home."

"What on earth has this to do with our wild adventure tonight?" asked Jim, cleaning the rain screen for the hundredth time.

"A whole lot," murmured Sooper. "I'm just beginning to enjoy this trip – I hope Lattimer has got his oilskin."

"Did you know why Brixton sent for you? I remember the man very well."

Sooper nodded in the darkness.

"I do know," he said. "And I know why he broke his appointment."

"But you said – " began Jim.

"I know what I said. I pretty well know why. But it's the how that's got me all temperamental."

The rain was pelting down, the lightning was so incessant that Jim had no need of his headlamps. He turned off the post road and struck a secondary that led to Great Pawsey village. That ancient hamlet was in darkness except for the light that streamed from the windows of the village inn, as he skirted the broad green and began the steep descent to the beach road.

Great Pawsey was separated from Little Pawsey by some five miles – by a whole universe in some respects, for Little Pawsey, as it appears still on the maps of the 'eighties, has long since dropped its contemptible prefix. The small fishing village has become a fashionable watering-place; its name, "Pawsey", is picked out in huge electric lamps on the face of the cliff. It has a winter garden and a parade and a pier. Bands play in its ornamental gardens, great actors appear in its mammoth theatre. It has hotels of such magnitude and importance that even the hall porters are called "Mister".

Two roads connect Pawsey with its poor relation. One, that crosses the downs parallel with the cliff, and the other the Lower Beach Road that runs by the side of the sea. The former is perfectly metalled and expensively illuminated; the lower is little more than a cart track. On the higher thoroughfare, the municipality and town council of Pawsey have lavished the taxpayers' money – its disreputable companion, being the object of a feud between the War Department, which owns a slip of the foreshore, and the city fathers, remains very much as it was in the days of our fathers. From time to time the local newspapers splashed a hectic headline "The Lower Road Scandal", and fiery statements were made at council meetings denouncing the War Department for its refusal to co-operate in the cost of repair, but the net result of all the speaking and all the writing was not visible in any kind of improvement.

"It's certainly a hell of a road," said Sooper, as the machine bumped and slithered down the rocky hill. "We'll park the car at the bottom, if you don't mind – there's a sort of old quarry there."

"You know the place?" asked Jim in surprise.

"Ordnance map," was the explanation. "Been studyin' all mornin'. The house is five hundred 'n' fifty yards from the foot of the hill an' two miles three furlongs from Pawsey. We ought to find Lattimer when we strike the level – dim those lamps of yours, Mr Ferraby."

Lattimer, a moist and shining figure, stood in the shelter of an overhanging "cut" – they would have passed him unnoticed if he had not stepped out of cover.

"Nobody has come to the house yet, sir," he reported, as they stepped out of the car.

"What! But Miss Shaw came here early this morning," said Jim.

49

"I'd have been surprised if she had," said Sooper. "In fact, I *knew* she hadn't come this mornin'."

Ferraby was staggered.

"That's deduction," said Sooper complacently; "deduction an' logic. Maybe it's psychology too."

"But how did you know that she hadn't come this morning?" insisted Jim.

"Because Lattimer 'phoned me an hour ago," was the calm reply. "That's proper police logical work: havin' a man on the spot an' gettin' him to 'phone. *And* deduction – I deduce that he's tellin' the truth. Put that car right back so that nobody can see it, Mr Ferraby – Sergeant, show your lamp...now all lights out, please."

The rain beat down mercilessly, though the thunderstorm had passed. Out at sea the white ribbon of lightning showed at intervals as they stumbled along the road, aided by occasional flashes from the sergeant's lamp.

Beach Cottage stood between road and sea, a squat stone bungalow, almost surrounded by a brick wall, breast high. At each end of the house there was a gap in the fencing to admit a rough carriage track.

"Sure there's nobody there?"

"Certain, sir; the door has a padlock on the outside."

"What's that building behind – a garage?"

Jim could see no building other than that which loomed before them, but Sooper had cat's eyes.

"No, sir; that's the boathouse. It's empty. When Mr Cardew used the place, so a boatman told me, he had a skiff, but that was sold."

Sooper tried doors and windows without result.

"Surely she can't be coming," said Jim. "Probably the storm scared her."

Sooper grunted something derogatory to the storm as a factor in Hannah Shaw's plans.

"I'm not saying that she'll come," he said. "Maybe I've been the'rizin': that's my trouble, I think too much."

Jim thought he had never seen a more desolate dwelling. On one side was the sea; on the other, beyond the road, the grim escarpment of the cliffs, only to be guessed at in the pitch darkness of the night.

"The place is honeycombed with caves," said Lattimer, "most of them quite inaccessible."

They had withdrawn to the road and were walking slowly towards the place where the car was concealed.

"I don't wonder that there's not a rush to rent Cardew's summer cottage," said Jim.

"What's the matter with it?" asked Sooper. "It's the kind of place I'd like to retire to when I take my pension. I'll bet it's a peach of a house in the sunlight; and anyway, what's there to do at night but to sleep?"

He dived into his clothes, and Jim saw the phosphorescent glow of his watch dial.

"Eleven, as near as makes no difference," he said. "We'll give her till twelve, and then I'll start apologizing."

"What did you expect to find here?" asked Jim, putting into words the question he had been asking himself all that evening.

"That's goin' to be difficult to say," drawled Sooper. "Only...when a middle-aged spinster gets keen on marriage, and when she says what she's goin' to do if she don't get married, I'm entitled to be interested in her. Maybe I expected to get a stronger line than I look like gettin', maybe – "

He clutched suddenly at Jim's arm and drew him to one side.

"Behind that rock, quick!" he hissed.

THE KITCHEN

On the road had approached two dim lights, the lamps of an approaching car.

Jim tripped and stumbled towards the cliff and found cover, Sooper crouching at his side, Lattimer flat on the ground behind them. The car was moving quickly. It was abreast of them before Jim imagined it was possible on that rough road. As the little machine flashed past he had a fleeting vision of a dark silhouette – a woman with a wide-brimmed hat, bent forward as though to meet the rain that swept along the beach.

In a few seconds the car had turned into the opening in the wall and had come to a standstill before the door of the house.

"She's opening the door," whispered Jim, as the squeak and grind of a key turning in the padlock was borne to them on the wind.

Sooper said nothing. Presently they heard the door slam, and then he rose.

"No conversation," he warned them under his breath, and led the way towards the bungalow.

The car stood squarely before the door. Moving like a cat, he crept to its side, felt the radiator and was satisfied. The windows, he knew, were shuttered. He passed round the house to the back. There was no sound from within; no light showed. Coming back to the door, he found the padlock loose and, bending forward, listened. His efforts were unrewarded, and he came back to the man he had left by the wall.

"Somebody else is coming," he said. "She's not here for the night – she's left the car running. She's certainly heavy on juice!"

They went back to the rock that had served them for a hiding place and settled down to their vigil. A quarter of an hour, half an hour passed, and then they heard the door open and close again, and there came to them the sound of the padlock being fastened.

"She's not stayin'." Sooper was surprised: his hurt tone was that of a man who had been cheated. "Now why in thunder – get under cover, she's taken the dimmers off!"

From the little car, invisible until then, shot two rays of strong white light, but only for a second. They were dimmed again almost immediately, and so remained until the machine shot through the second opening and turned towards them. They had just time to drop out of sight when the headlamps glared out of the darkness. Again they caught a glimpse of the bowed head and the wide-brimmed hat, and then the car was gone and only the faint rear lamp gleamed dully.

Sooper rose with a growl.

"I'm apologizin'," he said. "Both deduction an' psychology are punk. She goes in and she comes out and she disappeareth no man knows whither. With a bit of luck we ought to be able to pick her up and trail her to the place where she *really* lives."

But they had some distance to travel before they could reach Jim's car, and then the inevitable happened. One of his tyres was down, and though the wheel was changed with the least possible delay, they did not pick up the Ford or see the machine again.

In Great Pawsey they surprised the village policeman, who had no information to give. He had seen the two cars go through, but until they had arrived none had returned.

"I'm leavin' you here, Lattimer – maybe they'll put you up at the cooler. I want somebody on the spot."

They came back into the storm near Horsham, and the thunder was rolling heavily when a weary Jim pulled up his car before Sooper's office.

"Come in and drink coffee," said Sooper, who had been a very silent man all the way back to town. "Maybe I can think better out of the rain. I'm certainly feeling very temp'ramental over bringing you on this fool job, Mr Ferraby. Big Foot – humph! We ought to have passed that flivver. Don't like it very much."

He sat, a bedraggled, harsh-faced man, in his chair.

"Don't like it! She couldn't have gone into Pawsey – I looked for wheel tracks as we passed. She didn't strike Great Pawsey – the intelligent officer on the street hadn't seen any Ford, an' strangely I believed him. He's an honest man – I had him with me on a case when I was at the Yard. And she didn't go into Pawsey, I'll swear. We passed the end of the road and I stopped you, didn't I? The road's all lit up and there wasn't a car track. Lattimer may send me news – I've asked him to phone."

The desk sergeant came in at that moment.

"Somebody at Great Pawsey wants to speak to you, Super-intendent."

Sooper slipped out of his chair and dashed to the old-fashioned wall phone in the charge-room.

"It's Lattimer speaking, Super: I've found that Ford car."

"Where?"

"On the top of the cliff – it must have turned off the road that leads down to the beach – Sea Hill we call it."

"Lights on or off?" asked Sooper quickly.

"Off, sir – queer thing about it that, written in chalk across the back of the car, are two words – 'Big Foot'."

"Big Foot, eh? Anything else? Nobody with it, of course?"

"No, sir."

Sooper thought quickly.

"Wake up the local sergeant and phone the chief at Pawsey. You might search the top of the cliffs and the undercliff to see if you can find anybody. I'll be right down. You've kept the house under observation? Good!"

He hung up the receiver and repeated the gist of the officer's information.

"I'm going to see," he said, "but I'll have to fix it with the Yard. I'll call up a commissioner. Go an' find Cardew an' get the key of the bungalow. Bring it back just as quick as you can."

Mr Cardew had a very small flat near Regent's Park, a *pied-à-terre* for him when he wished to spend a night in town.

Jim was fortunate, for the outer doors of the flats are locked at midnight, and it is impossible to secure admission except by waking every one of the dozen families which occupy each block. But his arrival coincided with the return of a cheery party from one of the dance clubs, and he got past the outer door and mounted to the third floor, where the amateur criminologist had his habitation.

Mr Cardew was a light sleeper, and as Jim knocked for the second time, a light appeared in the passage and the door opened to the length of the chain that held it.

"Good heavens, Ferraby!" he said, as he fumbled with the chain. "Come in – what on earth brings you here at this hour?"

In the fewest words Jim told him of the night's adventure.

"I'm sure that in the circumstances you'll forgive me," he said, "but I had to tell Minter about the threatening letter and I think he takes a serious view of the matter."

Mr Cardew rumpled his hair, which was already in a state of disorder.

"She didn't arrive until late at night?" he asked in a tone of bewilderment. "But she left Barley Stack soon after eleven. Where is she?"

"That is exactly what Minter wishes to discover," said Jim. "The car has been found abandoned, with the words 'Big Foot' written across the body. Sooper thinks that there has been foul play – in fact, the local police are at this moment searching the beach and cliff for – well, not to put it too delicately, her body."

Cardew could only shake his head.

"I can't believe it – it is too – too ghastly. I have duplicated keys, but they are in my chambers at the Temple. Just wait whilst I dress – have you a car here? If not, you had better get a cab."

He was not longer than a few minutes changing, and when he joined the caller he was dressed for a long journey.

"Of course I must go with you," he said quietly. "I couldn't possibly rest until I knew the truth about Hannah."

The machine brought them to the gates of the Temple, and Mr Cardew went quickly through the postern and returned in a few minutes with a bunch of keys.

"They are on this ring: I did not wait to search them out; we can do that later."

If Sooper was surprised to see the despised amateur he did not betray his emotion.

"Nothin' has been found on or under the cliff," he said. "Find me the keys, Mr Cardew."

With little difficulty, the lawyer discovered and detached three from the bunch.

"Are there any others than these – I mean any other duplicates?"

"No – there have never been more than two sets. One that I give to people who rent or use the cottage, and the other which is kept in my office. These, by the way, have never been used."

Just before they left on the southward journey, Sooper took the young man aside.

"I sent a feller up to Hill Brow to locate Elson. He went out at nine last night and hasn't returned. He took his two-seater Rolls, and his chauffeur did not go with him. I'm tellin' you this – maybe you'll hear more about it when the case comes up to the Prosecutor's office. Know Cardew's gard'ner?"

"You were asking about him the other night?"

"Yuh," said Sooper, and did not pursue the subject.

Jim took the wheel and again the long car roared along the Horsham Road, but this time with less caution, for the road was empty, the streets of Horsham itself a place of the dead. The storm had finally passed, stars showed between the cloud wrack, and in something over the hour the machine had stopped before the tiny building that served as lodging for the village sergeant and a lock-up for the infrequent tramps who outraged the laws of Great Pawsey.

The sergeant was waiting for them, and two detectives from the more important Pawsey.

"We've found nothing, sir," reported the sergeant, "but one of our villagers saw a woman walking towards the sea road and go down the hill."

"When was this?"

"About two hours ago. He said she came from the direction of the railway station – Pawsey Halt, which is midway between here and the town. The last train from London stops at the Halt but I haven't been able to find the station man."

"She wasn't coming from the railway at all," said Sooper. 'She may have been trying to give that impression. Do you ever use the Halt, Mr Cardew?"

"I have got down there once during the war," said Cardew; "usually if I come by rail, I go into the terminus at Pawsey and drive out by a station fly."

"Has Hannah Shaw been in the habit of coming by rail?"

Cardew shook his head,

"Not since 1918," he said. "We spent a very considerable time here during the war: during the weekends when air raids were likely we came down here for quiet."

The derelict car had not been moved, the sergeant told them, and they found the machine in the position described by the policeman. It was easy to understand why they had passed it on their way to Great Pawsey. The car had been driven up a gentle bank and down into the steep of a hollow on the other side. It was out of sight from the hill road, which in the last fifty yards ran through a cutting.

With the aid of his lamp Sooper examined the machine carefully. The chalked inscription on the back, though it excited Mr Cardew, did not seem to interest the old police officer.

"It isn't white chalk – it's green!" said Cardew. "Billiard chalk?"

"Maybe we'll find her in a billiard saloon," snarled Sooper. "Let us look for the cue!"

Whereafter Mr Cardew preserved a dignified silence.

Sooper's most thorough inspection was of the car's interior. He inspected the hood inch by inch and presently lowered it before, standing on the running-board, he brought the light of his torch slowly along the floor and the seat, both in the driving and the passenger space.

"The seat is scratched…recent scratches too, the canvas shows, and it is quite clean. No mud on the foot brake or clutch. There's nothing here of consequence."

They came back to Jim's machine.

"Have you been down to the bungalow, Sergeant?" Sooper asked, and Lattimer answered yes.

"Nobody is there; the place has been watched since you left – there is a man watching now."

Sooper stepped into the car by Jim's side, and the local officers, finding what accommodation they could on the footboard, the car went down the hill and struck the beach road. This time it went on to the house and the men descended.

"How horribly eerie!" said Cardew with a shiver. "I have never realized how lonely and desolate this place of mine is!"

The car had been stopped, at Sooper's suggestion, so that the light of the headlamps fell on the door.

"The padlock is on; she's not here."

Sooper was unmoved by the discovery.

"Never expected she was," he said. "But she was here. She came for something. Did she have any kind of belongings here, Mr Cardew?"

The lawyer shook his head.

"None, except those she may have brought today," he said.

"She brought nothing today," replied Sooper emphatically. "Did she keep anything in a cupboard or wardrobe?"

"Nothing, so far as I know."

Sooper fitted the key in the padlock and the lock turned easily enough. There was a lock to the door, and when this had been dealt with and the door opened, Sooper flashed his lamp into the dark interior.

It was a small lobby. Beyond was a second door, the upper half of which was panelled in glass. It opened at a touch and he found himself in a narrow passage that ran from the front to the back of the house.

"Stay where you are," he warned them. "I'm goin' to make a search an' I guess I'd like to be alone."

The two rooms opening from the passage on the right were first explored. They were bedrooms, very plainly furnished. The beds had been stripped of clothes, and he guessed that the linen was in the locked presses that he found in each apartment.

He went back to the front of the house and examined the first room on the left. It was a dining-room, and a quick examination revealed no remarkable feature. In one wall was an opening covered by a shutter, evidently a servery communicating with the kitchen, which was the only room now left unexplored. He tried the kitchen door: it was locked, and he went back to the waiting men.

"Have you got the kitchen key?" he asked.

"No," said Cardew in surprise. "There is a key to the kitchen – but it is never taken away. Isn't it in the lock?"

Sooper returned and tried the handle, but the door was fast. And then he began to sniff, and called Jim.

"Smell anything?" he asked. "Seems like somethin' burnin' to me."

Ferraby could detect a peculiarly pungent odour that was queerly familiar to him.

"Cordite!" he said suddenly. "A rifle or revolver has been fired here – and recently!"

"Thought it was," said Sooper calmly. "Got an idea I knew that hot-iron smell. Door's locked from inside."

He went back to the dining-room. The shutter of the servery was fast – he found a small keyhole and this time called Cardew.

"Yes, it locks but I have no idea where the key is. It was there during the time my secretary was here, Miss Leigh, and its loss has not been reported. It fastens with a spring catch, and if it were closed by accident it could not be opened without a key. I never had a duplicate. Can't you get into the kitchen?"

"No – that's fastened on the inside."

"Then break the shutter," suggested Cardew, and guided Lattimer to a little outhouse where a few rusty tools were kept.

A small case-opener was found, and Sooper, fixing the claw between shutter and wall, worked at the lock. Presently, with a crash, it broke, and he slid back the cover. Now the rank smell of cordite was marked – even Cardew began to sniff.

"What smell is that?" he asked, but Sooper did not hear him.

Leaning through the opening, he was searching the room with his lamp, and suddenly the white circle of light, moving slowly along the floor towards the door, revealed a boot. The toe was pointing to the ceiling…the light moved…another foot, the edge of a dark skirt.

A woman sat with her back to the door, her head sunk forward drunkenly on her breast. Sooper could not see her face, but he knew it was Hannah Shaw, and he did not need the evidence of the rivulets of blood on the floor to know that she was dead.

THE VISITOR

Sooper withdrew his head slowly from the aperture.

"Everybody had better stay here," he said. "Sergeant, go find a doctor... Mr Ferraby, you can drive the officer...no, I guess you'd better stay. You may be concerned in this case."

Lattimer volunteered to drive the car to the village, and, after a whispered consultation with Sooper, departed hurriedly.

"Not that any doctor's goin' to be any use."

"What has happened?" asked Cardew tremulously. "My God...not Hannah?"

Sooper nodded.

"I'm afraid it is, Mr Cardew," he said gently.

"Hurt...dead?"

Again Sooper inclined his head.

"Yes: you'd best stay here. Follow me, Mr Ferraby. Use a chair to stand on."

With an unexpected agility he wriggled through the hole in the wall, and Jim followed.

"Pull the shutter close: I'm going to light the lamp."

Sooper lifted the glass chimney of a small kerosene lamp that stood on the kitchen table, and lit it carefully, laying the matchstick on the table.

Jim Ferraby was gazing awe-stricken at the inanimate figure by the door.

"Is it suicide?" he asked, almost in a whisper.

"If it is, we'll find the gun," replied Sooper. "She's dead...that's a fact. I'm sorry I got so fresh with her. She wasn't a bad woman – as women go."

He stooped down and peered into the colourless face.

"Not suicide," he said, almost cheerfully. "Never thought it was. Murder – but how? Here's the door locked on the inside – see the key? And the servery shutter locked, key on the inside – notice that too?" He tried the heavy shutters that covered the window: they were bolted.

On the table was a woman's handbag, which had evidently been turned out, for a medley of small feminine belongings and a packet of paper money was scattered on the table.

"Fifty-five pounds English and two thousand dollars in American bills," said Sooper, counting. "What's the brick mean?"

It was a red brick, well-worn on one surface. Attached to this was a circle of rubber, which in turn was attached to a string.

"The floor is of red brick," said Jim.

"Yes...noticed that."

Sooper took up the lamp and stooped, searching the floor. Immediately under the centre of the table was an oblong cavity that the brick exactly fitted.

"The rubber is what we used to call a 'sucker' when I was a boy," meditated Sooper. "They call 'em 'vacu-ums' nowadays: that's how he or she pulled out the brick."

Going down on his knees with the lamp at his side, he peered into the shallow hole.

"There's been something hid here," he said; "that's what she came down to get. I wondered why she only stayed a little while."

"But how did she get back...the front door was padlocked from the outside?"

Sooper shook his head.

"Got a lot of things to think about just now," he said. "Anyway, we did come down for *something*!"

Again he squatted down before the quiet figure, his unlighted pipe clenched between his teeth, a frown of anxious concern adding to the lines of his forehead.

"Can't move her till the doctor comes," he said, getting up again. "She was shot at close range – he must have stood on this side of the table…somewhere about here," he pointed. "Probably an automatic, though I can't see the shell anywhere. She was standing to the right of the door: see the mark on the wall. Then she walked a step and slid down by the door. Bullet went through the heart, I think, and dead people often walk a pace or two. Left glove on an' right glove off. She never intended stayin'. Do you notice anything, Mr Ferraby, anything very remarkable?"

Jim shook his head helplessly.

"There are so many things that are remarkable that I can't differentiate," he said.

Sooper's nose wrinkled.

"Cardew would have seen it before I did," he said. "She's got no hat on – *and* no coat."

It was true the figure was bareheaded; there was no sign of coat or mackintosh.

"An' look at that clothes peg on the wall…see anything on the ground?"

"Water," said Jim.

"Ran off her raincoat. She hung it up when she came in the first time, anyway. Where did she leave her coat and hat?"

"Probably they are in one of the other rooms," suggested Ferraby, and the old man showed his teeth.

"They're not in the house. I didn't comb the rooms, but I had a good look at 'em. And those clothes are not in this house!"

His tone was exultant. It was as though he had achieved some great personal triumph.

"There's the doctor," he said. "He'll have to come through the hole in the wall, an' if he's fat he'll hate it."

The doctor proved to be a young man, who made light of the business of entering the kitchen.

There was never any doubt what the verdict would be.

"No, I could not say how long she has been dead. Certainly over an hour. I have 'phoned for an ambulance. Sergeant Lattimer told me what had happened."

Sooper looked at his watch: it was half after three.

"I'll wait till she's gone before I do any more," he said.

When, a few minutes later, the motor ambulance had arrived and the pitiable object had been removed, Sooper unbarred the shutters and opened the window. Only Jim and he remained of the party. Mr Cardew had been taken away in a state of collapse, and Lattimer had gone away with the ambulance to make a search.

"And a pretty good thing too," said Sooper heartlessly. "I couldn't have stood for his psychologizin'. It's pretty dark for close on four," he said, looking out of the window, "but it's still rainin'. Fine English summer weather. Look at that." He laid on the table a long yellow envelope. "Found it under her when she was moved," he said.

Jim examined the cover.

"Empty," he said, and read the typewritten address and gasped.

DR JOHN W MILLS,
Coronor of West Sussex,
Hailsham, Sussex.

"Then it was – suicide?"

Sooper folded the envelope before he replied.

"Dr Mills hasn't been coroner of West Sussex since five years," he said, "that bein' the amount of time he's been dead. I happen to be certain about that because I went to his funeral."

"But whoever wrote that didn't know?"

"They certainly didn't know," said Sooper, with a touch of his old mysteriousness.

Jim watched him prying about the kitchen, peeking into ovens, opening cupboards, pulling out drawers, and the realization of the tragedy began to grow on him. It had been so terrifically sudden and unexpected that he could not absorb its true significance. And, strangely enough, his first thought was the effect which this tremendous happening would have upon Elfa Leigh. She would be shocked beyond measure, pained more because she disliked the woman.

"It's certainly a wonderful murder," said Sooper, with an ecstatic sigh, as he stopped to light his pipe. "I'm glad I called up the commissioner. He's a good feller an' maybe he'll let me hold the case. That man knows when a thing's in good hands. He's intelligent. I wonder why they keep him at the Yard. If he puts another man in charge, he ain't fit for his job – few of these guys are. They get pushed into jobs because their wives have got a pull with the Secretary of State…" he proceeded libellously.

"No weapon of any kind in the place," he went on, "no shell on the floor. Nothin' but an empty envelope addressed to the coroner…did Miss Shaw use a typewriter, do you know, Mr Ferraby?"

"I believe she did: Mr Cardew told me that she had an old one."

"It was written by an amachoor," said Sooper, taking the envelope from his pocket, "and somebody who hasn't written 'coroner' very often – it's spelt wrong. Few people can spell on a typewriter. I got to have that raked for fingerprints."

He had dug the bullet from the wall, a bent steel cylinder, and it lay on the table.

"That's a .42 automatic," he said, as he put away the envelope. "Same calibre as those in the magazine we picked up on the lawn. Not an unusual size of gun, so don't draw conclusions: they are only made in two sizes. She couldn't have owned one; women are afraid of firearms, and besides, Cardew would have known."

"Where has he gone?" asked Jim.

"Into Pawsey – to the Grand Hotel." Sooper chuckled quietly. "When the'ry gets into the ring with fact, he takes the count in the first round. Here's a big fact – death by violence. To sit around in a comfortable armchair an' play a fiddle an' th'rize is one thing; to come up against the smell of blood an' general nastiness is another…"

He stopped and bent his head, listening. Through the open window came the ceaseless "hush hush" of the waves striking the sandy beach.

"There's somebody fumblin' at the door," he said, and, picking up the lamp, walked softly into the passage.

Jim heard it now and his flesh crept. A soft scratching sound, the swish of hands passing over the panels, and then the door handle turned a little.

Sooper looked at Jim and his nod was an instruction. Jim Ferraby crept forward, turned the key quickly and pulled open the door.

Standing on the step was a slim figure, rain-drenched, dishevelled. She stared at the young man stupidly.

"Help me," she muttered, as she stumbled forward into his arms.

It was Elfa Leigh!

"Don't move – listen!"

Sooper hissed the words, and Jim stood motionless, the unconscious girl in his arms. From somewhere in the darkness and from far away came the mournful cadences of a song:

> "The Moorish king rides up and down
> Through Granada's royal town,
> *Ay de mi Alhama!*"

"Hell!" roared Sooper, as he put down the lamp and dashed past them into the night.

ELFA'S STORY

Day had broken greyly when he came back to record his failure.

"He must have been singing from the top of the cliff," he grumbled. "That musical tramp gets an engagement first time I reach within gunshot of his nibs! Now, what about this young lady?"

"I've built a fire for her in one of the bedrooms," said Jim. "She is quite recovered."

"Have you told her anything?"

Jim shook his head.

"No, I didn't think that was wise in her present state. Poor girl, she's had a terrible time."

Elfa heard the voices in the passage and opened the door an inch.

"Is that Mr Minter? I will be out in a little while."

She appeared in a few minutes, wrapped in Jim's mackintosh, her bare feet thrust into a pair of old slippers which she had found in the linen press.

"Where is Miss Shaw?" was the first question she asked. "Has anything happened? Why are you here?"

"Well, we just came down to have a look round," said Sooper calmly. "Got an idea of takin' the place for the summer."

"Where is Miss Shaw?" she asked again.

"She's gone away," said Sooper.

The girl looked from one face to the other, trying to read the grim riddle of their presence.

"Something *has* happened."

"It seems to have happened to you, Miss Leigh, anyway," said Sooper good-naturedly. "How did you come to be around here in the middle of the night?"

"Miss Shaw sent for me," was the unexpected reply.

She went back to the bedroom and returned with two telegraph forms covered with writing. Sooper adjusted his pince-nez and read. The telegram was addressed to Elfa at her lodgings in Cubitt Street.

I want you to do me a very great favour. As soon as you receive this come to Mr Cardew's cottage on Pawsey Beach. If I am not there wait for me. However late you arrive you must come. Have never asked you favour before but your presence will have an influence on my life. I want you to be witness to a very important matter. I appeal to you as one woman to another.

It was signed "Hannah Shaw". The telegram had been dispatched from Guildford, Surrey, at six o'clock the previous night.

"I received it soon after seven," said Elfa, "and I really didn't know what to do. The fact that I do not like Miss Shaw very much made my task all the more difficult. At last I decided I would go, and after dinner I caught the last train at ten o'clock, and got down at the station Halt – "

"Then it was you the villagers saw crossing from the direction of the station?" interrupted Sooper. "Of course! That removes one of the stumbling blocks to my theory. Go on, Miss Leigh. What were you doing between then and the time we found you?"

"There is a footpath down the face of the cliff which cuts off much of the road," the girl continued. "I know every inch of the ground and have explored the cliffs as far as Pawsey, so I didn't have any doubt about finding my way, the more so since I brought a little pocket-lamp with me, and that helped considerably. There was another reason why I came down the cliff path: it was a terribly stormy night and the cliff gave me cover from the rain. What I didn't know was that there had been a landslide here last summer, and halfway down the path had been swept out of existence. The first knowledge I had was when I stepped on a loose stone and found myself sliding down, as I thought, to certain death. I found myself lying on a narrow ledge of chalk, and, not daring to move, I lay there, waiting for the light. I saw two cars come along the road: one went to the cottage, which was quite visible from where I lay, and the other didn't seem to pass much farther than the end of the sea road. I shouted in the hope that I would be heard, but the wind must have carried my voice away. You can't imagine how desolate I felt when I saw the two cars disappear and I was left alone. I was terrified. I think I must have got hysterical, for I imagined the strangest things happening." She shuddered as at an unpleasant memory.

"Did you see anybody?"

"No, nobody."

"No tramps or anything?"

"No. I lay quiet till, two or three hours later, a car appeared – I suppose it was yours – and stopped at the door. And then I grew desperate, and tried to crawl inch by inch across the face of the slope. And of course I failed. I went down, down…oh, it was dreadful! And yet it wasn't so terrible after all, for I landed at the bottom without hurt and within a few yards of the house. I don't know how I walked to the door."

Sooper took the telegram from her hand and read it again.

" 'I want you to be witness to a very important matter,' " he read, and scratched his chin.

"Where is Miss Shaw?" she asked again.

She read the answer in Sooper's eyes and shrank back, white-faced.

"Not…not dead?"

He nodded.

"Naturally? Or…oh, no!"

"She was shot – there." He jerked his head towards the kitchen. "Now listen, Miss Leigh; you are going to be an important witness, because you lay in sight of the cottage all night. No other cars came but those you have described?"

"None – I'm sure of that."

"Did you see anybody walking along the road on foot – did you see Miss Shaw return?"

"No. I would not in any circumstances. It was very dark indeed. I only saw the cars because of their lights – I should not have seen or heard them otherwise."

Sooper was disappointed.

"Everything depends now on that commissioner: if he keeps me on the job, I can see daylight. But if he sends any of them long-nosed the'rists, justice is goin' to get a jolt. I've got the locals in the holler of my hand…it's these anthr'pologists I'm scared of."

Jim knew that the decision as to whether Scotland Yard should be called in was largely determined by the wishes of the local authorities. Except in the area of London, Scotland Yard has no official position. Local authorities may, and generally do, ask the help of the Yard when they consider that they have a case too big to deal with. Outside of London the local police make arrests even when a criminal is "wanted" for an offence in the Metropolis.

Elfa sat shocked to speechlessness by the news. Hannah Shaw dead! She could hardly believe it possible.

"As soon as your clothes are dry I'll get Mr Ferraby to take you back to town," said Sooper. "I suppose there's nothing more you can tell us?"

"Nothing," she said numbly. "How terrible, how terrible!"

"You use the typewriter, don't you? Did you type this?" He showed her the envelope.

"No, that is not my work," she said. "It wasn't even typed on my machine. I believe Miss Shaw had an old machine of her own that she used – in fact, I know, because she once asked me to recommend her a good book on typewriting."

It was broad daylight now, and though the skies were grey, the rain had ceased to fall. Leaving the girl to dry her clothes, the two men walked out of the front door, and Sooper scrutinized the cliff with interest.

"Just as Lattimer says, the face of the cliff is honeycombed."

He pointed to the hundreds of little black gaps that showed in the white chalk.

"If anybody's there, it's goin' to be difficult to find them," he said. "At the same time, logic an' deduction tells me it's just as hard for a fellow who lives there to *get* there. I don't think it's goin' to be possible or practicable to make a search of any except the lower caves, and I'll have the police workin' on that today."

As he turned his head to look up the road, Jim's car, with Lattimer at the wheel, swung into view. Lattinier pulled up the machine near his chief and jumped out.

"I only found one thing of any importance," he said, "and this is it."

He took out of his coat packet a small chamois leather bag, a little bigger than a postage stamp, which was attached to a thin gold chain.

"This was round her neck," he said, as he put the find into his chief's hand.

Sooper pulled open the neck of the bag and shook out on to his palm a bright gold ring.

"Looks to me like a wedding ring," he said. "No marriage certificate?"

Lattimer shook his head.

"Nothing, sir. In fact, we did not find a document of any description."

Sooper looked at the glistening object on his palm.

"A wedding ring, and a new wedding ring," he said thoughtfully. "The question is, did she ever wear it? It looks as if she didn't. The man who put this on knows considerably more about this murder than we shall ever learn."

They walked leisurely by the side of the house towards the beach. The tide was coming in.

"It's a pretty lonely spot," admitted Sooper, "and I think I'll take back all I said about this bein' the place I'd like to retire to."

Far out to sea was the trailing smoke of a steamer. Nearer at hand, a fleet of red-sailed fishing boats were making for Pawsey Harbour.

Behind the bungalow was a patch of garden, but the fence which surrounded it was broken and the little gate hung crazily. Weeds grew in rank profusion where Mr Cardew had fought a losing battle against wind and spindrift.

"At the same time," Sooper said, "it's not a bad place for a feller who likes sea bathin'."

They ploughed through the sand to the gate. Here the sand was firmer.

"Not a bad place for a bit of sea bathin' for those who like it," murmured Sooper again, and said nothing more.

Jim saw the look of bewilderment which came to the old man's face, saw his jaw drop.

"Suffering snakes!" said Sooper.

He was looking down at a footprint, half obliterated by the rain, but all too distinct. It was the print of a huge, naked foot, some eighteen inches in length, and broad in proportion.

"Christopher Columbus!" muttered Sooper, staring fascinated.

He turned his eyes towards the sea, and slowly walked in that direction. The prints were clearer as they reached the hard sand, and they went in one direction, towards the house.

Big Foot!

Those words meant something, after all.

Not until they came to the sea's edge did they stop, though the prints persisted, and they saw them again in a shallow pool, lately made by the incoming tide. Sooper looked at Jim.

"Got any the'ries or deductions?"

"I'll admit I haven't," confessed Jim.

"That's too bad, because I haven't either, not at the minute. Merciful Moses! but this has got me properly temp'ramental!"

He sent Lattimer into the town to get some plaster of paris, and they spent an hour making moulds of the more distinct of the footprints.

And all the time, from the mouth of one of the inaccessible caverns which pitted the sheer cliffs like a disease, a brown-faced, bearded man lay full length on the floor, watching them out of bright eyes that sparkled with foolish laughter. And as he watched, he sang softly to himself the tale of Alhama.

THE SEALED ENVELOPE

Though Jim Ferraby was half dead for want of sleep, he was compelled to listen to the man who sat by his side as he drove the car towards Pawsey. For Sooper was brighter and more garrulous than Jim ever remembered him. He might have risen from a long and refreshing sleep, he was so very alert.

"It takes years to make a good *pukka* detective. Take Lattimer now: you'd think he knew the game thor'ly. But does he? No, sir. He didn't find that wash-leather bag with the ring in it. An' yet he must have seen it because he knocked it on the floor when the search was goin' on, an' the ring wouldn't have been found at all only one of the locals remembered takin' the chain off an' searched around for it. There's too much deduction about these young officers an' not enough look-see. Tired?"

"Damnably," replied Jim.

"Try to think you're enjoyin' yourself," said Sooper. "Fancy you're dancin' with the girl of your heart – sent her back to London by the first train."

"Who?" asked Jim, startled. "You mean Miss Leigh…what do you mean by 'girl of your heart,' Sooper?"

"I'm naturally disconnected in conversation," said Sooper gently. "If I've made the forks pass I apologize."

"Forks – oh, you mean *faux pas?*" smiled Jim. "Your French is horrible, Sooper."

"It's nothin' to my English," said Sooper, and sighed. "Poor soul! she was always throwin' that up into my face – that I was short on

74

class. An' now she's dead an' I'm alive. Which shows that education's nothin' but an illusion. Is that psychology?"

"Sort of," said Jim.

"Maybe it's ant'ropology," suggested Sooper. "This place is certainly gettin' more an' more like an amusement park every time I see it! An' to think that it was once an honest-to-Peter fishin' hole that didn't know the difference between a cabaray an' a consommy!"

Pawsey in the bright sunlight, with its gilded domes and its magnificent stucco fronts, was almost impressive. Its wide promenade was already crowded with holiday-makers, its yellow beach speckled with loungers.

The car drew up before the Grand Hotel, and a resplendent porter fussed forward and assisted them to alight. Mr Cardew had had the good fortune to find a vacant suite facing the sea, and he was in bed, but very wide awake, when the two men came in.

"Is there any news?" he asked, almost before the door closed behind them. "Poor Hannah is dead?"

Sooper told him of the wedding ring that had been found, and Mr Cardew sat bolt upright in bed.

"Married? Hannah married? Impossible!" he said vigorously. "I don't care what information you have, or what you have discovered: Hannah Shaw is not married!"

"Why are you so certain, Mr Cardew?"

The pale face of Gordon Cardew was puckered in thought, and it was a little time before he answered, and then in a less agitated tone.

"I have acted as Hannah's lawyer for many years," he said. "She had no secret that I do not know. She might have felt some affection for a – a certain person, and I have been contemplating the possibility of her marrying for some time; but she could not get married without my consent!"

Even Sooper was dumbfounded.

"But why?" he asked, and Cardew's explanation was a simple one. When his wife died, she had left Hannah Shaw an annuity – a very considerable sum – on condition that she did not marry without her husband's consent.

"My poor wife could not bear the idea of my being left alone without somebody to look after me," said Cardew. "That was the object of the legacy, the conditions being that she remained in my employ, and, as I say, that she did not marry."

"How much was the annuity?"

"About two hundred pounds a year, a considerable sum to Hannah. With one exception," he went on, after a second's hesitation, "Hannah Shaw told me all her secrets, the exception being that, about three years ago, she gave me a large sealed envelope, which she asked me to keep for her. I very naturally asked what these documents were that she had given to me for safe keeping, but here she resolutely refused to supply information. Naturally I did not press her, because her history had been a very unhappy one. We took her from a charity institute, and there was some mystery about her parentage, which I have never been curious enough to investigate or attempt to investigate. She, on the other hand, never ceased to make inquiries, and I have an idea that the envelope contained the results of her search."

Sooper nodded.

"That certainly is highly mysterious," he said, "and of course I shall have to get that envelope. Where is it kept?"

"In my rooms in King's Bench Walk," said Cardew. "If you care to send up today, you will find it in a small black japanned box, marked 'H S'. It is one of the very few deed boxes that remain in my office. There are certain other papers which include, if I remember aright, a copy of the clause in my wife's will, the correspondence we had with the manager of the orphanage, her birth certificate and similar documents, more or less unimportant."

He reached out and pulled his clothes from a chair, and handed the superintendent a bunch of keys.

"Here are the keys of the office." And then, "You have made no fresh discoveries?"

"None," said Sooper. "How she came back and got in, with Lattimer practically sitting on the doorstep, is certainly one of the most remarkable pieces of conjury that has ever been known in a murder case."

"Lattimer was there all the time?" asked Cardew quickly.

"All the time, sir," said Sooper emphatically.

Mr Cardew fingered his unshaven chin.

"I have my own theories, but I would like to test them before I put them to work," he said.

He saw Sooper's lips curl, and, in spite of his distress, smiled wanly.

"You are not a great believer in theories? Yet I will swear that my theory as to how the murderer escaped from the kitchen is accurate."

"Let's hear it," said Sooper, a little coldly.

"The two went into the kitchen – poor Hannah and the murderer. Either he or she turned the key. The murder was committed, and she fell against the door. The man hadn't the nerve to move the body, and decided to escape by way of the servery. The key in the lock must have given him that suggestion. Once he was in the dining-room, it was a simple matter to pull the shutter close, and as it is a spring lock..."

Sooper smacked his knee.

"That's it, that's just it!" he agreed with some reluctance. "That's certainly a wonderful piece of the'rizin', and I wouldn't be surprised if you're nearly right. But how did he get in and get out without Lattimer seein' him?"

"There is a back door – " began Cardew.

"Bolted and locked on the inside," replied Sooper promptly. "All the windows are shuttered and the shutters are covered with bars, and nobody got in or out that way. If the murderer escaped by the back door, how did he bolt the door behind him? No, Mr Cardew, that's no solution.'

Cardew nodded slowly.

"I agree," he said, "and I'll admit that that wasn't my idea at all. Perhaps some day I will outline a hypothesis that will be acceptable even to you, Superintendent."

On the way down the stairs, Sooper said: " 'Hypothesis' is a new one on me. When these fellers start talkin' Latin I'm sunk! But he's surely right about the way the murderer escaped from the kitchen, and

I'm disappointed. I thought he'd the'rize a secret panel in the wall, or a subterranean passage under the floor; or one of them cleverly concealed doorways that looks like a bookshelf, and you've only got to touch a spring, or maybe two springs, and it turns round or stands up or turns in, as the case may be, and there's a long flight of stairs with an earthy smell."

"Sooper, I believe you've been reading popular literature," laughed Jim.

"I read everything except the finance columns, and I'd read them, only they're so full of figgers."

For same extraordinary reason, Jim no longer felt tired when he took his place at the wheel and guided the car through the crowded streets of Pawsey into the open country. And if he were tired, Sooper would have kept him awake, for the old man was unusually talkative and devoted the first twenty-five miles of the journey to London to a discourse dealing with the advantages and disadvantages of popular education.

"When I joined the force, readin' an' writin' an' figgerin' were all that a chap needed. If you pinched more burglars and tea-leaves* than any other detective officer, you got promoted, even though you mightn't know the least thing about the differentious – what's the word? Something about calculation – "

"Differential calculus," suggested Jim.

"That's the feller. No, you didn't need to know anythin' about bot'ny, or whatever department that diff'rential thing belongs to, or zoology or psychology or nothin'. The only thing you had to do was to keep your eyes skinned and catch the lad in the act. If you pinched a feller that was bigger than you and he started somethin' rough, you were expected to know somethin' about anat'my, such as the proper place to hit him with your stick. But that was practically all the science there was in the old days. I never used a microscope except to examine my pay. And test-chubes and things like that, which the swell detectives use to find out whether the stain on the cuff was blood or

* London thieves' argot for their own profession.

beer, were never seen in any police station that I've frequented. Look-see and catch-hold was the shining motto of the police force. I'm not disparaging education. Personally, I'd like to speak six languages and be able to converse graceful in Swahili. But I've got on pretty well without these accomplishments. I'm going up to Cardew's office to take a look at that envelope of Hannah Shaw's: maybe you'll come along with me?"

The worshippers were streaming out of Temple Church when the mud-stained car stopped before Cardew's chambers. Jim, who knew the place, led the way up the stairs to the big oak outer door. In the Temple every set of chambers has a double door: the "oak" which, when closed, means that the inmate does not wish to be disturbed, and which stands open in his office hours; and the inner door, which, open or closed, is an invitation to enter. The "oak" was unfastened; the detective was slipping the big key into the keyhole when he felt the door yielding to his pressure.

"It's not locked," he said, and walked in.

They were in a narrow passage, a door on the right leading, as Jim knew, into Elfa Leigh's office. This door was closed, but that which opened into Mr Cardew's sanctum was wide open.

Sooper stood in the doorway, silently surveying the room for a minute. Then: "Looks as if we've come rather late," he drawled.

The few deed boxes that the office contained lay on the floor, their contents scattered in all directions. Cardew's roll-top desk was wide open and its surface littered with papers.

"Certainly looks as if someone's been here before us," said Sooper again.

He turned the open boxes over one by one.

"Here's the 'H S'," he said, "and it's empty."

LATTIMER'S UNCLE

He looked round slowly until his eyes rested on the grate. It was filled with blackened ashes, which must have been carefully stirred so that the last vestige of writing was destroyed. The drawers of the desk had been pulled out and thrown on the floor, and when a systematic search of the papers was concluded, no trace of any envelope, or, indeed, of any document affecting Hannah, was discoverable.

Sooper picked up the black box marked "H S" and put it on a table, drawing table and box to the light of the window.

"No damage here," he said. "It was opened with a key."

He put down the box and, crossing to the fireplace, knelt down and began to lift out the ashes delicately. He was ten minutes at his task before he rose and dusted his knees, and then he began to look round the floor. Presently he stooped and picked up a scarlet match-stalk, which he examined curiously.

"I ought to be able to say right off who made this match, and how many people in London use the brand. All I *can* say is that it was struck to light the paper in the grate and not for purposes of illum'nation."

He scrutinized the windows, pulled gingerly at a blind and drew it down. As he did so, a piece of paper that had been caught up on the roller fluttered to the floor. He stooped and picked it up. It was a tradesman's receipt for a small sum.

"Blown against the blind on a windy day," said Sooper, "just as the blind sash had been released. Ain't nature wonderful? And that's deduction. We'll have to notify the City Police about this, and I'll go down tonight to see old man Cardew, and break it to him gently, and if I know anything about him, he'll be almost as much upset by the burglary as he was by the murder. That's the worst of being a lawyer: it breaks your heart to lose papers."

Jim accompanied him to the City Police office, and at last, glad to be released, he went back to his home, and, without troubling to undress, lay down aim his bed and fell instantly to sleep.

It was past sunset when he awoke, and his first thought was of Elfa Leigh. He did not risk telephoning, but, finding a taxi, drove to Cubitt Street, and, by great good fortune, met her on the doorstep coming out.

"Have you seen Mr Minter?" was her first question. "He left a few minutes ago."

"Doesn't that man ever sleep?" asked Jim in amazement. And then: "Did he tell you about the burglary at the office?"

She nodded.

"He came for that purpose this afternoon," she said, as she walked by his side. "Apparently the burglars didn't go into my office at all, for the door was locked. Do you know about Big Foot?" she asked suddenly.

Jim wondered why Sooper had told her of this discovery – he had carefully kept the alarming intelligence from Mr Cardew.

"He wanted to know whether I had ever heard the name used," she went on, unconsciously answering his unspoken question, "and of course I had not. What is the association, Mr Ferraby?"

He told her.

"No, I have never heard of Big Foot. It is all very terrible and mysterious. I can't believe that it's true that Miss Shaw is dead: it is too horrible to think about."

She was walking towards Holborn, and Jim was speculating as to what had brought her out at that hour of the evening, unless she was on her way to the park. She stopped at the corner of Kingsway.

"And now I'm going to unravel a little mystery of my own," she said with a faint smile, "and it is so very unimportant that I wouldn't dare to ask your assistance, although it is mysterious."

"The smaller the mystery, the more useful I shall be," said Jim eagerly, "and the only reason I suggest you should go, wherever you're going, by taxi, is a purely selfish one: I can smoke."

"You can smoke on top of a bus," she said, as he called a cab. "Taxis are bad habits."

Nevertheless, she made no other protest, and gave an address in Edwards Square.

"I am going to see my tenant," she explained. "That sounds very grand, doesn't it? When daddy died, he left me the house we had been living in. It's a very small property, but much too large for me. I have put it out to rent, and the income, small as it is, is very acceptable. I'm not afraid of losing my tenant, because house property is at a premium; but the poor little man is getting more and more nervous about the eggs, and I'm afraid if something isn't done he will find another house."

"The eggs?" said the puzzled Jim.

She nodded solemnly.

"Eggs; sometimes potatoes; occasionally a few cabbages. But eggs constitute the principal mystery, because they come more frequently. Mr Lattimer treated it as a joke, of course – "

"Lattimer?" interrupted Jim. "Is he any relation to the gallant sergeant?"

'His uncle. I only discovered today, when Sergeant Lattimer was bringing me up to town, that Mr Bolderwood Lattimer is a very well-to-do provision merchant and a bachelor. I don't think that the sergeant and he are on speaking terms; at any rate, they're not very friendly, because Sergeant Lattimer said he had never been to Edwards Square, and that his uncle disapproved of his being in the police; he thought he was lowering the family standard."

She laughed softly.

"But please tell me about the eggs."

"And the potatoes!" she added. "The whole thing is so absurd that I thought it was a joke when I heard about it first. Ever since Mr Bolderwood Lattimer has been living at 178 Edwards Square, these extraordinary gifts have been arriving. Usually they are found on his doorstep in the early morning, and, as I say, the donations range from eggs to carrots! Sometimes there will be a dozen potatoes, wrapped in a dirty old piece of newspaper, but invariably during the summer months these gifts are accompanied by flowers. Mr Lattimer's servant opened the door on Friday morning and found the top of a lilac tree, with a dozen sticks of asparagus! It has lasted too long to be a practical joke, and it seems to be getting on my tenant's nerves. I'm rather glad you came, because you may find some solution."

Edwards Square is a secluded and jealously preserved atom of late Georgian London: a place of small houses, of green forecourts. Here the laburnum drops its golden tassels to the sidewalk, and window-boxes blaze with flowers.

Mr Bolderwood Lattimer saw the cab stop and came down the little path to meet them. He was short and stout and bald. He had the austere countenance and the rubicund complexion of one (as Jim mentally decided) who might conceivably be a churchwarden with a taste for port.

"Come in, Miss Leigh," he said, and graciously inclined his head in acknowledgment of Jim's presence. "You got my note? I am sorry to have bothered you, but really, this thing is becoming an intolerable nuisance."

He led the way to a mid-Victorian drawing-room, an apartment in which flower-bordered carpets seemed strangely in harmony with stiff, horsehair-covered furniture.

"The truth is," he said, "that I was almost inclined to complain to the police. Hitherto, I have regarded these extraordinary marks of attention in the nature of a practical joke, or possibly an attempt on the part of some poor creature I have helped to reward me, in his humble way, for my charity."

He was pompous and oracular; had a trick of pointing his arguments with the end of his pince-nez.

"I have now reached the conclusion, and I think that there is justification for my view, that the almost weekly appearance of these articles is nothing more or less than the act of some ill-balanced vulgarian, to remind me that I am, in fact, a tradesman. A successful man makes enemies," he went on. "There are certain people, whose names I would not wish to mention, who bitterly resented my election to the Town Council of the Royal Borough of Kensington: members, I regret to say, of my own church. I do not profess to be engaged in any other profession than that of commerce. These insults are, therefore, a little superfluous."

"What time are these things usually left on your doorstep?" asked Jim, after he had been introduced.

"Between midnight and three o'clock in the morning," was the reply. "I have sat up several nights in the hope of catching the scoundrel in the act, and of demanding an explanation, failing which I should, of course, send for the nearest policeman and give him in charge. But so far my – um – vigils have been unrewarded."

"It seems a fairly innocent sort of offence, Mr Lattimer," smiled Jim. "After all, you have the advantage of receiving marketable commodities!"

"Suppose they were poisoned?" asked Mr Bolderwood Lattimer icily. "I have sent several of the articles to the public analyst, and though I admit no trace of any deadly drug has been discovered, yet what is more likely than that the first series of so-called gifts should be free from danger, in order that I should be lured on – "

"That seems to me to be fairly unlikely also," said Jim. "Have you spoken to the police?"

"I have spoken to two officers who are on night duty, and have enlisted their help to capture the man who is annoying me, but I have not addressed any official complaint to the officer in charge."

"You might do worse than discuss the matter with your nephew. I understand Sergeant Lattimer is a relation of yours, Mr Lattimer?"

A look of pain passed over the provision merchant's face.

"John Lattimer and I are not exactly friends," he said; "in fact, we are scarcely acquainted. In his early youth he declined a very excellent offer I made him to enter my counting-house – in a humble capacity, to be sure, but then, one must work upwards from the very bottom. That is an American method – one of the few American methods of which I approve. And he refused, sir. For my dear brother's sake I endeavoured to persuade him, but no, that kind of life had no interest for John. And to emphasize his ingratitude, he took the extraordinary step of joining the police force. An admirable body of men," he added hastily, "without whose guardianship we should be in a very bad way. But not exactly the profession one would have expected my brother's son to adopt."

"It's a very honourable profession," said Jim.

Mr Lattimer shrugged his shoulders.

"One hears extraordinary stories," he said vaguely, "and one scarcely knows what to believe…the pay of a sergeant of police is not sufficiently large, it seems to me, to enable him to dine at the most expensive restaurants. And yet, less than a week ago, I saw John with my own eyes at the Ritz-Carlton, entertaining, and most expensively entertaining, a party of four men, one of whom, I understand, was a millionaire! Remember, I make no charge," he said, shaking his finger in the face of the dumbfounded Jim. "I merely say that one hears things. And although I'm sure our police force is incorruptible…well, dinners at the Ritz-Carlton cost a considerable sum of money!"

For a moment Jim was too astonished to find a rejoinder. Lattimer! That quiet, courteous and well-behaved man! And yet it was impossible that Bolderwood could mistake his nephew for anybody else.

"No, I do not think I shall consult John. I wished to see Miss Leigh, because I thought that possibly she might have been able to throw some light upon the subject. She occupied this house for many years…"

He looked inquiringly at the girl, but she shook her head.

"We never had anything like that happen, Mr Lattimer," she said, "and I can only suggest that you report the matter to the police."

"It worries me," said Bolderwood Lattimer, who was one of those people loath to hand the burden of conversation to anybody else, "it plays on my nerves. I am naturally an imaginative man: you have probably read some of our ads., every one of which is prepared by me?" he added, with unconscious humour. "And I cannot help feeling that possibly I am being the object of a vendetta. Eggs, potatoes, cabbages! Why on earth should they pick me out for their infernal charity?"

"Do these things come in any great quantity?" asked Jim.

Mr Bolderwood Lattimer shook his head.

"There are generally as much as a man could carry in his pocket – the lilac bush was an unusual gift. I am an omnivorous reader, and I have read a great deal about the mysterious warnings which are sometimes given to the intended victim of these black-hand gangs. Do you think, Mr Ferraby, from your wide experience, that these articles come into that category?"

"It is unlikely," said Jim, keeping a straight face with an effort. "Take my advice and consult the police. They will probably relieve your annoyance."

Mr Lattimer pursed his lips thoughtfully.

"I am very comfortable here and I do not wish to leave the place. In fact, as Miss Leigh knows, I have made her several offers for the purchase of the freehold. But recently I have seriously considered whether it would not be advisable for me to move my residence, to see whether I am still pursued by my tormentor."

"That seems a fairly cumbersome method of making the discovery," smiled Jim, "and rather like burning down the house to roast the pig. No messages come with these gifts?"

"None whatever. The nearest approach to a clue, if I may use a police expression, that I've had, came with the lilac. There were some words pencilled on the paper which surrounded the stalk, but they were perfectly meaningless to me."

"Have you got the paper?" asked Jim, with sudden interest.

"I will see."

Mr Lattinier disappeared, and did not come back for some time.

"Do you really think it's somebody playing a joke on him?"

"It rather looks like it. And yet apparently this thing has gone on for years at odd intervals. The paper will tell us something, perhaps."

When Mr Lattimer returned, it was to tell them that the "clue" had been used to light the kitchen fire.

"I don't think that the words would have told you anything," he said. "They meant nothing whatever to me, and I should imagine that they had either been written with the idea of throwing us off the scent, or else they were on the paper when it was used to wrap up the flowers, and have no meaning at all."

That practically concluded the interview, and Jim's preoccupied silence during the drive back to Bloomsbury had nothing whatever to do with Mr Lattimer and his unknown benefactor.

"You're very quiet: do you really think there's anything sinister about the wretched potatoes and eggs?" asked the girl, as they were passing through the park.

Jim started.

"The eggs? No, I wasn't thinking about those. But that story he told us about Sergeant Lattimer is very curious."

"Why shouldn't the poor man dine at the Ritz-Carlton?"

"For the excellent reason that poor men do not dine at the Ritz-Carlton," said Jim quietly, "and police headquarters are suspicious of detectives who have money to burn."

SOOPER INQUIRES

Sooper had the gift, which is the blessing of all great leaders, of being able to sleep in odd places at odd intervals; and when he plussed the nap in the train on his way back to his station with the two hours' sleep he took in his office chair he considered himself to have rested adequately.

The bells were ringing for evening service when he summoned Lattimer, and that officer, a little hollow-eyed and undisguisedly wearied, heard the summons with a groan.

A tall, muscular man was quiet Lattimer. Impressionable young women described him as "distinguished", and the prematurely grey hair at his temples, the somewhat Napoleonic nose and firm chin deserved this description.

Sooper looked up sharply over his spectacles as his subordinate came in.

"Just been having a phone talk with Mr Ferraby," he said. "Somebody's been bombarding your uncle with garden truck and eggs an' lilac – bet it's the first time anybody threw flowers at him, but the eggs must seem like ol' friends."

Sooper said nothing about the dinner at the Ritz-Carlton.

'I hope some of them got on the target," said Lattimer viciously. "He's a sanctimonious old gentleman, as mean as a duke and about as human as a kitchen stove."

"Seems a nice feller," mused Sooper. And then, abruptly, as was his wont: "Elson's back. Got to Hill Brow at 5.53. Car covered with mud, one of his lamps smashed and both fore mudguards all ways."

88

A long pause.

"Thought I'd go up and see him," said Sooper, looking out of the window. "If the active and intelligent officer I put up to watch the house had had the brain of a gnat, he'd have pinched him for speedin' or drunk or sump'n' and pulled him in. I like to get a feller well inside before I start investigatin'. That's the old-fashioned way; it doesn't appeal to you youngsters. Put the key on 'em!"

He sighed and rose.

"I'll just leap up to Hill Brow: you hang on to the office for any message that comes through from Pawsey — I'm in charge of that case: heard from the commissioner two hours ago. You might break it gently to that pudd'n'-headed inspector from Pawsey that he's nothin' 'n' less than nothin' in this case."

Sooper "leapt up" to Hill Brow on his ancient machine with a thunderous leap that frightened children, that interrupted servants, that distressed the sick and lame, for his motor-cycle was at its worst on the Sabbath, when most of the world noises are hushed.

He was surprised when the door was opened by Elson's valet and he was invited in.

"Mr Elson is expecting you," said the man. "I'll show you the way."

They went up the broad oaken stairs, along a red-carpeted corridor to the end room. It was furnished as a sitting-room, and had the obvious advantage of combining a view across the country with a more immediate observation of the drive, up which visitors must come to reach the house.

Elson lay sprawled on a big settee; he was unshaven, grimy; his boots, Sooper noticed, were thick with dried mud, and his unprepossessing appearance was not enhanced by the strip of sticking-plaster which ran from temple to jaw. As Sooper came into the room, he was holding a large glass, half filled with amber fluid, and an open decanter stood on the table within reach of his hand.

"Come in, Minter," he said shakily. "I wanted to see you. What's this story about Hannah Shaw being killed? I saw it in the Sunday papers —"

"If it was in the Sunday papers I'd like to know the feller that wrote it," said Sooper calmly. "We didn't discover the murder till daybreak this morning."

"I saw it somewhere – maybe I heard of it," said Elson, and pointed a trembling finger to a chair. "Sit down, won't you? Have a drink?"

"Teetotaller from birth," said Sooper, seating himself with the greatest care. "As it wasn't in the Sunday papers, you must have heard of it."

"It was in the later editions of the Sunday papers: I saw it in London," said Elson doggedly. "What's the idea? Think I know anything about it?"

There was a defiant note in his tone. Sooper shook his head gently.

"Last person in the world I should have thought knew anything about it was you, Mr Elson," he said. "Didn't even know Hannah Shaw, did you?"

Elson hesitated.

"I've seen her at Cardew's house, that's all."

"Maybe she came over here once or twice?" said Sooper ingratiatingly, almost apologetically. "Housekeepers sort of run round when they get short of things. I'll bet she's been over here once or twice?"

"She's come over once or twice," admitted Elson. "How did it happen?"

"Been over to see you once or twice, hasn't she?" persisted Sooper. "Got an idea I've seen her comin' out the front door – perhaps comin' out of your room. Got a sort of memory of it."

Elson looked at him suspiciously.

"She came over once to ask me" – he hesitated again – "a question about her – about some business. That's the only time she's been here. And if any of these damned servants say that she has been oftener, they're lying!"

"Haven't talked to the servants," said Sooper in a shocked tone. "Never discuss a gen'leman's business with his servants! She'd come over to talk business, wouldn't she? What kind of business would that be?"

"It was her private affair," said Elson shortly, and gulped down the remainder of the whisky in the glass. "Where was she killed?"

"Where was she killed? Why, down at Pawsey. She went to spend a weekend there, and…she was killed."

"How?"

"I've got an idea she was shot," said Sooper, screwing up his face as though he were making a tremendous effort to remember something that had been casually mentioned to him. "Yes, I'm pretty sure she was shot."

"At the bungalow?" asked the other quickly.

"It was a kind of bungalow," admitted Sooper; "a sort of summer cottage belonged to Mr Cardew. Know it?"

The man licked his dry lips.

"Yes, I know it," he answered curtly. And then, to Sooper's surprise, he leapt to his feet and shook a clenched fist at the window. "Hell! If I'd only known…"

He stopped suddenly, as though conscious of the detective's curious eyes.

"Yes, I'll bet if you'd only known it'd have been different," said Sooper sympathetically. "If you'd only known what?"

"Nothing," snapped Elson. "Look at my hand."

He held out his hand and it was shaking like a leaf.

"This has got me!… Shot like a mad dog, that's what!"

He strode up and down the apartment, his hands clasping and unclasping in his agony of mind.

"If I'd known!" he said huskily.

"Where were you last night?" Sooper put the question without violence.

"Me?" The man spun round. "I don't know. I was drunk, I guess. Sometimes I get that way. I slept some place – Oxford, was it? Lot of students in caps and gowns wandering about the streets. Yes, I guess it was Oxford."

"Why did you go to Oxford?"

"I don't know…just went…had to go somewhere. God! how I hate this country! I'd give that hand and that hand" – he shook them both before Sooper – "and three parts of my money to go back to St Paul!"

"Why don't you go?" drawled Sooper.

The man glowered down at him.

"Because I don't choose," he said harshly.

Sooper fingered his bristling grey moustache.

"What hotel might you have stayed in at Oxford?" he suggested.

Elson stood squarely before him.

"What's the great idea?" he asked. "Think I know anything about this shooting of Hannah Shaw? I tell you I was at Oxford, or maybe at Cambridge. I lost the way and went to a big heath where there's a race track – Market something."

"Newmarket," Sooper nodded. "You were at Cambridge."

"Call it Cambridge – what does it matter?"

"You'd stay at a pretty big hotel, and give your own name, Mr Elson, wouldn't you?"

"I may have done; I don't remember. How was she killed – tell me that? Who found her?"

"I found her, and Mr Cardew found her, and Sergeant Lattimer found her," said Sooper and saw the man wince.

"Was she dead when…?"

Sooper nodded. Again Elson resumed his restless pacing. After a while he grew calmer.

"I know nothing about it," he said. "I've certainly met Hannah Shaw: she came here to ask me a question which I answered to the best of my ability. A man wanted to marry her, or she wanted to marry a man. I don't even know who he was, but I believe they got acquainted on one of her car trips."

"Is that so?" Sooper received the news with every evidence of polite interest. "On one of her car trips, eh? Now, isn't that too curious? I've been deductin' and the'rizin' over this case, and that was just the conclusion I came to, that she met him on one of her car trips."

"Then you know about it?" asked the other quickly.

"I only know a little bit; just a soopsong. That's a foreign expression, which maybe you've heard, Mr Elson." He slapped his knee, a preliminary signal to his rising. "Well, I won't be keeping you much longer. A lovely garden you've got, almost as good as Mr Cardew's."

Glad to be off a subject which was uncomfortable to him, Elson crossed to the window.

"Yes, it's pretty good," he said, "But people come up from the town and steal things. Someone took the top of that lilac bush the other night – just cut it right off." He pointed, but Sooper did not look. He was thinking very intensively.

"Top of the lilac bush, eh?" he murmured. "That's certainly queer."

After the police officer had left, Elson went into his room, changed his mud-stained clothes and indulged in the luxury of a hot bath and a shave. He ate a meagre meal – he was usually a hearty eater – and spent the last hour of the declining day wandering aimlessly about the grounds, his hands in his pockets, his chin on his chest. At exactly half-past nine he walked down the garden slope, through an extensive rosary, and came at last to a small door set in the high wall which surrounded the garden. Here he waited, listening. Presently there came a gentle knock, and he pulled back the well-oiled bolt and swung the green door open. Sergeant Lattimer walked in, and, waiting till the door was rebolted, asked sharply: "What in thunder have you been telling Sooper about that lilac bush?"

"Aw! shut up!" growled Elson. "Come up and have a drink. The servants won't see you from this part of the house."

THEORIES AND DEDUCTIONS

At an abnormally early hour the Deputy Commissioner of Police made a call at the Bureau of the Public Prosecutor, and it was Jim's good fortune to be the senior officer on duty, for his chief was nursing an attack of hay fever, and the sub-chief was at the Hereford Assizes, assisting justice in the case of a wife-poisoner whose trial was proceeding.

Sooper never spoke of Colonel Langley in any other way than as "that long-nosed Deputy", sometimes with and occasionally without violent expletives. The Deputy seldom referred to Sooper save in terms of admiration and awe; for the feud which (according to Sooper) raged between him and headquarters was largely imaginary.

"Sooper's the luckiest devil on our business," said Langley enviously. "He tumbles into cases as easily as a fly falls into milk. And when he begged to be sent to 'I' division I thought he was in his dotage."

"Sooper always gives me the impression that he was exiled to 'I'," Jim remarked.

"Sooper is a liar," was the calm response. "Nobody dare exile Sooper: life wouldn't be worth living. We were jolly glad to see the back of the old hound. Living with Sooper is rather like living in a Seidlitz powder. But that's his pose – being exiled and shelved. He asked to go, and took Lattimer with him, and it was like his luck to fall into this case."

It was no part of Jim Ferraby's duty to take the Deputy into his confidence about Lattimer. He had told Sooper, and that was enough.

But he would not have been human if he had not asked a question about the sergeant's antecedents.

"I know very little about him – he went to a good school and is respectably connected."

Lattimer, however, did not interest him, and he came straight to the object of his visit.

"Sooper tells me that you were at Pawsey soon after that murder was committed? We had a conference at the Yard last evening, and I own that we're puzzled," he said. "And the big footprints are not the least mystifying feature of the case, for they only lead *towards* the cottage – Sooper had photographs taken and the proofs arrived late last night. Here are the facts, which I should be glad if you would check." He emphasized each point with a forefinger on the palm of his hand.

"Beach House, when you arrived before midnight on Saturday, was closed and locked. Lattimer had been on the spot for some hours, and he also had made an examination of the house and confirms Sooper's statement that the padlock on the door was fastened and that the door itself was locked. The door at the back of the house was also bolted on the inside; the windows were closed, shuttered and barred, and experiments which were made last evening, at our request, con- clusively proved that it was impossible to get into the house through any of the windows. The chimney is too small to admit a normal sized human being, and there is no other means of ingress which has yet been discovered.

"Shortly before midnight Miss Shaw arrives, driving an old car, and, pulling up before the door of the house, takes off the padlock, unfastens the door and goes in, locking or bolting the door behind her. Sooper tried the door when he examined the car, and found it fastened. From ten to fifteen minutes later, Miss Shaw comes out, locks up and drives away.

"Now, here is an important fact which must be kept in mind, Ferraby. If Miss Shaw had arrived earlier in the day with a companion, it is quite possible that she might have locked him in, though it would have been an unusual and suspicious circumstance. But she was not there the whole of that day, and the local police have convincing proof that no man was concealed on the premises before the arrival of Lattimer. On the evening before the murder, a police patrol, who keeps an eye on these isolated properties, came to Beach Cottage and, as is usual, got off his bicycle and examined the door. This is done because tramps and other worthless people occasionally break into these lonely places. He had seen a tramp loafing about one of the upper cliff paths, and he took the precaution of 'pegging' the door. As you know, the police carry little black pegs to which is attached a length of black cotton, and these they stretch across a doorway which they think may be forced, fastening the pegs into same crevice of the lintel in such a manner that it could not be detected except by some person who was looking for it.

"On the evening of the murder, just before sunset, after Lattimer had taken up his position, the patrol came along and stopped to look at the door of Beach Cottage and found the peg intact, which meant that nobody had passed through the doorway, or they must have broken the thread. This, as I say, is an elementary precaution which is taken in the case of every empty house, and the police patrol did, in fact, peg several other doors of empty dwellings in the course of his duty."

Jim nodded.

"That disposes of my theory that the murderer was already concealed in the house."

"Exactly," said the Deputy. "Now let me go on. Miss Shaw comes out of Beach Cottage, drives along the road and up the hill, and disappears. Her car is afterwards discovered on the top of the cliff; her mackintosh coat and hat were found by a constable hanging on to a bush halfway down the cliff."

"When was this?" asked Jim, in surprise.

"This morning; in fact, I heard just before I left the Yard. Our present theory is that Miss Shaw had arranged to meet a man at the cottage, but discovered that she was under observation. She may have seen your car parked in the quarry, or possibly may have caught a glimpse of one of you – I understand you were in hiding – as she passed. In order to lead you away, she returned to the top of the cliff, got out of her machine and came back by one of the innumerable paths which cover the face of the scarp. It is possible that at the place she left her car, the man was waiting and accompanied her back to the house."

"Why did she take off her hat and coat?" asked Jim.

"The mackintosh and hat were both light in colour. The dress beneath was black. It is likely that she took these off in order to escape observation, and may have stumbled and dropped them – they were found immediately under one of these by-paths."

Jim shook his head.

"You forget, Deputy, that Lattimer was left to keep the house under observation," he said.

"I have remembered that," said the Deputy. "Lattimer was left in Great Pawsey, which is some distance from the beach, and did not get back to the house for half an hour – at least, he states he did not. There was ample time for the woman to return to the cottage with her companion. It is a simple explanation, but in cases of this kind the simple explanation is usually the sound one."

His lips twitched.

"I have already offered my views to Sooper by phone, and although he was very polite, I couldn't help feeling that he was on the point of explosion. He did say that it was ridiculous to suggest that there was time for Hannah Shaw to climb down the cliff before Lattimer got back to the house, and I could not escape the feeling that he was exercising unusual restraint.

"Who was the murderer? Who was Big Foot, who had threatened this unfortunate woman? We come now to an incident of which I believe you were a witness. There was a dinner party at Mr Cardew's the night before, and Sooper says he saw a tramp standing under the shadow of bushes outside the window, and that the tramp was armed with a pistol, and that he subsequently heard him singing Byron's translation of a well-known Spanish song – '*Ay de mi Alhama*'. Now Sooper's description of the man," said the Deputy impressively, "tallies exactly with that of the local policeman who saw a tramp skulking about the face of the cliff; and further confirmation Sooper supplies himself. After the murder he heard this man singing the identical song that was sung in the plantation at Barley Stack. The man we want is the singing tramp. You agree?"

"Is that Sooper's view?" asked Jim cautiously.

For himself, he was inclined to accept the Colonel's theory without question.

"Sooper's? No. But then, you wouldn't expect Sooper to have the same view as headquarters. Apparently he is on another trail. We had an urgent request from him last night to put through inquiries to the Cambridge police – he wanted to know where a Mr Elson slept on the night of the murder. But that, as I say, is very like Sooper. According to him, Elson was acquainted with the murdered woman; though why he should suspect an American millionaire of killing a very inoffensive housekeeper he hasn't condescended to inform me. Apparently he has sent Lattimer to make inquiries, for one of my officers reported that the sergeant passed through London this morning on his way to Cambridge. Apparently Lattimer's inquiries were wholly unsatisfactory."

Jim did not expect that the sergeant would call on his way back, for there was no particular reason why he should do so. He was therefore surprised when Lattimer came into his room later in the afternoon, and at first he thought that the man had called with a message from Sooper.

"It occurred to me, Mr Ferraby, that you would like to know that Elson's alibi is proved."

"I wasn't even aware that he was suspected," smiled Jim.

"Well, he was, in a way," hesitated Lattimer. "When Sooper gets an idea into his head it is rather difficult to move. Elson was missing from Saturday afternoon till Sunday evening. It seems that he went on a jag, and spent the night at Cambridge. His name isn't on the books at any of the hotels, but I found a garage keeper who remembers putting up the car, and probably Elson found private lodgings."

"Not a very satisfactory alibi, is it, Sergeant?" suggested Jim, and Lattimer stiffened.

"I think it will satisfy the superintendent," he said coldly, and then, as if recognizing that his tone was unnecessarily sharp, he went on: "I haven't seen a bed since Saturday night, and I'm just about all in. Sooper doesn't seem to need sleep; he was out before daybreak this morning."

"You have made no fresh discoveries in Pawsey?"

Lattimer shook his head.

"I don't think there are any more to be made," he said. "Have you heard that we found her coat and hat? It was hanging on a bush, at one of the steepest parts of the cliff." The sergeant smiled faintly. "That was rather a blow for Sooper, who expected to find them somewhere else."

"Where?" asked Jim in surprise.

"I don't exactly know. It is very likely that he does not either!"

"After we left you at Pawsey, how long was it before you had the cottage under view again?"

"You mean on the night of the murder?" Lattimer considered. "About a quarter of an hour. Sooper says there wasn't time for Shaw to get back. I think there was ample time. I believe also that she slid down the cliff, the same as Miss Leigh did, and that is where she lost her coat and hat. But it's no use advancing theories to Sooper: he is a realist! When I suggested to him that the cottage may have been built on the site of an old smuggler's house, and that there are probably underground cellars, he was more offensive than I remember his being in the years I have known him. He won't listen to theories, and of course he's right."

"Why 'of course'?"

Lattimer looked at him strangely; there was a hint of a smile in his eyes.

"Because Sooper knows," he said dryly. "Nobody knows better than Sooper how that murder was committed – or why!"

Before Jim could recover his surprise, or fire another question at him, Lattimer was gone.

ELFA LEIGH'S HOME

Elfa Leigh had carried with her, from the house of the pleasant years in Edwards Square, all the intimate personal possessions which she had shared with her father. They had been great friends, this motherless girl and the dreamy, seemingly helpless man whom she called father; and when the curt intimation had came from the British Admiralty, prefaced by the mechanical expression of regret, that the US transport *Lenglan* had been torpedoed off the south coast of Ireland in a gale, and, with its escorting destroyer, had been sunk with all hands, the news had left her numb and unbelieving.

John Kenneth Leigh was returning from Washington, where he had been called into consultation with his chief. Throughout the war he had been a liaison officer between the British and American Treasuries, and had been largely responsible for the British end of the financial arrangements which had been made between the two countries. When America came into the war, he was transferred to the army department, and for twelve months Elfa had seen very little of her father. He seemed to spend his life moving between the two countries, and it was inevitable that the narrow escapes he had had should culminate in disaster. Elfa had to face a new life, and this she did with a courage beyond praise. She gave up the house in Edwards Square, moved to the three rooms on the top floor of 75 Cubitt Street, and started to build from the wreckage of her broken life.

She had some relatives in the United States, but she had preferred to remain in a city which was almost hallowed with memories of her father; and it was in the tiny suite on Cubitt Street that she regained some of her balance. The walls of her pretty sitting-room were covered with the prints and watercolours which her father, no mean connoisseur, had collected in his lifetime; the old chair he loved held the place of honour near the window; his pipe-rack was above the mantelpiece, beneath his sword – he had once served in the American cavalry.

Elfa had practically no friends of her own sex, and few acquaintances amongst the other. She did not encourage callers, but Sooper had become a privileged person, and when her landlady's maid brought his card on the Monday afternoon, she sent down a message inviting him up. Sooper climbed the three flights of stairs slowly, came into the pretty little sitting-room, hat in hand, on his face that substitute for a smile which so terrified the uninitiated.

"Gettin' old," he said, as he deposited his hat upon the piano. "Know the time when I could have come up those stairs in six leaps."

She could not guess from his manner whether he had come to give her news or to make further inquiries about the mysterious Big Foot. Perhaps Sooper's preliminaries, which seemed so aimless and so discursive, had their place in his system of interrogation, she thought, and was not far wrong.

"Pretty room you've got, Miss Leigh, and mighty comfortable. If you asked me to sit down, I'd sit down, but if you said: 'Minter, you can smoke,' I wouldn't dare do it – not with the kind of tobacco I use."

"You can sit down and smoke," she laughed. "The windows are wide open, and I like the smell of almost any kind of tobacco."

"There's a bit of a doubt as to whether this *is* tobacco at all," said Sooper, filling his pipe from an ancient pouch. "Some say one thing and same say another. I call it tobacco… Play the piano, Miss Leigh?"

"Yes, I play it sometimes," she said, amused.

"Nobody's educated until they can play the piano. Most anybody can play a gramophone. Got over your bad night?"

She nodded.

"If I'd laid out on the cliff in the rain, I'd have been dead," said Sooper. "You, bein' young, have got nothin' but rheumatics."

"I haven't even got rheumatics," said Elfa good-humouredly.

"But you will have," said the ominous Sooper. "You've got it, but you won't know it perhaps for twenty years."

He did not sit down, but wandered about the room, looking at the pictures.

"Pretty nice pictures, eh? Done by hand, Miss Leigh?" And when she answered laughingly that they were "done by hand": "You never know. I've seen machine pictures that looked as good as hand pictures – and better. You painted this yourself, I'll bet?" He pointed to a water-colour painting of a landscape.

"No, that was painted by a great French artist," she said.

"French people have got the knack of that sort of thing," mused Sooper, "and it's only a knack, putting the right colours in the right places. Anybody could do it if they were educated up to it. That's a fine lot of books you've got."

He fingered the volumes which filled three long shelves.

"Nothin' about anthr'pology? You haven't caught that disease? Or maybe psychology? I don't see a single book about crime."

"I'm not greatly interested in crime," said Elfa. "Those were my father's books."

He took out a volume, turning the leaves slowly. When he had replaced the book, he said: "He was killed in the war. I met him once."

"My father?" she asked quickly.

He nodded.

"Yes; one of the clerks in his bureau stole some money – he'd been playing the races – and I was called in. He seemed a very nice man – your father, I mean."

"He was the best man in the world," said the girl quietly, and Sooper nodded his approval.

"That's the way I like to hear children talk about their parents," he said. "There's too much 'governor-in' ' and 'old bean-in' ' and 'old top-pin'' about nowadays to please me. When I hear a lad call his father 'old horse' I'm glad I never married."

"Then you *are* a bachelor?" she asked, anxious to turn the conversation to a subject which was less sacred to her.

"Me? Why, yes. Only had one love affair in my life, and that wasn't exactly a love affair. She was a widow with three children, but she was temp'ramental, the same as me. There's no room in one house for two temp'ramental people, and there would have been five, for the children were the most temp'ramental of the lot – used to have their breakfast in bed, which is the most temp'ramental thing I know. Mr Cardew been to the office today?"

She shook her head.

"No, he telephoned me this morning. He is back at Barley Stack. I think he must have recovered from the shock of poor Miss Shaw's death, for his servant told me that he was very hard at work in his study."

"The'rizin' an' deductin'," said Sooper gloomily. "That's what he's at – the'rizin' an' deductin'! I made an early call on him before I came up this mornin', and there he was in the study, with books on anthr'pology an' soc'ology and logic an' everythin'; and he had a plan of the cottage and was measurin' it with compasses and tape measures and findin' out that it's twenty-six feet from the kitchen to the front door; and he had books of tide tables…but he hadn't got a microscope. That kind of disappointed me. And no test-chubes. Maybe he got 'em after I left. I brought away the plan of the cottage, but he won't want that. He's got the measurements, an' the tides an' a sample of the sand. We shall know who did the murder tonight."

In spite of the gruesomeness of the subject, she was laughing softly.

"You're not a great believer in the deductive method, Mr Minter?"

"Call me Sooper," begged the old detective. "You're wrong – I am, miss; I believe in science. There's not enough in the police force; that's what we're short of. She bought that hat at Astor's, in High Street, Kensington. She wanted that kind, though it was a year old. Funny thing, a woman wanting a hat that's out of fashion."

The transition from the detective's opinions on art to the mundane subject of clothes was so rapid and unexpected that Elfa was taken aback.

"You mean Miss Shaw? What kind of hat was it?"

"A big yellow straw with a curtain veil all round it – you know the kind that just comes down to your nose? She bought it on Saturday just before the store closed, and it didn't suit her. The girl in the shop said it didn't suit her. She must be honest. Very few shop girls would tell a customer that a hat doesn't suit her…but she said that was the kind she wanted, and she had it. Paid two pounds five and six and took it away in a bag. I didn't tell Cardew: news like that would rouse him to madness. He'd deduct that she bought the hat to wear on the Continent, and he'd be measurin' Paris with a foot-rule before you could say 'knife'."

Sooper was back at the bookshelf and was taking book after book in his hand, running his thumb along the pages, and giving the contents no more than a casual glance.

"Any more eggs and potatoes?" he asked suddenly.

"You mean in Edwards Square? No, I have not heard from Mr Bolderwood Lattimer."

"Can't understand why he calls himself Bolderwood. Thought only people named Smith wore mascots. Fond of flowers, Miss Leigh?"

"Very," she said.

Sooper scratched his chin.

"Who ain't?" he asked. "Flowers get me more temp'ramental than anythin' I know. Ever seen a field of buttercups…ever taken a good look at bluebells sort of shimmering in a dark wood? There's a bit of poetry somewhere:

> 'Such a drear bank of moss till, one grey morn,
> Blue ran a flash across an' vi'lets were born.'

Never think of those two lines without I get tears in my eyes. And that's temp'ramental. I've got a scrapbook full of poems about flowers at home – roses an' vi'lets an' primroses an' everythin'. It's funny nobody's written a poem about lilac."

She looked at him suspiciously.

"Mr Minter, you're coming in a roundabout way to the flowers that were left at Edwards Square. I could write a poem about lilac if I could write a poem about anything; it is my favourite flower."

"Mine's tulips," murmured Sooper.

He sat down slowly.

"Ever meet Mr Elson…like him? He's an American too, isn't he?"

"Yes," she said.

"He can read – just; and write – nearly. Keeps a secretary to run his correspondence, but can spell out a few words himself."

"Is that so?" she asked in surprise. "I thought there was nobody in the world who couldn't read or write."

"He's a nobody, in a manner of speakin'," said Sooper.

A few minutes later she went out of the room to order tea, and, coming back, found the police officer at the bookshelf again.

"You're very fond of books?"

"Readin' books I like," he admitted. "Studyin' books are about as popular with me as measles, scarlet fever and all the notifiable diseases. 'JKL'," he read on the flyleaf. "That was your father, Miss Leigh?"

"Yes, that was my father's name – John Kenneth."

"A nice man, I should think," said Sooper reflectively. "Not the kind of man who'd make enemies."

"He hadn't an enemy in the world," she said. "Everybody loved him."

Sooper made a sympathetic noise.

"That's a thing that'll never be said about me," he remarked. "A list of the people who don't love me would fill that bookshelf, Miss Leigh, and there'd be enough left over to paper the room. All," he added modestly, "due to jealousy and genyus – their jealousy and my genyus. Bear that in mind, Miss Leigh: when a fellow's unpopular, it's due to jealousy, and if you don't believe me, ask the fellow himself. He'll admit it."

"I'm sure you're not so very unpopular, Sooper," she said, as she poured out tea.

"I ain't, but I'm goin' to be," said Sooper darkly. "You watch out, Miss Leigh. I'm goin' to be one of the most unpopular men in the force – and soon."

A LITTLE DINNER

Sooper, on leaving, told the girl he was going back to his station, permitting himself one of those unveracities which were wholly justifiable in his own eyes. He spent an uncomfortable time at the Yard, interviewing his superiors, but the discomfort was mainly theirs. In the space of two hours he demolished, in detail and in general, at least twenty-two theories and side theories. And this he accomplished with such a wealth of malignant comment and illustration that even the Chief Commissioner sighed his relief when the door closed upon him.

He left Scotland Yard and made for a fashionable picture theatre, not because he was tempted by the programme, but because at this particular resort the lights were not raised between the features, and Sooper slept best in the dark. For two hours he sat crouched in a chair, his head on his chest, his arms folded, and the terrific adventures of popular and well-paid artists flickered and gleamed before his unconscious figure. Men performed daring deeds; gallant heroes leapt abysmal chasms; fair maidens were rescued from heart-thrilling dangers; and Sooper slept on, till an attendant touched his shoulder and asked him if he would kindly stand up to allow a stout lady to pass him. Refreshed, he went into the theatre restaurant, drank three cups of coffee in rapid succession, ate a large wedge of indigestible cake, and went forth a new man.

His objective was Fregetti's, and in point of exclusiveness Fregetti's had nothing to fear from the Ritz-Carlton or from any other establishment, however magnificent. Fregetti's is in an unfashionable

108

quarter, being at the lower end of Portland Street, but is generally conceded amongst epicures that the restaurant is the best in London.

Sooper took up a position and waited. Car after car stopped before the glass awning and deposited its well-dressed cargo. But it was quarter after nine before a cab slowed at the door, and the two men for whom Sooper was waiting stepped forth.

The first was Elson: he was in a dinner jacket, and wore at the back of his head a shiny silk hat, which somehow seemed incongruous. There followed him from the cab a more elegant gentleman, who wore his well-fitting clothes with greater ease. He stopped whilst Elson paid the cabman, and then disappeared behind the glass doors of the restaurant, and Sooper grunted his satisfaction.

"I hope you enjoy your dinner, Lattimer," he said. "You're looking pretty spry for a tired man!"

Lattimer strolled through the palm court into the half-darkness of the restaurant. Beyond the dim illumination afforded by cornice globes, the only light in the room came from the table lamps, which brought to the saloon a strange sense of intimacy.

To Elson the half-darkness was welcome: he hated light almost as cordially as he hated company, and he made his way with quick if unsteady steps to the table in the far corner that he had booked by telephone.

"Where did you leave that old fool?" he growled, as he seated himself, and reached for the cocktail that stood waiting.

"Sooper? Oh, he's in London somewhere," said Lattimer, as he took a cigarette from a gold case and lit it. "You needn't worry about him."

"If you think I'm worried about him, why, you've made one big mistake," snapped Elson. "No, sir, I've no respect for the English police."

"Thank you," said Lattimer.

"You don't suppose I think a hell of a lot of you, do you?" demanded Elson savagely. "Where's that waiter?"

The waiter came at long last, and, having served them, melted into the darkness.

"Now what do you want?" asked Elson, putting down his fork and sitting back.

"I want another five hundred," replied Lattimer coolly.

"It doesn't sound much in dollars," grumbled the other, "but it's a whole lot in pounds! I gave you a hundred a fortnight ago: what have you done with that?"

"You lent me a hundred," corrected Lattimer carefully, "and I gave you a receipt. What I did with that doesn't matter. I want five hundred now."

Elson's face went dusky with anger.

"How long do you think you're going to milk me?" he asked. "If I went to that old guy and told him – "

"But you won't," said Lattimer softly. "And really, I don't know what you're making a fuss about. It's worth your while to keep on good terms with me. I've saved you from a heap of trouble, and I'm willing to go on helping you. I've got a big enough pull to help you out of almost anything except murder."

Elson shuddered.

"What's this stuff about murder?" he asked loudly.

Somebody at the next table turned their head to look towards him, and he went on in a lower voice: "I guess you'll be useful one of these days, and if you're not – well, it wouldn't look too good to your captain to see the receipts I hold of yours. I'm going to give you that five hundred, not because you've got anything on me, because you haven't, but because I kind of like you. I've nothing to fear from the police an' never had – "

"Except in St Paul," interrupted the other, with a twist of his lip. "You're wanted by the St Paul police on a charge of robbery with assault. You have served two terms in State penitentiaries for robbery and other offences, and if the extradition law works it isn't going to be difficult to pull you in at any time. Beyond that," he said, smiling into the scowling face of the man, "I've nothing on you."

"You're a blackmailer," said Elson between his teeth.

"And you're a fool," replied Lattimer, in excellent temper. "See here, Elson, or Alstein, or whatever your name is, I may be pretty useful to you – I've an idea I'm going to be. And you might remember that it isn't what I've got on you that counts – it is what Sooper has in his mind that matters."

"Does he know about that St Paul trouble?"

"It doesn't matter if he does," was the cool response. "It wasn't an extraditable offence…"

"How's that?" said the dumbfounded millionaire. "But you told me – "

"I've told you a lot that wouldn't pass on the witness stand: I'm telling you the truth now. So long as you remain in England you can't be pinched. And you needn't look ugly, because I didn't know about this until today." He leant across the table and lowered his voice. "Elson, there is going to be trouble over Hannah Shaw. Sooper sent me down to Cambridge to test your story, and it doesn't stand examination. I came back with a yarn that I'd found the garage where you put your machine for the night – but I never found any such garage. You weren't there!"

Elson moved restlessly in his chair.

"How do I know where I was? Didn't I tell you I was soused? I got an idea I was somewhere near a college, that's all."

Sergeant Lattimer's eyes were fixed on the uncomfortable man.

"Come across, Elson," he invited softly. "You've got something to tell – spill it, boy!"

The other man shook his head.

"I've nothing to spill," he said sourly. "What's the matter with you? You know it all – why ask me?"

"Who killed Hannah Shaw?"

Elson's eyelids narrowed till they were slits.

"Maybe you don't know anything about that!" he sneered. "Maybe you don't know where she was all afternoon."

"Why should I?" demanded Lattimer, with an air of unconcern.

"Perhaps you never met Hannah Shaw at the end of the lane after dark? And same days, when she went out riding in her flivver, you didn't meet her and go long rides together?" asked Elson, watching him closely. "I guess your Sooper doesn't know that."

"He doesn't know everything," was the cool reply.

"I'll bet he doesn't! Hannah Shaw and you were pretty well acquainted, it seems to me; too well acquainted for you to come and ask for information. She told me one or two things about you that wouldn't sound good before a judge. If it comes to a showdown, Lat, you're going to look pretty foolish. You've been playing Hannah for months. Sooper doesn't know, and Cardew doesn't know. I've been reading the papers this morning – at least, my secretary has been reading them to me – and it seems that when they searched Hannah's room no money was found. I happen to know" – he spoke slowly – "that when Hannah disappeared, she had four hundred thousand dollars. Never mind where she got it – I know she had it. Where is that money?"

Lattimer made no answer.

"You're a crook, Lat, like most fly-cops who've got ideas above their pay envelope. There's nothing you wouldn't do for money. You've been months trying to persuade Hannah to take shares in a dud syndicate. You told her a week ago that you'd do most anything to get ten thousand dollars. That looks mighty bad to me."

"Order another bottle of wine," said Lattimer, "and let's talk of something else."

It was past midnight when Elson's car came cautiously up the drive and stopped before the house. Elson got out and, swaying to the door, succeeded, after several futile attempts, in opening it. He got into the hall, steadied himself against the wall, and pushed the door close before he made his erratic way up the stairs, clinging to the balustrade. He succeeded in reaching the settee, and fell instantly to sleep. It was the sharp point of his dress collar that roused him to semi-consciousness. He woke, his head in a painful whirl, his legs so weak that they scarcely sustained the weight of his body when he eventually came to his feet.

Sleepily he tugged at the collar, and, after many attempts, tore it off. All the lights in the room were burning, and in a dim, fuddled way he realized that he might sleep better if they were extinguished. As he crossed the room with unsteady steps, he peeled off his coat, wrenched open his shirt, and, leaning against the wall before he turned the switch, kicked loose his shoes.

The change to the ghostly light of dawn partially sobered him. He went back to the settee, poured himself out a stiff brandy and soda and, drinking it down at a gulp, felt instantly wide awake.

The morning was warm: he walked to the window, pushed open the casement, and, leaning out, drank in deep draughts of the sweet dawn air. And then he became conscious that, almost beneath him, a figure was moving along the edge of the flower-bed, stooping now and again to pluck a bloom. His left hand already held a big bunch.

For a second, Elson thought that his eyes were playing him tricks, for the garden still lay under the shadow of the passing night. And then he heard the man humming a tune.

"Hi!" he shouted. "What are you doing here?"

The figure looked round. It was too dark to see his face.

"What are you doing here?" roared Elson angrily when the man made no answer.

As he spoke, the intruder leapt across the bed and ran rapidly towards the cover of the drive.

"I'll get you!" yelled Elson, in an insane rage.

And then, from the darkness of the trees, came the words of the song:

> "The Moorish king rides up and down
> Through Granada's royal town.
> *Ay de mi Alhama!*"

For a while Elson stood, grasping the window ledge, his face grey, his eyes staring.

> "*Ay de mi Alhama!*"

The refrain was dying away in the distance, but Elson did not hear. He lay in a heap on the ground, an unclean, shivering thing, croaking blasphemy and supplication, screaming in terror, for he had heard a voice from the grave.

But there was, within the very shadow of the house, one whom that song galvanized to life. Sooper, keeping his watch at the end of the lane, heard the song, caught a momentary glimpse of the singer as he flitted like a shadow across the road, and in another instant his crazy motor-cycle was exploding like a machine-gun as he drove down the lane to intercept the night wanderer.

The tramp saw him, broke back across a field, and dived into a wilderness of bush and woodland which formed the corner of an adjoining estate. Sooper's noisy machine turned, and he flew down the main road and swung round an angle of an old wall just as the tramp broke cover.

The man ran like the wind, still grasping in his hand the flowers he had picked; and just as Sooper came abreast of him, he turned at right angles, leapt a ditch and sped across a meadow. Sooper made a quick calculation, sent his cycle along the road at a remarkable speed, slowing to take the corner of a cart track which he knew ran parallel with the meadow across which he had seen the man running, and his manoeuvre was successful. As the tramp staggered out on to the road, Sooper leapt from his bicycle, caught him under the arms, and gently lowered him to the ground.

"Steady, my friend!" said Sooper.

The tramp looked up with a queer smile on his bearded face. "I'm afraid I've given you a lot of trouble," he said faintly.

His voice was the voice of a cultured American, but for that Sooper was prepared.

"No trouble," he said cheerfully. "Can you stand?"

The tramp climbed to his feet shakily.

"Think you'd better walk with me to the station and have some food," said Sooper kindly, and the other obeyed without demur.

As they walked slowly along the road towards the town, Sooper expressed his inward satisfaction by an inevitable garrulity.

"A week ago I'd have treated you rough, I admit it. Got an idea you were a pretty bad man."

"I'm not at all a bad man," said the other simply.

"I'll bet you're not," agreed Sooper. "No, sir! I've done a lot of the'rizin' an' deductin' about you, an' I guess I've got you right. I know your name."

The man smiled.

"I have so many names. I wish I knew the right one," he said.

"I'm going to tell you the right one," replied Sooper. "By logic an' deduction an' the'ry, I've decided that your name is John Kenneth Leigh, of the United States Treas'ry!"

SOOPER'S SENSATION

Mr Gordon Cardew put down his compasses, took off his glasses, and stared open-mouthed at his visitor. Having produced his sensation, Sooper did everything except purr.

"But I understand from the young lady that her father was killed in the war?"

"He's alive," said Sooper unnecessarily, "and in a nursing home."

Mr Cardew looked from the plan of the cottage to the detective, as though he were not quite sure in his mind whether the news was sufficiently startling to justify the interruption in his work.

"I am very glad," he said at last, "extremely glad. I have heard of such cases, but never dreamt that one would come within my personal experience. That, of course, explains why Miss Leigh did not come to me when I wired for her."

And there, so far as Mr Cardew was concerned, he was prepared to let the matter end. For whilst the advent of a lost father more or less might be interesting to Sooper in his official capacity, Mr Cardew was only mildly intrigued, until:

"There's no doubt he was the feller that did the singin' on the night of the murder," said Sooper. "Got an idea that he lived in one of those caves high up, an' had a rope ladder which he let down at night when he came out, an' took up in the mornin' when he got back. He practically told me so."

"The tramp!" gasped Cardew. "Not the man who was in the garden the night you dined here?"

Sooper nodded.

116

"But a tramp… Miss Leigh's father! It is incredible! What on earth was he doing?… A tramp!"

He was shocked.

"Just what tramps do," said Sooper; "loafing around, picking up things. He must have remembered, in a wild kind of way, where he lived, and I think he had a crazy notion that his daughter might be starving. He used to collect things, like eggs and potatoes, and leave them on her doorstep. Sometimes he left flowers."

"Isn't he – quite right in his head?" asked Mr Cardew anxiously. "I should not like to think that that was so. These derangements are frequently hereditary."

"He's right in his head and yet he's not right in his head," was the unsatisfactory explanation which Sooper offered. "The doctor thinks there's a pressure, a bit of bone – there's a four-inch scar on his scalp. Somebody gave him a crack that he won't forget in a hurry."

The lawyer put the tips of his fingers together and looked up at the ceiling.

"Possibly it was a splinter of shell: I have heard of such cases. But in that event, I can't understand how he came to be a tramp. It must have been a very pleasant shock for Miss Leigh to have discovered her father was still alive. I hope you broke the news gently, although joy does not kill."

"Yes, sir, I broke it tactful," nodded Sooper. "I got her on the phone and told her I didn't think her father was as dead as she'd calculated. And that sort of prepared her for the news."

Mr Cardew pursed his lips dubiously. He was really not interested in the remarkable recovery, except in so far as Leigh's presence at Pawsey on the night of the murder brought a new element into the case.

"I understand you had a theory that this man was associated with the crime?" he said. "In fact, if I remember rightly, you thought he might be Big Foot?"

"I never thought anything of the kind!" snarled Sooper, who resented nothing so much as having views attributed to him which he did not hold. "I just didn't think anythin' of the kind. You're the 'rizin',

Mr Cardew." He looked down at the plan, criss-crossed with innumerable straight pencil lines. "Got the whole thing worked out?" he asked sardonically. "Murder committed by a left-footed man?"

Mr Cardew could afford an indulgent smile.

"I have done nothing quite so clever," he said. "But I have learnt a very important item from the city surveyor of Pawsey. He tells me that the bungalow was built on the site of an old cottage, and beyond doubt there are cellars somewhere beneath the floor of the kitchen…"

Sooper sighed.

"For the love of Mike!" he said softly, "won't they forget those cellars? And how did the feller escape – through a crack in the floor? Or maybe through a worm-hole? And ain't there anythin' about secret springs – maybe the whole house revolves like the trap in the shop of Sweeney Todd, the barber."

"At any rate, I am so far convinced that no harm can be done by excavating," affirmed Mr Cardew, "that I am perfectly willing to give my permission, and since the house is my property, I don't see what objection there can be – I will pay for the work."

"Know my sergeant?" interrupted Sooper in his abrupt fashion.

"Lattimer? Yes, I know him. He has been here on several occasions," replied Cardew in surprise.

"Has he ever tried to be friendly?"

Mr Cardew hesitated.

"No," he said. And then, "I don't think that I should speak about the man to his superior officer, but…"

"But what?"

"Well, he once hinted very broadly that he'd like to borrow a little money."

"Huh!" grunted Sooper. "He did, eh? Did you lend it?"

"No, I did not. I was rather annoyed, as a matter of fact. One does not expect a responsible officer of police to make that sort of suggestion. I never told you about this before, Superintendent, because, as I say, I have no wish to get the man into trouble."

Sooper ruminated on this, then pointed to the plan again.

"Got all your the'ries properly fixed?" he asked, and Cardew laughed aloud.

"I don't mind your gibes, Superintendent," he said good-humouredly, "because I realize there's no malice in them. But if I were a betting man, which I am not, I would wager that I am nearer to the truth about that murder than you."

He walked with Sooper to the front door, and again the old policeman went off at a tangent.

"Mr Elson's ill," he said. "Had a fit or sump'n. Sounds like booze to me. That fellow is a soak of soaks. I asked the doctor this mornin' if it was delirium trimmings, but he didn't give me any satisfaction: these doctors are closer'n oysters."

"Where is your tramp?" asked Mr Cardew at parting.

"Mr John Kenneth Leigh, of the United States Treas'ry," said Sooper carefully, "is in a nursing home, being nursed. That's what nursing homes are for."

"And his daughter?"

"Miss Elfa Henrietta Leigh – she's with him, tryin' to get him to talk about his experience, but all he does is to sing that foolish song about the King of Spain ridin' up an' down. 'Oh, dear, Alhambra' or sump'n'. It may be a mighty fine song, but it don't thrill me. But it was his favourite song apparently – I saw it on the top of her piano when I was makin' a call on the young lady. Also books on Spanish poetry. That's what made me start deductin'. If you get any crackajack ideas about this bungalow murder, Mr Cardew, you know my telephone number – I'd be interested. The London police told me that they've got no new clue about the burglary at your office."

"I am hardly surprised," said Mr Cardew dryly. "Yet the connection between the murder and the burning of poor Hannah's documents must be fairly clear, even to Scotland Yard."

"Nothing's clear at Scotland Yard," said Sooper unkindly.

Mr Leigh had been removed to a nursing home in Weymouth Street, London, and Sooper found time later in the morning to call and inquire after his patient. The girl, who came down to the reception-room, had undergone a subtle transformation. There was a new colour in her cheeks, a new brightness in her eyes that still showed signs of tears, which had almost changed her appearance.

"He's sleeping now," she said.

"Does he know you?" said Sooper.

She shook her head.

"Not really," she said. "I must have changed a lot in the last six years. He asked me if I knew his little girl." Her lip trembled. "If I'm a fool and cry, shake me, Sooper. Isn't it wonderful – finding him again?"

"I found him," said Sooper.

She took his rough hand between hers and squeezed it.

"Of course you did," she said softly. "Nobody else would have connected the song with daddy. And the queer thing is that I heard him singing that night when I lay on the cliff. Then I thought I had been dreaming."

"Didn't you know about this tramp who sang Spanish songs?"

She shook her head again.

"No," she said, "if I had, I should have been certain it was daddy, although I believed he was dead. Poor darling!" she said softly. "It was he who left food on the doorstep in Edwards Square. He must have remembered something of the past. What I can't understand is why he never came to the house or made himself known. He has been hiding for all these years – why?"

Sooper's ferocious grin was the answer.

"That's just what I've been the'rizin' about for a long time," he said.

A few doors from the nursing home was the house of the great surgeon whom Sooper, on his own responsibility, had summoned to make a superficial examination. It was Sooper's good fortune to find the doctor at home, and the report he received was distinctly encouraging.

"I wouldn't describe him as insane, although obviously he's not responsible for his actions. Every symptom points to pressure, and there's a chance, if that is relieved, Mr Leigh will become normal. It is by no means certain, but the operation is justified. I have had a visit from an official of the American Embassy, and no expense is to be spared."

"When will you operate?" asked Sooper.

The great surgeon shook his head.

"That I can't tell you. The man at the present moment is not fit to endure the shock of a big operation. We must build up his vitality."

"Do it soon, Doctor," said Sooper; "I want to get this case finished before the Long Vacation – there's an Old Bailey Sessions in six weeks: maybe I could make it."

He took a little diary from his waistcoat pocket and consulted it.

"Yes, they'd get the trial over in June, and they'd be hung in July, in time for my holiday – never like to go on a vacation till I've got my man properly dead. What with these courts of appeal and pleas of insanity and unconscious v'lition, you're never sure of your man till you've got him on the drop."

He left the mystified surgeon undecided as to whether he had been drinking or was suffering from sunstroke.

There was no need for Sooper to introduce himself to the desk sergeant at Marylebone Lane police station, and he secured an interview with the officer in charge by the simple process of walking into his room and shutting the door behind him.

"I want a day and night watch on 59 Weymouth Street," he said. "There's a member of the American Embassy there named Leigh, and here's a list of the people who mustn't see him."

He laid a paper on the officer's table.

"I've told the matron that he's to have no food but what comes from the kitchen; no fancy truck, chocolates, grapes or any other vegetables donated by kind an' lovin' friends. All I want your man to do is to see that nobody gets into the house after nightfall."

He then proceeded to explain at greater length the importance and seriousness of the charge that was committed to his care. Most divisional inspectors would have resented the appearance of a "foreigner" from another division, and grown a little apoplectic at his peremptory tone. But Sooper was Sooper, and he strode forth into the sunlight of Marylebone Lane, satisfied that his instructions would be carried out to the letter.

His work completed, he could indulge in the luxury of a friendly call on Jim Ferraby; and such was his extraordinary memory for the habits and characteristics of his friends that Sooper arrived simultaneously with the object of his search on the steps of Jim's club.

Jim almost fell upon him in his anxiety to procure news.

"I've been trying to get you all morning," he said. "Miss Leigh phoned me the wonderful news, and since then I've been unable to get in touch with her. The tramp is her father? It doesn't seem possible."

"None of the coops I bring off seem possible," said Sooper, who throughout his life had resolutely refused to give any but an English pronunciation to the French words that have crept into our speech. "Thought I'd call on you; restaurants are pretty expensive in London, and the cooking here's good."

It was not until lunch was finished and they were sitting over their coffee in the smoke-room, that Sooper revealed his mind.

"That Spanish song didn't mean a thing to me," he said, "though it told me that the tramp was a different kind to the usual run. So I got on to the trail of this feller, picked up information from all over the country, through the local police, and discovered that this singing tramp was pretty well known – he'd been in prison for a week at Canterbury, on a charge of vagrancy. Wonder is the prison doctor didn't spot the fact that he was nutty. But it was the news you gave me on Sunday about the eggs and potatoes bein' left on the doorstep of Miss Leigh's old house that got me thoroughly interested. To my mind that could mean only one thing: that somebody was fond of Miss Leigh, but didn't know she had left the house, was dropping these little gifts. That could only mean somebody who had a crazy notion she was starving; and the only person who'd feel that way would be her father. So I called on the young lady, and it was a pretty simple bit of th'rizin' to link up the tramp. The doctors think that an operation may bring him to his senses, and then we're goin' to learn a whole lot of romantic things that you don't dream about."

"Such as...?" asked Jim suggestively.

"Remember that feller I told you about – Brixton, the City alderman?"

Jim nodded.

"A close, mean sort of feller."

"Well, what about him?" asked Jim.

"Noth'n'," replied Sooper casually. "I just wondered if you remembered my mentioning him."

"What has he to do with the tramp?"

"A considerable lot," said Sooper, "*and* with the murder. You mark my words, that feller, Sir Somethin' Brixton, is going to be a highly interesting witness."

He took out his pocket-book, laid it on the little table where their coffee had been deposited, and, groping in its capacious depths, produced a folded envelope.

"Remember that?"

Jim nodded. It was the envelope that had been found on the kitchen floor on the night of the murder.

"Only two people know about that," he said, "you and the young lady. Even Lattimer doesn't know. The man who wrote the letter that was inside this here envelope was the man who killed Hannah Shaw. That's certain. He may have come down the chimney, he may have come up from the subt'ranean depths of the earth, out of secret cellars and other remarkable places; or he may have leapt through the front door, or he may have leapt through the winder; but the man that typed that" – he tapped the envelope impressively – "pulled the gun that killed that unfortunate female. Maybe she's not so unfortunate as some people think. Personally, I've got an idea she's well out of it."

"Out of what?" asked the puzzled Jim.

Sooper waved a comprehensive hand.

"Everythin'," he said. "If you want to order me a liqueur, I'll have an old brandy – I don't like the stuff with sugar in it."

He gave Jim the address of the nursing home, and, retrieving his motor-bicycle from the garage at Scotland Yard, where it had been an object of wonder to many young constables, he exploded himself back to his headquarters.

Lattimer was not there. He had sent him, earlier in the morning, to Pawsey to make inquiries. The inquest was on the following day. Sooper had his case to prepare, and it was no easy task to disentangle the evidence he could give in open court from that which, in the interests of justice, must be suppressed.

From time to time he lifted his head, put down his pen, and indulged himself in certain malignant reflections, amongst which appeared most frequently the knowledge that Mr Cardew must be torn from his work of criminal investigation and kick his heels in a stuffy little coroner's court.

Lattimer returned towards night, and reported the result of his investigations.

"I followed the field path south of Pawsey for three miles," he said. "It would be impossible for a car to go that way. The track is narrow, and there are two stiles. It joins the London–Lewes Road, as you suggested."

"As I knew," corrected Sooper. "A car couldn't get that way, eh? I'd have been disappointed if it could."

Lattimer opened his eyes.

"Why, I thought you expected – "

"I'd have been mighty disappointed if a car could have got that way," said Sooper with satisfaction, and, as Lattimer turned to go: "That man Elson's better, they tell me."

"Didn't even know he was ill," said Lattimer indifferently.

"I don't know whether delirium trimmings is illness or whether it's just experience, but he's better," said Sooper. "You might shoot up there tomorrow mornin' an' make a few tender inquiries. I'd send him flowers, only it seems premature. And, Lattimer, I want you at court tomorrow."

"Very good, sir."

Adjoining the police station was a small cottage, which was Sooper's habitation. It possessed a microscopic garden, two bedrooms and a sitting-room all on one floor, whilst at the back of the house was a little field, wherein his priceless Buff Orpingtons lived on the fat of his neighbours' land, for they were chronic trespassers, and seldom came home except to sleep. Such was the magic of Sooper's name, however, that complaints were few, though his feathered brigands raided corn-fields and gardens for sustenance. There were other marauders, however, who respected neither Sooper nor his chickens. From the copse on the hill came brown, slinking shapes at nights – Sooper discovered the way the foxes came, and set a spring gun, with disastrous consequences to the local hunt. It was a good spring gun, home-made but good.

It was dark when Sooper went out to the small shed wherein his motor-cycle was stored. He had promised himself a tightening up of certain bolts and the cleaning of a carburettor, and some time after midnight was his favourite hour for effecting repairs.

Though his eyesight was excellent, he invariably guided himself to the shed by the simple process of putting up his hand and running his finger along the overhead flex which connected the house with the shed. Sooper was not a very good electrician, and he had fixed the lighting apparatus of the shed somewhat crudely.

When he put up his hand, he found, to his surprise, that the wire had gone. Stooping, he groped and found it trailing limply on the ground. There was nothing remarkable about a broken wire, except that, when Sooper had seen it in the daylight, it had stretched tautly, and there was no means by which the connection could have been destroyed.

Sharply he turned and went back into the house, carrying the loose end, and disconnected the plug through which the current was supplied. Under the light of a table lamp, he examined the flex. It had been cut: he saw the unmistakable pressure marks of pliers.

"Dear me!" said Sooper mildly.

If there was one thing more certain than another, it was that no practical joker dared play a trick on Sooper. The wire had been cut for a good and sufficient reason, and the object could not be to his advantage.

Going into his bedroom, he pulled a box from under his bed and took out a large and heavy Colt revolver, loaded it, and, after a search, discovered a police torch. Thus armed, he returned to the yard, and with cat-like steps moved silently towards the hut. No sound broke the stillness of the night save the distant sleepy cackle of a hen. Mentally he reconnoitred the position. The danger lay in the hut.

Sooper had fixed the electric light in the hut, but had forgotten the switch until the work was completed. In consequence, the switch was outside, protected from the weather under the eaves of the roof. The door was never fastened. It was a simple matter, both to gain admission to the yard and to enter the hut.

He walked cautiously forward, lighting his way with the lamp, and his hand touched the latch of the door. Keeping to one side, he suddenly jerked the door open. There was a deafening explosion, followed by the sound of breaking glass. When the smoke cleared away, Sooper peered through the crack of the door.

He knew the spring gun: it was his own. But he had not set it on the floor of the hut, with the barrel pointing towards the door, nor had he fastened the trip wire by a cord to the door. When he had seen that spring gun last it was some hundreds of yards away, cunningly concealed between two bushes.

He heard someone calling and went back to the house, to admit Lattimer.

"Hullo!" he said. "Thought you were in bed?"

"I heard an explosion: what was it? It was too near to be the trap gun." Lattimer was unusually agitated.

"Come right in," said Sooper. "Here's an opportunity for the younger school of detectives to figger out causes and effec's."

"Has any damage been done?" asked Lattimer breathlessly.

"Three panes of glass smashed, twenty-five high-class chickens woke out of their beauty sleep, but that's about all."

A cloud of smoke hung in the heavy air, and the not unpleasant smell of burnt gunpowder pervaded the cottage. Lattimer followed his chief into the hut and inspected the spring gun, a primitive arrangement, made all the more crude by Sooper's amateur workmanship.

"Did you leave the gun in the hut?" asked Lattimer.

Sooper made an impatient clicking noise.

"Certainly I did," he said sarcastically, "*and* tried to commit suicide. Sort of hobby of mine."

He looked owlishly at the reeking weapon and then shook his head.

"Gosh! he's getting scared!" he said.

"Who?" demanded Lattimer quickly.

"The feller that laid this little trap for me. Plumb scared. I'll bet he's just the sickest dog for miles around. He knew I'd turn on the light before I opened the door, and thought I might see the gun in time, so he cut the wire. He's the cutest little thing, that Big Foot. Now I'll tell you sump'n', Sergeant: if that man Elson had kept in bed, this wouldn't have happened. No, sir. If he'd been put in a strait-jacket and tied down so as he couldn't go wanderin' around, that spring gun would be right up by the covert."

"Do you think Elson did this?"

"No, sir, I don't," said Sooper, "and I never said so. Don't go puttin' words into my mouth that I didn't use. I merely remarked that if that guy had been put into a padded cell, I shouldn't be in the position tomorrow of payin' good money for new glass. I thought you were in bed, Sergeant?" he said again.

"No, I don't feel so tired as I did. I was walking up and down the road smoking, when I heard the shot fired. This case is getting on my nerves."

"You're temp'ramental," said Sooper.

He slouched back to the house, the sergeant just behind him.

"Go sleep, my son. You'll lose all your pretty colour."

He waited till Lattimer had gone back to his quarters, then he returned to the yard with a lamp, and began a systematic search of the grounds. There were a dozen ways by which his murderous-minded visitant might have secured admission, but traces of his enemy were non-existent. The ground was dry and hardened. The intruder had left no trail.

"I might have got one of those well-known bloodhounds," said Sooper next morning, as he shaved. "Most all detectives use bloodhounds. I'd have got one myself, only I don't know one hound from another."

"Do you think," asked Lattimer, "that somebody put the gun there with the intention of killing you? It may have been a joke."

"It doesn't take a lot to make me laugh," said Sooper, screwing up his face as the razor rasped round his chin, "but that sort of joke wouldn't get a single ha-ha from me, not in a million years. Or ten millions," he added.

"Where did you see the gun last?"

"At the far end of the field, near the hawthorn bushes. I put it there to discourage fox-huntin'. Suppose I'd opened that door without knowin', what would people have said? They'd have said: 'That old fool Sooper put the gun back in the shed an' forgot it was there.' Verdict of accidental death, with a vote of consolation for the widder, which, as I'm not married, would have been superfl'ous. Can't understand where juries get that sentimental stuff. There'd have been a three-line par in the dailies, maybe four. And possibly a line or two in the back-chat gossip. Lattimer, when I pass out at the hands of miscr'ants and roughnecks, I want a column, with a pitcher. I know what I'm entitled to. When I think about the dirty dog who put that gun in the shed, I get all flushed and hectic. The explosion might have done fearful harm to my machine. As it is, the paint around the handle-bars is all cockled up and blistered. I'll have to put a new coat on Firefly – how does a deep orange strike you, Sergeant?"

"All of a heap," said Lattimer.

Sooper stropped his razor with a far-away look in his eyes.

"Elson's better. He'll be walkin' about the grounds tonight. I've phoned the war department to send me a tank. At least, I haven't, but I'm thinkin' of doing so."

Jim Ferraby, who was one of the witnesses at the inquest, had arranged to bring his car to pick up Sooper and Lattimer on his way to Pawsey. He found the old man in a very agreeable, even jocular, frame of mind, and certainly could not have guessed from his demeanour how narrow an escape from death he had had in the early hours of the morning. Whilst he was waiting outside the station for Sooper to deliver one of his eleventh-hour orations to the officer in charge of the station, he saw Cardew's machine pass and the lawyer stopped the car.

"No, thank you, I've arranged to drive Sooper to Pawsey," said Jim to the kindly invitation.

Cardew smiled grimly.

"I hope to have the pleasure of driving him back," he said. 'I believe I can give him a definite line as to how the murder was committed. It came to me in the night when I was half asleep, and the more I think of it the more certain I am that I've found the true solution for what seemed an inexplicable mystery. What is more," he went on impressively, 'I have turned up a case almost parallel – the Starkie murder which was committed in 1769, and which was fully reported in one of the old calendars. It appears that a man named Starkie…"

But Jim had neither the time nor the wish to listen to the details of a hundred-and-forty-year-old murder, and excused himself as Sooper appeared on the station step, pulling on the second of a pair of gloves which were so patently misallied that Jim attributed the queer effect to Sooper's absent-mindedness.

"One isn't as bad as the other," said Sooper, as he settled himself by Jim's side and stretched his legs luxuriously. "I always lose the left hand of my gloves – wonder nobody ever thought of selling gloves singly: there'd be a fortune in it. There goes old Cardew in a cloud of dust, his mind filled with hypotheses and conjectures! He's got what they call a legal mind – in other words, he can't see straight."

"He has a theory to expound to you," said Jim, as the car, gathering speed, rapidly overhauled the slower limousine in front.

"I should say he had," said Sooper comfortably.

"It came to him in the middle of the night."

"Too ashamed to be seen around in the daytime," said Sooper. "Gosh! I wouldn't have that man's mind for ten million pounds! It's full of atmospherics – a term," he explained, "that I've picked up from studying the wireless. No, sir, I can tell you in advance what his the'ry's goin' to be – he won't have the nerve to pull that secret cellar stuff on me. His the'ry is that Hannah Shaw was murdered by Miss Leigh."

"What!" almost shouted Jim, and in his agitation he sent the car swerving across the road.

"Forgive me if I holler," said Sooper, who did not indicate any desire to "holler". "My nerves are not what they used to be. But that's his the'ry, I'll bet! Miss Leigh met Hannah Shaw – didn't she wire for her? – that there was a quarrel, and that Miss Leigh shot her, got out of the house and locked the door."

"But that's preposterous!"

"Of course it's preposterous," said Sooper cheerfully," but that's the kind of the'ry that a highly romantic man like Mr Cardew would get."

"He never struck me as romantic," smiled Jim, as, with a warning blare from the electric horn, he swept past the subject of their discussion.

"He's romantic," said Sooper; "otherwise, what does he read all these books about anthr'pology for? If there's anythin' more romantic than deduction, show me to it!"

A little later he mentioned casually, as it were a matter of no great importance, the incident of the spring gun.

"Scared me a bit. But not so much as the price that window man Isaacs asks for puttin' in new glass. He says there's a glass trust, and all the prices are up. He was lying likely enough: Isaacs couldn't tell the truth to a Rabbi."

He looked back over his shoulder. Mr Cardew's machine was a long distance away.

"When a professional man gets the fever for publicity he never knows where to stop. There'll be pitchers of him in all the papers tomorrow, and none of these newspaper men will ask me as much as to smile. Personally, I like to work without publicity. I'm one of the strong silent types that you read about in books. Ever noticed that?"

"No," said Jim truthfully.

"It's a fact," said Sooper. "I hide away from these reporting lizards. The *Surrey Comet* once said: 'Superintendent Minter likes to work in the dark' – I've got six copies of that paper; I'll show it to you one of these days."

Sooper's modesty was not very apparent when they reached the Town Hall where the inquest was to be held, for Jim noticed that he instantly attached himself to the largest group of reporters, and soon after disappeared at the head of the gang in the direction of the Royal Hotel. The group returned in time for the opening of the court, and Sooper justified himself.

"I just set up one round for the boys. I didn't want 'em to mention me, so I thought I'd better tell 'em so. Nothin' like gettin' on the right side of the Press if you want to keep your name out of the papers."

It was rather remarkable, Jim noted that evening, when he was skimming the report of the inquest, that, in spite of Sooper's precautions every newspaper not only mentioned him by name, but had a most flattering reference to his perspicuity, his genius and his many admirable qualities.

The proceedings were longer than Jim anticipated. Sooper's evidence was a marvel of condensation, but it took some considerable time to give. He himself was on the stand for half an hour, whilst Cardew's evidence took an hour to hear, and it was well into the after-noon before the court again adjourned.

"Did you hear that feller Cardew givin' evidence?" asked Sooper bitterly. "I knew he'd drag in measurements – he did it to spite me. When that fool coroner thanked him for his very valuable data, he almost bust himself with pride."

They had tea at the hotel before they began their journey back to town, and Mr Cardew, uninvited, joined them, though he might have known, by the steel in Sooper's eyes, that it was neither the moment nor the opportunity for exposing his hypothesis. Jim tried to switch him on to a fresh track, but Mr Cardew would not be denied.

"I mentioned to Ferraby this morning, Superintendent, that I'd hit upon what I feel is the solution of this remarkable mystery."

"Listen to this, Lattimer," said Sooper, with ominous politeness. "A young officer can't know too much. And when you get a gen'leman like Mr Cardew pullin' out the'ries, you ought to listen. It may be an education. On the other hand it may not. You never can tell. Sit up an' listen!"

But Lattiiner had needed no such injunction: he was listening intently.

"As I understand the evidence," Mr Cardew began, "you three gentlemen were concealed on the beach road when poor Hannah made her appearance. You saw her as she passed silhouetted against the sky; you noticed her hat and her figure; saw her stop before the door. You did not see her get out."

"Perfectly true," murmured Sooper. "That's a bit of deduction you ought to be proud of."

"Well, you *said* you didn't see her get out," said the other good-humouredly. "And if you did not see her get out, you did not see the man who was concealed in the back of the car, crouching down to escape observation. He had probably jumped on to the car unknown to Hannah, and, waiting until she had opened the door, sprung on her, silenced her cries, and dragged her inside. The locked kitchen almost proves that he was using that place as a prison."

"The door shut behind him – I heard it slam," said Sooper wearily.

"He could have closed it with his foot," was the quick response. "What happened in the kitchen we shall never know. It is certain that they had not been there very long before this murderous scoundrel shot the poor woman. What did he do then?"

"Ah! what *did* he do?" asked Sooper.

Cardew looked at him face to face.

"He put on her coat and hat," he said slowly, "came out of the door, locked and padlocked it, got into the car and switched on the lights. You say they were on for a few seconds and then turned off, and the reason is obvious: when he put on the lights they would fall upon the wall immediately in front of the headlamps, and light would be reflected back and would reveal to any person who happened to be within sight the fact that it was not a woman but a man, in spite of the woman's hat he was wearing."

Sooper was silent.

"He then turned the car up the road," Cardew went on, evidently enjoying the mild sensation he had created, "came to the top of the cliff, threw away the coat and hat, and made his way on foot to where a car was waiting – probably a small car, easily concealed."

Sooper was staring blankly at the lawyer.

"That's one of the most remarkable the'ries I've ever heard," he said at last, and Jim knew that he was not being sarcastic. His eyes were wide open, his ugly mouth gaped; his very moustache seemed to bristle. "That's one of the most remarkable the'ries I've ever heard! By gosh, you're right!"

There was a dead silence. Then Sooper rose slowly and extended his huge hand and grasped Cardew's.

"Thank you," he said simply.

Not a word did Sooper speak on the journey from Pawsey to his station. He declined Jim's invitation to sit by his side, and huddled himself up in the back with Lattimer, and only once on the journey did Jim hear him so much as grunt. At parting he broke his silence.

"I'm taking back a lot I said about Cardew – not all, but a lot," he said soberly. "I never thought lawyers of that kind had much use except to write letters to people who haven't paid the coal bill. But that Cardew's done sump'n' that no other feller could do, Mr Ferraby." He poked his long finger in Jim's chest. "He's given me confidence in myself! He's shown me that I'm cleverer than him, and a man that can do that is what I might term a public benefactor."

"But in what way are you cleverer than he?" asked Jim in amazement.

"He didn't mention Big Foot. Now I" – he tapped himself in turn – "I know who Big Foot is! Know him as well as I know Lattimer." He glared round at the sergeant. "And I know it without the'ries, deductions, hypotheses, or any other book stuff. For days I've had Big Foot in my office. I could introduce you to Big Foot just when I like."

"The murderer?"

Sooper nodded.

"Big Foot was certainly the murderer."

"And he came in through the back door of the bungalow?"

133

Sooper nodded again.

"Yes, sir; he came in various ways, but he certainly came in by the back door of the bungalow."

Jim was bewildered.

"But did Hannah Shaw know him?"

"No, sir, Hannah Shaw never heard them feet of his, never saw them. She was dead before Big Foot came."

"But, Sooper, you said she was murdered by him?"

"So she was," said Sooper, turning to enter the station. "The'rize on that, son. And, Sergeant, get me an evening paper; I want to see what those stenographic criminals have been sayin' about me."

THE PASTRY

The privilege which had been exclusively enjoyed by Sooper was extended to Jim. He was permitted to stay half an hour in Elfa Leigh's little flat, and hear the latest report on her father.

"They would not let me stay the night at the nursing home," she said, "and perhaps they are wise. He is quite cheerful and happy in his way, and really most tractable. It all seems like a dream to me, a pleasant and yet unpleasant dream. It is dreadful to think of those years when he was wandering about the country, without anybody to care for him."

Jim had also seen the great surgeon; the date of the operation had been fixed. The doctor and his assistant were hopeful of the result and had recited a very cheering list of similar cases that had made good recoveries.

"No, I'm not worried about the operation," she said quietly, when he asked her. "I'm not really worried at all, because the Embassy are doing everything for him. They have been most sympathetic and kind, and have offered me an income until he recovers, so that there's really no necessity for my going back to Mr Cardew at all."

"Have you heard from Cardew?"

"Yes, he telephoned me this morning," she said. "He was awfully kind, but very vague. I had the impression that he is so absorbed in the problem of poor Miss Shaw's death that he really cannot bring his mind to bear on my affairs. He is rather a dear."

"Who – Cardew?" Jim smiled. "I know one man who doesn't share your view."

"Sooper? Of course! But then, Sooper is a law unto himself, for one cannot imagine Sooper – how easily one falls into the habit of using that nickname! – holding views remotely resembling ordinary people's! He is a dear too. Is he really as tough as he seems – he talks so queerly?"

"Sooper is one of the oldest officers in the force," said Jim. "I could never quite make up my mind whether his education is as deficient as he pretends. But then, Sooper has so many poses that it is difficult to keep track of them…"

The telephone bell rang at that moment, and the girl took up the instrument and listened, with a gathering frown.

"No, I sent nothing…yes, I'm sure. Please don't give it to him. I will come round."

She put down the instrument, and her face wore an air of concern.

"I can't understand it," she said. "The matron of the nursing home called me up to ask if I had sent a small cherry pie for my father. Of course I haven't. A messenger brought it, with a note supposed to have come from me."

Jim whistled. "That sounds queer," he said.

When the girl went hurriedly into the room to dress, he bethought him of Sooper, and in a moment of inspiration called that gentleman on the phone. By great good fortune, Sooper was within a few feet of the instrument when it rang, and listened without comment whilst Jim told him of the call from the nursing home.

"Tell 'em to hold that pie until I come. And after you've seen Miss Leigh to her apartments, wait for me outside the nursing home. If you see an officious young man who's interested in your loafing around, mention my name."

It was the first intimation Jim had had that the home was being watched.

When they arrived at the place where the sick man was lying, they were admitted to the matron's private room. On the centre of the table, wrapped in grease-proof paper, was the suspicious confectionery.

"I didn't like to give him any until I was absolutely sure you had sent it," said the matron. "Mr Minter was very emphatic on that point."

"Did you say there was a letter?"

The matron gave her an envelope. At the first glance at the superscription, Elfa said: "This is not my writing."

Nor was the brief note inside. It was on plain paper, her address in Cubitt Street being written at the top, and was a brief request that the pastry might be given to her father.

"Do you know the writing?" asked Jim.

She shook her head.

"I have never seen it before," she said. "But why send the pie at all? Is it — oh no, that can't possibly be." Her face went white.

"Probably some well-meaning friend," Jim endeavoured to soothe her.

"But who would wish to harm father?" she asked. She looked down at the innocent-looking pastry fearfully.

"What am I to do with this?" asked the matron.

"Keep it, please," said Jim quickly. He glanced significantly at the girl, and the woman understood.

Though he made light of the incident, Elfa had no doubt in her mind as to its significance.

"I heard you telephoning Mr Minter," she said, as they were driving back to Cubitt Street. "Is he coming to town?"

"He'll be there when I get back. You're not to worry about this, Elfa."

She noticed the more intimate term of address; it seemed very right that he should call her "Elfa".

"There is so much behind my father's absence that is inexplicable, that I don't think I'll try to disentangle the skein," she said, with a hopeless gesture. "I shan't go to bed just yet. Will you telephone me if anything is discovered?"

With this assurance he left her and returned to take up his post outside the nursing home. As Sooper anticipated, no sooner had he paused by the doorway than out of the darkness from the opposi side of the road appeared a stranger, who, without preliminary, asked him his business. Nor was Jim's explanation too readily accepted, for the detective is by nature sceptical. Fortunately, in the middle of the argument there came, from the direction of Cavendish Square, the sound of a machine-gun being fired at irregular intervals and a few seconds later Sooper, on his loud machine, came into view.

"Hit her up to forty on Barnes Common," said Sooper with illegal satisfaction. "Traffic cop tried to stop me at the railway crossroads, but he might as well have tried to take two big handfuls of a flash of lightnin'."

Propping the machine against the kerb, they went into the house, and the pie was brought out for his examination.

"Yes, it looks good," said Sooper. "I'll take it away, if you don't mind, miss. I suppose you couldn't remember what station the district messenger came from?"

"I think it was from Trafalgar Square," said the matron. "In fact, I'm sure."

They stopped only long enough to deposit the pastry at the police station, with instructions that it should be sent in a sealed jar to the public analyst the first thing in the morning, and went on to interview the messenger. Jim persuaded Sooper to leave his alarming vehicle at the police station, and it was by taxi that they travelled to Trafalgar Square.

There was no difficulty in confirming the matron's story. The parcel containing the pie had been left apparently by a nondescript individual, who was evidently a messenger of the real sender.

"A loafer picked up in the streets for a few pence," said Sooper. "We shan't find him without advertisin', and then, with the natural cunnin' of the criminal classes, he'll not turn up."

"He may not be a member of the criminal classes."

" loafer, an' all loafers are criminals," said Sooper, who had a ⸳⸳ping generalities.

Trafalgar Square and stood on the side of the Nelson's Monument thoughtfully.

"Wish I could run across Lattimer. He's in town somewhere and he's the very feller to put on to trail this loafer – Lattimer has got a natural affinity for people who won't work. I'll have to report this to the Yard, and I hate doin' it," he said. "That long-nosed Deputy will probably put another feller into the case, and that will get me all wrong."

With seeming reluctance he went down Whitehall, and had the satisfaction, when he got to the Yard, of discovering no one of sufficient importance on duty to take the case out of his hands, yet one having enough authority to deal immediately with the inquiry.

There was little to tell, yet Jim telephoned to the girl, relating the results of the investigations.

"Do you think it was poisoned?" she asked.

"Sooper isn't sure. We shall know for certain tomorrow."

It hurt him to hear the anxiety in her voice.

When he rejoined Sooper, that genius made a strange confession.

"Got an idea I'd like to go back in comfort. Where's that old bus of yours?"

"My car is garaged quite close here, and I'll take you down with pleasure. But I thought you were wedded to your infernal whizz-bang."

"I'm scarcely wedded," Sooper said.

Jim went off in a taxi to the garage and picked up Sooper at the police station. The old man had the cycle waiting, and lifted it on to the back of the car.

"Queer how ideas come to you, isn't it? Like Mr Cardew's, in the middle of the night. I've just had an idea that made me feel very joyful."

He refused, however, to share his joy with Jim.

The run back was quick and eventless.

"Come inside," said Sooper. "I won't keep you a minute. Maybe there's a spot of news."

News there was; the desk sergeant reported that he had received a visit from a motor-cyclist.

"He says that somebody fired two shots at him on the road a mile out of town," he said, and Sooper sighed happily.

"They didn't hit him, eh? I guess they misjudged the rate he was travelling. He's probably one of these drivers who can't get more than twenty-five out of his machine. Now, if I'd been on Firefly, doing my forty, they'd have got me sure."

"You!" gasped Jim. "Were they shooting at you?"

"You bet they were shooting at me," said Sooper calmly. "You talk about my being wedded to Firefly – that's just what I want to be. I'd hate to know that Firefly was a widder."

Jim understood now why Sooper had seemed anxious to return by car. Supposing that the explosion of the previous night had not been an accident, and that his life had been attempted, he would be an easy mark for an ambuscade. The noise of his strange machine could be heard for miles (it afterwards appeared that the cyclist who had been fired at was also astride a particularly thunderous engine).

"I shouldn't be surprised at anythin' happenin' now," said Sooper philosophically. "But they've got to be quick – Lattimer back?"

"No, sir," said the station sergeant, "he's in town."

But here he said that which was not true. At that identical moment Lattimer was sitting on a fence between two high bushes on the dreariest part of the London road, a large automatic pistol in his hand and a very resentful feeling towards his chief in his heart. For he had not seen Sooper pass.

SMOKE FROM HILL BROW

It seemed the most natural thing in the world to Jim Ferraby that he should call at Cubitt Street in the morning, wait till the girl came down, and drive her the all too short distance which separated Cubitt Street from Weymouth Street. He had not the excuse that it was on his way; it was, in fact, so much out of his way that it doubled his journey. This aspect of his service was pointed out to him on the first morning, and was emphasized at night when he called for her at Weymouth Street. Mr Leigh had had a good day, sleeping most of the time. The nurse reported that it was in the night that he was most wakeful.

"He must have got into the habit of sleeping by day and moving about in the dark," she said. "I have an idea that he recognized me this afternoon. He looked in such a puzzled way, as if he was trying to recall something or somebody. Just before I came out he asked me if I could not take him to the sea. He said he wanted to look after 'three' and 'four'. According to the matron he made the same request to her last night. Who are 'three' and 'four'?"

Jim shook his head.

"I must pass that piece of information to Sooper. Did you see the doctor?"

She had interviewed the surgeon, and the operation was fixed for Saturday. He had made certain tests and was satisfied that Leigh could be restored to normal health.

Her first question that morning was about the pastry and Jim ha answered glibly that the analyst had discovered no sign of poison. S did not seem convinced. On the way back to Cubitt Street she asked again.

"I got through to Sooper, and he told me that there was no poison," he assured her, but Elfa Leigh's scepticism was not dispelled.

"I have been wondering today whether father witnessed the murder, or knew the murderer," she said. "At lunch time today I went to King's Bench Walk and saw Mr Cardew, and he is quite certain that, if an attempt was really made upon father last night, it was because he had seen things happen at the cottage. Daddy lived in a cave within view of Beach Cottage, you know that, of course? Sooper told me this morning that the cave had been explored by the police, and there's proof that he must have been living there for years. He used to let himself down the cliff face by a rope ladder at night and climb up before daybreak, pulling the ladder after him. It was so white with chalk that Mr Minter said it could have escaped notice, even in the daytime."

"You've seen Sooper, then?"

Sooper had apparently made a very brief call at Weymouth Street, but with some skill had avoided discussing the analyst's report on the pastry.

After Jim dropped her at the door of her flat, he lingered awhile, waiting the invitation to enter.

"I'm going to be inhospitable and let you go home without a cup of tea," she said. "I'm so awfully tired."

Again he urged the recuperative value of tea in the park, with a Guards' band playing. She did not even grant that request.

"I wish it was all over," she said. "I have a feeling…such a horrid feeling of danger…as though something terrible was going to happen."

"You sound as if you were a perfect subject for tea in the park," ` enticingly, but she smiled her farewell and the door closed

`ᵉ end. He had kept himself free for the evening, rk waiting for him at home, the very thought ⸀f mental nausea.

It was a fine evening; he did not feel inclined for a solitary dinner, and mechanically he turned his car westward. His first inclination was to visit Sooper, but when he arrived he found that worthy gentleman had gone away to an unknown destination. Even Lattimer was invisible. Jim sent the car up the hill to Barley Stack, and had the satisfaction of surprising the amateur criminologist, who was pacing his lawn, his hands clasped behind him, his high forehead corrugated in thought. At the sound of the whining engine he turned and waved a cheery hand.

"If there is one man I wanted to meet tonight, that man is you, though I have no particular reason except...well, I suppose I'm suffering from the reaction of poor Hannah's death. It still seems so unreal that every minute I expect to hear her domineering voice" – he hesitated – "I don't want to be unkind...poor Hannah!" He sighed heavily. "The servants, I am sorry to say, do not show the amount of sorrow one would have expected for a hard task-mistress. Hannah was hard, but then, there was a lot of good in her that nobody understood."

They had walked to the far end of the lawn, along the smaller grass plot that ran at right angles, and from here they had a view of Hill Brow. There was something sinister about that great red house, Jim thought. And then he heard an exclamation from his companion.

"It is rather a warm evening for fires, isn't it?" he asked.

From one of the tall pseudo-Elizabethan chimneys, a cloud of white smoke was drifting.

"I happen to know," said Mr Cardew slowly, "that that chimney connects with Elson's furnace. Now why on earth has he lit his furnace on a night like this?"

The two men stood in silence, watching the strange phenomenon. Evidently the furnace was being very incessantly fed, for the smoke did not diminish in volume.

"Perhaps they are burning garden refuse," suggested Jim.

Mr Cardew shook his head.

"There is an incinerator in the grounds for that purpose. Besides, at this time of the year everything is so green, and the leaves have not begun to fall."

Jim watched the chimney, not quite certain in his mind whether the spectacle was as remarkable as the lawyer thought.

"He may be making a clearance of old papers," he suggested. "I have that kind of urge once a year, and I never stop to consider whether it is appropriate weather."

Mr Cardew smiled mysteriously.

"I do not know our friend very well," he said, "but he never struck me as being a man with a tidy mind – I wonder what he is burning?"

He looked round and summoned the surly-faced gardener whom Jim had seen on an earlier visit.

"I want you to take a note over to Mr Elson," he said, and disappeared into the house to write it.

When the man had gone on his errand, Cardew explained his subtle scheme.

"I've asked Elson to come over to dinner tomorrow," he said. "Not that I want him! But I have an idea, when Frederick gets to Hill Brow, he'll find Elson alone in the house."

"Which will prove…?" asked Jim.

"It will prove nothing, except that for some very pressing reason Elson has sent away his servants whilst he indulges in this orgy of burning," said Cardew. "And now I would like to show you something very interesting."

Jim followed him to the study, and he guessed what the "something" was, when he saw a bulky object on the library table. It was covered with sheets of paper, and these Mr Cardew removed, revealing a perfect model of Beach Cottage.

"I had it constructed by a model-maker in twenty-four hours," he said, with pardonable pride. "The roof comes off" – he lifted it as he spoke, revealing the tiny rooms beneath. "The man didn't get the colouring, but that is unimportant; and I have had to rely upon my memory for the position of the various articles of furniture. This," said Mr Cardew, indicating a space with a penholder, "is the kitchen. The model is drawn to scale; you will observe the bolts on the back door. And here is the servery." He slipped back a tiny panel, and showed the connection between kitchen and dining-room. "Now, here is a remarkable fact," he said impressively; "from the time Hannah Shaw went into the house until she, or somebody else, came out, is considerably less than five minutes. It is clear that she or they went immediately into the kitchen – why?"

"To get the letter," said Jim, and Cardew gaped at him.

"The letter!" he squeaked. "What do you mean by letter?"

"There was a letter addressed to the coroner of West Sussex; Sooper found the envelope and a loose brick in the kitchen immediately under the table, where this document had evidently been concealed."

Mr Cardew's distress was comical.

"A letter?" he said. "That didn't come out at the inquest. This upsets my theory to a very considerable extent. I wish to heaven that old man wouldn't be so infernally reticent!"

"I probably shouldn't have told you about the envelope at all," said Jim.

Mr Cardew sat down, eyeing the model gloomily.

"It may fit in," he said at last, but some of the confidence had gone from his tone. "I did not allow for there being another motive for the murder," he said. "The envelope was addressed to the coroner; is it suggested that this was a case of suicide?"

"Even Sooper wouldn't suggest that," smiled Jim.

He was already blaming himself for betraying Sooper's mystery to the rival.

"It is a queer thing that the idea of suicide occurred to me, but then, of course, no weapon was found, and that makes it impossible."

"Added to which, the doors were locked on the outside," suggested Jim, and Cardew nodded.

"Yes, I've got to start all over again. But I'm determined to find an explanation. I respect Superintendent Minter, who works on what I would describe as the rule of thumb method, which certainly does produce roughly good results. But I am convinced that this is not a case where the rule of thumb system can be successfully applied."

He took a folder from his cabinet and turned over the leaves, and Jim was amazed at the industry of this investigator. One page was covered with times and measurements. On another was a rough plan of the sea-front covered with lines which indicated the height of the tide at certain hours. There were innumerable unmounted photographs, showing the cottage from various angles. Yet another was a survey map of Sussex, over which Mr Cardew had scrawled in red ink what Jim supposed were possible routes of escape which the murderer might have taken. They were examining this when the gardener returned.

"I gave Mr Elson your note, sir," he said.

"Did he answer the door himself?" demanded Cardew eagerly.

"Yes, sir; it was five minutes before he came up. I think the servants must be out."

Cardew leant back in his chair with a smile.

"How was he dressed, Frederick? Tell me that. And did you notice whether Mr Elson's face and hands were – er – normal?"

"Normal" was a word outside the gardener's vocabulary.

"They were black," he said. "Looked as if he'd been sweeping the flues. He only had on his trousers and shirt, and he looked very hot to me."

Mr Cardew smiled again.

"Thank you, Frederick," he said, and, when the door closed, his eyes met Jim's.

"There *is* something doing," he said. "I was sure of it! And in how far is his recent curious behaviour connected with poor Hannah's death? Remember," he waved the penholder at Jim, "that he knew Hannah, and had met her secretly. I know from servants' gossip which has come to me since her death that she was a frequent visitor to Hill Brow. Now this is a fact that since that tragedy Elson has not been sober. He drank heavily before, but now he has thrown aside all restraint. Two of the maids left yesterday, and his valet is leaving him this week. He wanders about the house at night, and has had more than one fit of screaming terror."

He rose and replaced the roof of the model, covering it carefully with paper.

"Hitherto my investigations have been in the region of the abstract. I will now venture into a new field, for which neither my years nor my physique qualify me."

"In other words?" said Jim.

"In other words, I am going to find out the secret that Hill Brow holds," said Mr Cardew.

THE WARNING

Sergeant Lattimer waited for darkness to fall before he strolled out of his lodgings and, taking a circuitous but secluded route, made his leisurely way towards the American's home. He did not enter by the front gate but found a gap in the hedge, familiar enough to him, and, penetrating a thicket, came to the little green gate in the wall. This time Mr Elson was not there to meet him, nor was his presence necessary. Lattimer fitted a key, passed through the door, closed and locked it behind him, and, after a brief reconnaissance, walked noiselessly across the gravel drive to the front door. He did not knock. He had certain work to do, and this he performed rapidly. From his pocket he took a sheet of white paper, the back of which was evidently gummed, for when he licked and pressed it to the centre panel of the door, it adhered. This done, he half-circled the house, and, coming to a pair of French windows which opened on to the lawn, he tapped gently. For a time there was no response, and he knocked again, and heard the creak of a chair, saw the heavy curtains pulled aside, and Elson's frightened face peering out into the darkness.

"You, is it?" growled the man.

"Me," said the other laconically. "And you can put your gun back in your pocket; nobody is going to hurt you."

He pulled the curtains close after him, and, dropping into a chair, reached out his hand mechanically to the open cigar-box.

"Sooper's gone to town," he said.

"He can go to hell so far as I'm concerned," snarled the other.

The mark of his heavy drinking was visible; his face was scarcely recognizable to those who had seen him a week before; his hands were shaking, his loose lip quivered at the slightest provocation.

"I dare say... Sooper would go to most places if he could get a good killing."

"He'd better be careful..." began the man in a loud voice, but Lattimer's raised hand and pained expression silenced him.

"There's nothing to shout about."

"He's got nothing on me."

"Maybe he thinks he has," said Lattimer, biting off the end of the cigar with his strong teeth. "You never know what's at the back of Sooper's mind. I've been wondering if he suspects me. He gave me a long lecture this morning on the advantage of turning State's evidence. He said he'd go a long way to help any member of a gang who was prepared to spill it."

Elson licked his lips.

"I don't see how that affects you or me..." he began.

"Don't let us slide into personalities," said Lattimer lazily. "I'll take one small nip at the whisky; it'll be all the less for you – been having a bonfire tonight?"

"Me? What do you mean?"

"I saw your old chimney smoking. It seems a pretty warm night to have the furnace going."

Elson considered before he answered.

"I was getting rid of a lot of old junk," he said shortly.

They smoked without a word for five minutes, then Lattimer asserted, rather than asked: "You went into town this morning."

The man looked at him suspiciously.

"I wanted to get out of this cursed place. No harm about me going into the City, is there?"

"What sort of a cabin did you get?"

Elson jumped; his jaw dropped.

"The CPR route is a pretty comfortable one. I suppose you didn't like risking the direct line into New York?"

"How did you know?" gasped the other.

"I guessed you were flitting. I've had that feeling for a long time. And naturally, it's worried me," said Lattimer lazily. "I don't like to see a source of income slipping away."

"I thought you called the money 'loans'," sneered the other. "Why I gave you anything I don't know."

"I am useful," said Lattimer. "I may be more useful next Saturday. Naturally, you don't want anybody to know that you're leaving the country. I suppose, when you're safe in Canada – "

"I'm safe anywhere," exploded Elson violently. "I tell you, the police have nothing on me!"

"You've told me that so often that I almost believe it," laughed Lattimer. "Now come across, Elson; what's the hurry?"

"I'm tired of England," said the other doggedly. "Since Hannah was killed, my nerves have gone. Say, Lattimer, what has happened to that tramp?"

"The fellow Sooper pinched? Oh, he's in London somewhere. Why?"

"I don't know – just interested," said Elson huskily. "I saw him in my garden the morning he was pinched – the chauffeur was on the road when Minter took him. That tramp sort of rubbed me raw. Nutty, isn't he?"

"Mad? Why yes, I think he is – at least, Sooper thinks he is. I haven't got a licence to think when Sooper's around."

"Listen, Lat" – Elson leant forward and dropped his voice to a hoarse whisper – "you know the law of this country…nobody'd take notice of what a nutty fellow said, would they? I mean, the law? Supppose he starts something – sort of charges people with – things? The law wouldn't fall for that nutty stuff, would it?"

Lattimer was eyeing him steadily.

"What are you afraid of?" he asked.

"Afraid of nothing," snapped Elson. "Did I tell you I was afraid of anything? Well! Only I'm curious; I've got a hunch I've met that fellow in America somewhere. Maybe down in Arizona, when I was – I was farming and did him dirt – I've done a lot of people that way; you see what I mean? That's the only thing I'm scared of."

150

He was lying, and Lattimer knew he was lying.

"I guess they wouldn't take very much notice of what a madman said – I hope they wouldn't anyway. But he's not going to be mad very long. Sooper told me there is to be an operation and there is every hope of his recovering."

Elson leaped to his feet, his face livid.

"That's a lie! A lie! He couldn't get right! God, if I had known – if I had known!"

Lattimer was watching him unemotionally. Not a line of his saturnine face moved.

"I thought so; he's the fellow that has got the pull on you. You can make your mind easy. John Leigh will be days and weeks before they let him talk – if he ever talks."

The other man was calmer now, and something in Lattimer's tone arrested him as he turned to the half-empty decanter by his side.

"What is he to you, anyway?" he asked.

The sergeant shrugged.

"He means nothing to me," he said.

Still Elson made no attempt to move. His swollen face was thrust downwards towards Lattimer.

"Suppose he's not as mad as you think he is? They say he's got a cave or something up in the cliffs near Beach Cottage. It is likely he wasn't so far away when Hannah went out. How would that affect you?"

Lattimer laughed and sent a cloud of smoke up to the ceiling.

"How would it affect you?" he asked significantly. "You're wrong if you think that I know this man Leigh. I've heard of him, naturally, but I'd never seen him until Sooper put him into the cooler – I don't know that he was even in the cooler; when I saw him, he was in Sooper's office, drinking tea."

He saw Elson's hand raised, enjoining silence. The man was listening intently. Presently he pulled out his watch.

"My servants are back," he said.

"Will they come in here?"

"Not unless I ring for them."

Almost as he spoke, there came a tap at the door. Lattimer rose quickly and slipped behind the curtains, as his host went to the door and unlocked it. It was his valet.

"Excuse me, sir," said the man, "I didn't want to disturb you – "

"Well, why have you?" asked Elson harshly.

"Well, I was wondering, sir, if you'd seen the notice on the door? I couldn't get it off; it was gummed on tight."

"Notice on the door?" demanded Elson, in a different tone. "What are you talking about?"

He dashed past the servant and ran across the hall, the lights of which were now burning. Jerking open the door, he saw the white square of paper pasted on the panel and read it slowly, unbelievingly.

FIRST HANNAH SHAW.
YOU WILL BE THE NEXT TO GO.
BIG FOOT.

His hand went up to his throat; he tried to articulate, but nothing escaped but a thin whine of anguish. Staggering back to his study, he slammed the door and locked it.

"Lattimer!" he gasped. "Lattimer!"

He jerked aside the curtains, but Lattimer was gone the way he had come.

TEA IN THE PARK

There came from Sooper's backyard a "chicka-chick-bang!" which was fairly familiar to everybody who lived within a radius of one mile. The proprietor of the local picture house had once hired Sooper's bicycle to produce the effects in a great battle scene, and that was about the only time that the engine of Firefly (he called it The Hawk in those days) had been known to run without producing sounds suggestive of a trench raid. Once a party of admirers had subscribed to buy him the latest and the most silent of machines; the presentation had been made in the presence of the Mayor, the Corporation and the local ministry. Sooper kept the machine for exactly a week, and then it disappeared. He told a thrilling story of it having been smashed up, but it is an open secret that he sold it by public auction, and out of the proceeds of the sale added an incubator to his poultry yard, a new coat of paint to Firefly, and a not inconsiderable sum to his account at Barclay's Bank.

It was very early in the morning, before most citizens were abroad, though it could not be said with truth that anybody within range was sleeping. He had mounted the machine upside down on a kitchen table, and was engaged in regulating a piece of mechanism which was only complicated because it was Sooper's own repair work.

A respectful officer stood by in his shirt-sleeves. This policeman had some knowledge of mechanics, and he was invariably employed, on such occasions as these, to agree with all that Sooper said. He remained a mechanical authority just so long as he adopted this attitude.

"Noise is nature, Constable," said Sooper, plying a spanner. "Never heard that anybody put a silencer on thunder, did you?"

"No, sir."

"The sheep make noises, and the cattle within thy gates, to quote that well-known expression."

"I only suggest, sir, that you could put a better silencer on the machine," said the officer respectfully.

"It would be a waste of money, Constable. Besides, people like the sound of Firefly. They just turn over in their beds and they say: 'Everything's all right; Sooper's around.'"

At that particular moment, many people were turning over in their beds without experiencing a glow of satisfaction that he was on hand.

"But, Sooper, isn't it a bad thing; suppose a farmyard robber hears you coming – "

"They'd never hear me coming," said Sooper, glaring at the officious man. "This machine's highly ventriloq'al. You think you hear it coming in one direction when it is really coming in another. What's the matter with you this morning, Constable? You're arguin' an' arguin'. Gosh! I can't get a word in edgeways!"

Thereafter the constable remained discreetly silent.

Sooper finished his work to his entire satisfaction, lit his pipe and examined the morning sky, and found it good. Disappearing into the hut, he came back with a large bag of chicken-feed, which he slung over his shoulder and carried to his clamouring children. The inspection of hen-houses and collection of eggs being concluded, Sooper went in to perform his toilet, and had reached the stage when he was hissing into his rough towel, when Lattimer reported for duty.

"Where were you last night, Lattimer?" asked Sooper, growling over the edge of the towel.

"It was my night off, sir."

"There used not to be such a thing as a night off in my days," grumbled the old man. "Bring my letters."

Lattimer came back with a small wad of official correspondence, and Sooper sorted his mail accurately.

"That's a bill, that's a complaint about Firefly, that's a hue-and-cry, that's a letter from that smart Alec in the Pay Department," he muttered rapidly, as envelope after envelope passed through his fingers. "And that's what I want."

It was in a plain envelope, Lattimer noticed, and the letter had some sort of printed heading which he could not read.

"Humph!" said Sooper, when he had scanned the contents. "Ever heard of aconite?"

"No, sir. Is it a poison?"

"Slightly poisonous. As much as would go on the head of a pin would kill you, Lattimer, though it wouldn't kill me, bein' more robust an' not spending my nights jazzin' an three steppin' with a parcel of girls."

"Is the letter from the analyst, sir?" asked Lattimer.

"It is. You might put through an inquiry and find out if anybody's been buyin' aconitine. It's not usually sold. Ask the Yard. Never heard of aconitine, eh?"

Sooper was fastening his collar, his twisted face upturned to the ceiling.

"No, sir, I've never heard of that drug."

"I'll bet you old Cardew, the famous amateur sleuth, could tell you a dozen cases where it's been used."

"Very likely," agreed Lattimer.

"I don't like poisoners," mused Sooper, tying his cravat with unusual care. "They're about the meanest kind of murderers; they never confess. Did you know that, Lattimer? A poisoner never confesses, not even when he's toeing the 'T'."

"I didn't know that, sir," said the patient Lattimer.

"I'll bet old Cardew knows. I'll bet he's got books about murderers and about poisoners that would make your hair curl. I must get a subscription to one of these scientific libraries; I'm so far behind the times that it's catching me up in the first lap."

He concluded his official correspondence in a very short time, and, mounting his machine, began a round of important calls. They would not appear to be very important from any other viewpoint than

155

Sooper's. He was a quarter of an hour in the telephone exchange, interviewing another kind of superintendent; he was nearly two hours at the village stationer's in the High Street, and during that period obtained a very considerable knowledge of writing papers, their watermarks and characteristics. At the typewriter agency, his stay was brief but informative. But it was not until he had left his district far behind him, and was wandering around the side streets that lead from the Strand, that his really important inquiries could be said to have begun.

Jim saw him quite by accident, as he and the girl were driving along Whitehall on their way to Green Park. A little to his distress, Elfa insisted upon stopping and running back nearly a hundred yards to overtake the long-striding old man.

"We're driving to Kensington Gardens; won't you come?" she asked.

Sooper looked round at the distant car.

"I don't suppose that young feller will be wantin' me, Miss Leigh. I'm not, an' never have been, the sort of man that'd come, so to speak, between two young lovin' hearts."

"Our hearts are young, Mr Minter, but they are not loving," said Elfa, going very red. "Mr Ferraby has been most kind to me."

"Who wouldn't be?" murmured Sooper. "You're sure he won't mind?"

"Of course he won't mind," said Elfa, slightly annoyed. "Why should he mind?"

Sooper got on board with a show of reluctance.

"I was just sayin' to this young lady that far be it from me to go buttin' in when two young people want to be alone."

"We're very glad to see you, Sooper," said Jim stiffly.

"I always say that young people have got plenty of time to canoodle an' hold hands an' do things of that kind, and there's no sense in gettin' sore when some old feller walks into the parlour without coughin' or knockin'. I've never been in love myself," he reflected sadly. "There was a certain affair between a widder woman – did I ever tell you about that temp'ramental widder?"

"I expect she missed you when you left her," said Jim viciously.

"She did – by inches. The plate hit the wall too near to be comfortable."

It was the only reference he had ever made to the cause of his breach with the temperamental widow.

"I like to see people marry young," he rambled on. "By the time they're old enough to be divorced, they've settled down."

"You're not exactly cheerful this evening, Sooper," said Jim, laughing in spite of himself.

"I never am cheerful at this time of the day."

As they passed the magazine in Hyde Park, the sentry on duty came stiffly to attention and presented arms. Sooper took off his hat solemnly.

"He was saluting the officer on the other sidewalk," explained the girl.

Sooper shook his head mournfully.

"I thought appreciation had come at last," he said. "If I had my due, the church bells'd ring every time I came into London."

Over a third cup in the alfresco tea ground, he made a passing reference to the business which had brought him to town. And then, with characteristic abruptness: "That pie had been doctored, young lady. I'm not going to pretend that it hadn't – anyway, you wouldn't believe me."

"You mean poisoned?" she said, going pale.

Sooper nodded vigorously.

"Got an idea somebody doesn't want your father to get his mind clear. Maybe he saw too many things from that little cave of his. In fact, I am inclined to think that it is somethin' which he saw before he went – before his mind changed. It's no use askin' me who did it, because I'm not at liberty to tell you, and if I told you, I haven't got evidence to arrest him."

His eyes wandered over the surrounding tables.

"When I was a young officer, I never dreamt of walkin' about like a gentleman, eatin' ice cream," he said.

So rapid was the transition from one subject to the other that the girl was bewildered, but Jim, who knew Sooper's queer habits, followed the direction of his eyes.

At a table on the outskirts he saw a familiar face.

"Did you bring Lattimer here?"

Sooper shook his head.

"Eatin' ice cream!" he said bitterly. "Like a young girl! Now, when I was his age, I'd have been takin' a sociable and manly glass of beer."

"Has he seen you?" asked Jim, dropping his voice.

"You bet he's seen me. That Lattimer sees everythin'. He's like the well-known spider with forty million eyes, or maybe four million."

Yet, if Lattimer saw him, he made no sign. He was indeed engaged in the operation of consuming a plate of ice cream, and did not betray any proper shame when Sooper came over and sat down facing him. Looking across, Jim saw the old man speak, and from his expression he guessed that Sooper was in his most vitriolic mood, for as he came stalking back, Lattimer summoned the waitress, paid his bill and disappeared somewhat hurriedly.

"I gave that feller strict instructions not to leave the station," he said, "an' here he is eatin' ice cream like a young lady! Got the time on you, Mr Ferraby? I don't carry a watch myself. There was some talk of presentin' me with one, but it fell through. If you ever find yourself with an old watch you don't want, maybe you'll shoot it down to me?"

When Jim had told him the hour, he got up.

"I'll have to go now; I've left my joy-waggon in the Bayswater Road; it's only a step from here."

With a nod to the girl he was gone, before she could ask even one of the questions she had made up her mind to put to him.

From where they sat they could see the road and the bridge leading across the lake. As Sooper strode off, Jim saw a man cross the road and follow at a respectful distance. It was Lattimer.

"I wonder what he's doing. Sooper said he'd sent him back to his headquarters, but he doesn't seem to be in any hurry."

They waited for half an hour, talking aimlessly, then strolled off to the car, which was parked by the side of the road. Jim was getting in when somebody addressed him by name.

"Excuse me, Mr Ferraby," said a voice.

He looked round, and his eyes fell upon an unknown face that he yet seemed to know. From his gaping boots to his battered straw hat, "tramp" was legibly written on every garment.

"Remember me, sir? Sullivan. I was the gentleman you was good enough to prosecute at the Old Bailey."

"Moses!" said Jim softly. "You're the brute that ought to be doing time!"

"That's right, sir," said the man, unabashed. "Haven't got the price of a bed about you, have you, sir? I've been sleeping out for a week."

Jim, who had no sentiment in matters of this kind, looked round for a policeman, but evidently Sullivan had taken the precaution of reconnoitring the ground for the same purpose. Jim saw the smile trembling at the corner of the girl's mouth and turned to her hopelessly.

"This is the 'poor fellow' to whom you once referred, Elfa. You remember I prosecuted him?"

"And you did it well, too, sir," said Sullivan ingratiatingly.

And now Jim saw, coming round the bend, a very welcome sight. It was a mounted police patrol. Sullivan saw him also.

"If you give me a couple of shillings, sir," he said rapidly and earnestly, "you'll be doing me a great favour. The only money I've earned was a shilling I got last night from a gent to take a pie to Trafalgar Square."

The keen-eyed patrol was coming forward at a trot as Sullivan turned to fly, but Jim's arm kept him.

"Come here, my friend. What's this story you tell me about carrying a pie? Who gave it to you?"

"Some fellow – I've never seen him before. He came up to me on the Embankment and asked me if I'd like to earn a shilling – I won't lie to you, sir, it's truth – by taking a parcel to the district messenger office."

"Did you see his face?" asked Jim quickly.

Sullivan shook his head. By this time the patrol was abreast of them and, bringing his horse to a standstill, was eyeing the vagrant unkindly. Jim stepped out into the road, and in a few words introduced himself and told the gist of the tramp's story.

"Yes, sir, we've had that inquiry in station orders," said the patrol, and beckoned to Sullivan. "You can come a walk with me," he said. "If you try to run I'll murder you."

That evening, Sullivan was taken down to an interview with Sooper. His story had many disappointing features. In the first place, he had not seen the stranger's face, and in the second, he was not prepared to identify him in any other way.

"He talked very sharp and official, sir. I thought he was a busy at first – I mean a detective."

"Say what you mean, bo'," said Sooper gently. "I'm sufficiently acquainted with the common talk of the lower orders to know what a 'busy' is. Sounded like a detective, did he?"

"Yes, sir, the way he ordered me about."

Sooper turned to the Central London man who had conducted Sullivan to the station.

"He's been identified by the district messenger, has he? Good! I seem to remember Mr Ferraby telling me that he asked him for the price of a bed? He's goin' to get one tonight, and it's goin' to cost him nothin'. Put him in the refrigerator where he'll freeze to death," said Sooper, with a lordly gesture, and Sullivan made a complaining exit.

CHLOROFORM

Mr Gordon Cardew was an omnivorous reader, and since he had retired from the practice of the law, he had devoured more books than the average gentleman's library contains. It was his practice to take a book to bed with him, for he was not the best of sleepers, and to resume in the early hours of the morning where he had left off the night before. Of late years his studies had been exclusively directed to that department of science, the mention of which never failed to arouse Sooper's derision. Yet anthropology can be a fascinating subject, and the bald records of dead criminals more thrilling than the most modern of romances. Cardew had discovered that not a day passed which did not increase his store of knowledge and widen his outlook upon the criminal, his method and his psychology.

He was still in bed, with Mantegazza's well-intentioned but misguided treatise on physiognomy set against his knees, and his mind divided between the theories of that great criminologist and the adjourned inquest which would be resumed in a few days' time, when the maid brought him his morning tea, and set it on the table beside the bed.

"Mr Minter is downstairs, sir."

"Minter? Good heavens!" said Cardew, jerking himself up. "What time is it?"

"Half past seven, sir."

"Minter, at this hour? Tell him I will be down in a few minutes."

161

He scrambled into his dressing-gown and slippers, and, carrying his tea in his hand, went down to find Sooper sitting bolt upright on a hall chair.

"I've got a feller in the cooler named Sullivan," said Sooper, coming at once to the point. "I don't suppose you remember him. He tried to break into Elson's house…"

"I remember the circumstances. Of course, he was the man whom Mr Ferraby prosecuted."

"That's why he got off," said Sooper unkindly. "He was pulled in last night. I don't mind tellin' you that I'm pretty worried, Mr Cardew, and I wouldn't have come out here because, honest, I don't think there's anythin' in the'rizin' or anthr'pology or any of that truck. But you're a lawyer and I'm an ignorant old man, and I've got an idea that this feller's keepin' somethin' from me, that he knows more than he'll say. I've tried every way of persuadin' him, short of beatin' his head off, but he won't spill what I want him to spill. Now to tell the truth," said Sooper, with an obvious effort, "I've always guyed your ideas an' notions, because I'm an old-fashioned policeman with old-fashioned ways; and all that magnifying-glass and Chopping's Sonata stuff doesn't mean anythin' in my young life. But I'm a broad-minded man and I've never stopped learnin'." He paused, and seemed to expect Mr Cardew to say something.

"Well, what do you want me to do?"

"You're a lawyer," said Sooper doggedly. "You're used to gettin' fellers on the stand and turnin' 'em inside out…"

"And you want me to cross-examine him? But that's highly irregular. Why don't you get Mr Ferraby, who is in the Public Prosecutor's Department?"

"He publicly prosecuted Sullivan and Sullivan got off," said Sooper disparagingly. "Of course, you needn't come, only I got an idea. In the middle of the night," he added. "It is queer how ideas come to a man in the middle of the night."

"Precisely," said Mr Cardew eagerly. "If you remember, my theory as to the murder occurred to me at two o'clock in the morning."

"I don't remember the exact time, but I seem to remember that it did."

Mr Cardew considered the matter for some time.

"Very good," he said, "if you think there is no impropriety in my questioning the man, I will come, though I warn you that I am quite unused to criminal practice."

Sooper made no disguise of his relief.

"I've been layin' in bed worryin' about this Sullivan – a reg'lar grasshound he is; a lot of people think I wouldn't lower myself to ask advice, but I'm not that sort. You can pick up ideas from most anybody if you give your mind to it."

He seemed blissfully unconscious that his speech lacked graciousness but Mr Cardew was not offended.

"Now, tell me what offence this man is charged with, and what it is you wish to discover."

"Attempted murder," said Sooper, "accessory to, or before the act," and seeing the look of surprise that came on the lawyer's face, he expanded the charge, yet was brief in his elaboration.

"This Sullivan took a small cherry pie from a stranger on the Thames Embankment. He had to take same to the messenger office with a letter, and the whole lot was to be delivered at a nursin' home in Weymouth Street. In that pie was poison – aconitine. This Sullivan says he don't know the man who gave him the parcel, and he lies like a dog! An' clever as I undoubtedly am, I can't catch him out."

Mr Cardew pursed his lips.

"An extraordinary story," he said at last; "you are quite serious – you are not – er – fooling me?"

"I wish I was," said Sooper, "not that I'm capable of doing so, but I wish I was!"

The lawyer, with his chin in his hand, looked thoughtful.

"A remarkable story – it hardly seems possible that in the twentieth century, in the very centre and home of civilization…"

"An' cultcher," suggested Sooper, when he paused.

"That such things could happen. Very well, Superintendent, I will see this man, and such poor skill as I may possess will be at your disposal. You do not in any way connect this man with the murder?"

"I assuredly an' certainly do," said Sooper.

He went back to the station and aroused the slumbering Sullivan.

"Wake, bo', it's your last hour on earth!" he said. "Courage, *mon onfons* – which is French, you poor loft-lounger."

Sullivan sat up on the hard bench and knuckled his eyes.

"What's the time?" he asked drowsily.

"Time's nothin' to you, tramp – an' will be less," said Sooper evenly, "there's a firs' class lawyer comin' along to turn you inside out an' don't lie to him, bo', because he's a whale on psychol'gy an' he can see into your black heart. An' further, you'll tell him all about the man you met on the Embankment...*an'* the truth!"

"I don't remember the man," said the frightened Sullivan; "don't you think I'd tell you if I remembered?"

Sooper shook his head sadly.

"Never heard of brimston' an' fire, an' what happens to a feller that can't talk straight? Didn't you have a mother that taught you sump'n'?"

"I don't know, so I can't tell you," Sullivan almost screamed the words. "To hell with your lawyer!"

"You wait!" warned Sooper, and turned the key on his prisoner.

He strolled to the entrance of the station in time to see Cardew's limousine flying down the street. With a grinding of brakes, the car stopped and a dazed chauffeur leapt out on to the sidewalk.

"Superintendent, will you come at once... Mr Cardew has been chloroformed in his room..."

"Why didn't you phone?" shouted Sooper in a fury, as he jumped for the car.

"The wires have been cut," said the man, and Sooper showed his teeth.

"That Big Foot thinks of everythin'!" he said.

"I went back to my room and lay down on my bed to think out your unusual request," said Mr Cardew. He was the colour of chalk and had, in fact, been very sick.

He was stretched full-length on an ottoman, and the room was heavy with the sweetness of chloroform.

"I must have dozed... I didn't sleep too well in the night, and I have no recollection of anything happening until I felt my servant shaking me by the shoulder. He came into the room by accident and apparently saw me lying with a piece of folded lint over my face, and he must have disturbed my assailant, because he found the window wide open."

Sooper crossed to the window and looked out. He saw a shining object on the flower-bed immediately below and, going downstairs, went out into the open and retrieved it. It was a broken bottle, labelled "Chloroform BP". It had been newly opened, and now the fumes of its contents were rapidly destroying the flowers amidst which the bottle had fallen.

Sooper looked up at the open window. It was an easy drop. There were no footprints on the narrow flower-bed under the wall, but anybody jumping from the window must inevitably miss the bed and strike the gravel path.

He looked at the bottle label. It bore in the corner the initials of a well-known wholesale chemist, and would be difficult to trace. The telephone wire ran along the wall at this spot, within reach of a man of average height. It had been neatly cut.

"Same pliers that cut my wire," said Sooper.

Going back to the stricken lawyer, he found he had so far recovered that he was able to sit up in a chair.

"You hadn't seen anybody about the grounds – where was your gardener?"

"This morning he is in the potting sheds; none of the outside staff would be in view. I certainly heard a scraping noise as I was lying on the bed, but I gave no great attention to it."

"The window was open?"

"Half open and fastened with a hook which could easily be lifted from the outside. It was wide open when my man came in."

Sooper examined the folded lint. Though chloroform is one of the most volatile of liquids, the lint was still damp between the folds. He pulled away the pillow on which the lawyer's head had been resting and then looked under the bed.

Ill as he felt, Mr Cardew smiled.

"No, I didn't expect to find him there," said Sooper, impervious to ridicule, "I got an idea that I'd find…sump'n'. They didn't scratch your hands, did they?"

"Scratch my hands? What on earth…"

Sooper inspected the lawyer's hands, finger by finger, in his near-sighted way – he saw excellently in the dark, and there were many, Lattimer amongst the number, who regarded that peering habit of his as a pose.

"I thought they *would* have scratched your hands." He seemed disappointed. "That upsets one of my the'ries – I'm pickin' up the'ries pretty rapid. I'll have to give you police protection, Mr Cardew."

"You'll do nothing of the kind," protested the lawyer vigorously, "I am quite capable of protecting myself."

"Looks like it," was all that Sooper said.

THE WARRANT

The task that should have been Mr Cardew's fell to Jim Ferraby, peremptorily summoned from Whitehall, as he believed, for an important consultation. Officials of the Public Prosecutor's Department are not amenable to the autocratic demands of superintendents of police, even though a superintendent is a very important person indeed, and would in the United States be called captain. The irregularity of the proceedings occurred to Jim Ferraby on his way from town, and were emphasized by the coolness of Sooper's request.

"But, my dear man," said Jim irritably, "you do not give the third degree in this country! Sooper, you'll get me hanged!"

"I'm never goin' to rest until somebody's hung, Mr Ferraby," said the imperturbable man. "I wouldn't have troubled you, but the Feller That Thinks of Everythin' got at the grandest anthr'pologist of the age just as he was goin' to put it all over that low thief Sullivan."

"Mr Cardew? What has happened to him?" asked Jim quickly.

Sooper so seldom laughed that Jim stared in amazement.

"Big Foot got him – clever. That fellow's got brains as well as feet. General the'ry is that he was in the house listenin' when I was havin' a little conversation with Mr Cardew. And I've known that sump'n was goin' to happen to Cardew all this last week. I suppose I might have put on a squad to protect him," he mused, "but who'd ever think they'd catch a feller that's on speakin' terms with Lombosso, or whatever that Eytalian's name may be?"

Jim looked at him suspiciously. He was never quite sure how near to laughter Sooper was in his more solemn moments.

"Tell me what occurred," he said, and Sooper gave a very graphic description of Cardew's unhappy experience.

At the old man's earnest request he went into the cell and for an hour questioned and cross-questioned the angry tramp. Sooper left him to his task.

"I never thought you would," he said, when Jim reported failure. "Naturally, that feller's got a superior feeling towards you, Mr Ferraby. He bested you once. I never thought you'd get him to talk."

"But, my dear good man, Sullivan is speaking the truth," said Jim, nettled.

Sooper closed his eyes wearily.

"I suppose it sounds that way to you. It's a great pity." He shook his head again. "You're not going, Mr Ferraby?"

"Yes, I am," said Jim. "And really, Sooper, I don't know why on earth you brought me here."

Sooper looked up at the clock; the hands pointed to within two minutes to four.

"I've been strugglin' an' wrestlin' with myself all afternoon," he said. "Justice *v.* pers'nal ambition. An' justice has won."

He opened his desk and took out a blue blank, filling it in laboriously, and Jim watched him, wondering whether this was one of Sooper's gestures of dismissal.

"Don't go, sir. You're an officer of the Public Prosecutor's Bureau, and I think you can sign this."

Jim looked at the document which had been turned to him. It was a warrant for the arrest of Elson, on a charge of unlawful possession!

"Do you seriously wish me to sign this?"

Sooper nodded.

"Yes, sir. According to my knowledge, you're a Justice of the Peace."

"But unlawful possession of what?"

"I don't know till I pinch him," said Sooper. "Mr Ferraby, I'm taking a risk. I'll swear the information later. Give me that warrant now."

Jim hesitated for a second, picked up a pen and scribbled his name on the bottom of the blank.

"Good!" said Sooper. "Justice has won. You come up with me and you'll see sump'n'."

A servant answered the knock, and invited them into the hall before she went upstairs. They heard her tap at Elson's door, and presently she came down again.

"Mr Elson isn't in the house," she said. "He may be walking in the garden. If you will wait here…"

"Never mind, miss," said Sooper. "We'll find him. I know my way about these grounds."

There was no sign of Elson. The servant, who stood in the doorway waiting for their return, suggested that he might be in "the wilderness", a stretch of uncultivated bush land that had once assisted a singing tramp to make his escape. The wilderness, aptly called, lay at the foot of a gentle slope, beyond the red wall, and from the crest of the slope any moving object could be seen, for most of the bushes were no more than shoulder high.

"I shouldn't like to think that he's made a getaway," said Sooper.

"But what is really the charge?"

"I just want him, that's all," said Sooper. "I got an idea he'd flit this morning."

"Do you want him in connection with the murder?"

Sooper nodded.

"But you don't wish to charge him with the murder – is that right?"

"That's so, sir," said Sooper. "You're guessin' right almost every time."

Shading his eyes, he looked across the bush land.

"There's a path runs to the left," he said suddenly, "it'll do no harm if we walk to the end of the property."

What Sooper described as a "path" was no more than a foot-wide track, that twisted and turned mazily, sometimes running into hollows, occasionally marching parallel with the fence boundary.

"I don't think he's here," said Jim. "Do you really think he's gone away?"

Then, to his amazement, Sooper snarled round at him.

"What's the use of askin' me questions?" he demanded with sudden wrath. "Can't you see this thing's right on top of me?" And then, exercising his marvellous self-control, he showed his teeth in a grin. "Start kickin' me right away, Mr Ferraby, because I deserve it. I'm just temp'ramental today, as temp'ramental as I've been for years."

"I'm sorry I annoyed you," said Jim, "but I'm trying to get your mind."

"It ain't worth havin', Mr Ferraby," said Sooper.

Jim held up his hand to command silence. From somewhere in the wilderness came a peculiar sound – the "klop! klop! klop!" of an axe against a tree.

"He's cutting wood," he suggested, but Sooper did not answer.

After five minutes' walk, they turned the corner of the path, which led down to a saucer-shaped depression, and here it was necessary to push the bushes aside to make any progress. Sooper went through first and stopped, holding back the bush for the other to pass. At first Ferraby thought that this was an act of politeness, and then, looking ahead, he saw the crumpled figure in the path and the pool of blood in which it lay.

It was Elson! Sooper tiptoed forward and turned the thing upon its back.

"Shot one, two, three times," he said steadily. "Elson, I ought to have pinched you this mornin' an' saved your life!"

AMBUSHED

"For God's sake, who did this?" asked Ferraby in horror.

Sooper, kneeling by the figure, looked up with a bland expression which seemed shockingly callous.

"Who did it?" His voice was sunken so low that Jim had to listen intently to hear him. "The same man that chloroformed Cardew, the same man that shot Hannah Shaw, the same man that handed the pastry to that human fish in the tank – the same brain, the same hand, the same motive. He's consistent. I can admire a man who's that way. An' he thinks of everything. Don't go standing up, Mr Ferraby. I'm not kneelin' here for rev'rence but for safety. One of us ought to get back alive in the int'rest of justice."

A cold chill crept down Jim's spine.

"Is he here – in this bush?" he whispered.

Sooper nodded.

"Murder was committed less than ten minutes ago. Remember that 'plop-plop-plop!' we heard? You thought it was somebody cuttin' down trees. It wasn't. A gun an' a silencer, that's all."

All the time he was speaking, his eyes were ranging the immediate vicinity, his keen ears strained to catch the sound of breaking turf or rustle of leaf.

Presently, Jim, sensing the search the old man was conducting, saw him concentrate upon a patch of gorse – a golden splash of colour to the left front. His big hand came out stealthily, and the motion it made was towards the bush through which they had pushed their way.

171

"Jump!" he hissed, and as, his flesh like ice, Jim Ferraby stumbled and jumped to cover, Sooper flung himself face downward on the ground.

"Klock…klock!"

Something went "whang!" near Jim's head, he heard the staccato flutter of breaking twigs and severed leaves, and in another second, Sooper had plunged into the bush after him.

"Run! An' keep your nut down!"

They flew up the path to the cover of a new bush clump and on to the protection of a second covert.

"Slow down – he won't follow," said Sooper, dropping into a walk. "I wouldn't have seen him, only a bird was lightin' on that furze an' changed his mind quite sudden. I was always partial to birds. I got twenty chicks incubated this mornin' – it's not nature, but it pays."

The last thing in the world that Jim Ferraby wished to discuss was Sooper's poultry farm.

"Where is he now?" he asked, glancing back over his shoulder.

"Him – oh, he's movin' to safety. He didn't wait after he fired. I ought to carry a gun, but I'm old-fashioned. I'm givin' Cardew police protection tonight – I ought to have given it before."

"You think he is in danger?"

"Sure," said the other shortly. "I've always known he was in danger ever since he started to the'rize in public about how the murderer got into the cottage. His the'ry wasn't quite right, but near enough to be dangerous to him."

They reached the slope, and Sooper hardly paused to look back across the green tops of the bushes.

"He's gone," he said, and for ten minutes was fully occupied at Elson's telephone.

Almost as soon as he had finished his several conversations the police reserves began to arrive, by bicycle, by commandeered motorcars, and a large party in the hospital ambulance. A few of them were armed, and with this party, Sooper led the way back to the wilderness and to the place where he had found Elson. He had left the figure on its face, but the pockets had not been turned out, as they now were.

"We interrupted him when we arrived, and he went to ground hopin' to finish the good work. Anybody seen Lattimer?"

"He was not at the station when I left, sir," said a uniformed sergeant. "I left word that he was to come on here."

Sooper said nothing.

Crossing to the gorse bushes, he worked round them, his eyes on the ground. The exploded shells were there for all to see, but beyond motioning to an officer who followed him to pick them up, he paid them no attention. He was sniffing and snuffling for all the world like an old dog.

"Got a wonderful nose," he said, addressing Jim. "Smell anything?"

"No – except the gorse."

Sooper volunteered no further information; he was still looking for something, parting bushes, lifting sprawling tendrils, searching with his fingers amongst the debris that the seasons had left upon the ground.

"He must have taken it away," he said. "I banked on his leavin' it in his hurry. But he's too thoughtful."

"What did you expect to find?" asked Jim curiously.

Sooper sat back on his heels – he was kneeling at the time – and looked into Ferraby's face.

"Your latchkey, or – here it is, by gum!"

He scraped from under the bush a small golden object. Jim Ferraby recognized it instantly, though he had not seen the thing for a very long time.

"It is my sovereign purse!" he exclaimed.

It was a relic of the golden age, when money was metal.

"Remember when you lost it?"

Jim remembered perfectly. It was one Sunday two years before. He had called to see Sooper on his way to town and missed the purse from the end of his watch-chain.

"I thought I had dropped it in the car, and Lattimer searched the machine. The swivel was always a bit groggy – it is now – and I think

I must have lost it a dozen times before it finally disappeared. But how came it here?"

"He left it – the Big Foot man. He left somethin' at Beach Cottage. I guessed it would be a little souv'nir of yours… I wouldn't have been surprised if he's left a pair of Cardew's eyeglasses. But, lord! he wouldn't dare do it, not on *him*!"

"But what did he leave behind at Beach Cottage?" asked Jim.

"His feet," was the laconic reply.

A doctor was examining the body when they came back, and had already given orders for its removal.

"Come a little walk," said Sooper, and returned to the gorse bush. "He went this way." He pointed to a space between the blackberry bushes. "You just follow me and I'll give you an imitation of a bloodhound."

Jim was feeling physically sick. The sun was hot; there was in his nostrils the very aroma of death. Sooper, on the other hand, might have been discussing a game of tennis in which he had been beaten, so respectful was he to the man who had baffled him.

"Got an idea you ought to have police protection too, Mr Ferraby," he said, "an' I'm pretty certain that nobody wants it more than me. At the same time, there's a chance that, if I leave myself open, I'll catch Big Foot before the doctors get busy on Leigh."

"Does much depend upon that operation?"

Sooper nodded.

"If Leigh had got his mind back, the whole thing'd be so simple that a police recruit could clear up the case. As it is, I've got no proof, only suspicion. Juries don't like suspicions. What they want is two witnesses who saw the murder committed an' took a photograph of the feller while he was doin' it. And they're right. Know the hangman?" he asked abruptly, as he made his painful way along the bush path.

"I haven't the pleasure of his acquaintance."

"He's a good feller," said Sooper. "Got no side. I knew a hangman that wanted *patty de foy grass* for breakfast, but this new man's one of the plain beer and cheese kind. As modest a man as you could wish to meet. He keeps a barber's shop in Lancashire. Shaved me many a time."

Jim shuddered.

"If cases were brought into court on suspicion," said Sooper, continuing the thread of his argument, "that chap'd do nothin' but barberin'. And there's nothin' to be made out of that trade, especially in a coal-minin' village, where fellers only shave once a week. He told me that this safety-razor craze had taken pounds out of his pocket. He's a good feller; I'd like to find him a job."

Jim had learnt that, when Sooper was thinking, he talked, and that speech helped him pretty considerably. The subject on which he spoke, and that which was in his mind, were entirely different.

"It's curious," he went on, "that when a man commits a fairly clever murder, everybody says he must be mad. You'd expect to find Big Foot with straws in his hair – he turned off here," he said suddenly, and, lifting the branches of a young crab-apple tree, he crawled out into a grass-covered clearance. Before them was a plain wire fence. Leaning over, Sooper gazed up and down the sunken road which acted as boundary between the two properties.

"That's Cardew's field," indicated Sooper. "It's not so much of a wilderness… I wonder if he's still alive?" he asked calmly, and Jim was shocked.

"You don't think that…?" He did not finish his sentence.

"You never know," said Sooper, climbing over the fence and cautiously descending the steep slope to the dusty road. This he examined carefully.

"It's narrow enough to jump. At the same time, if we walked on the grass… Hullo!"

A man was coming leisurely down the road, the butt of a cigar between his teeth, a derby hat on the back of his head.

"Look at Lattimer comin' to work," said Sooper sourly. "You'd never think that the factory bell had been ringin' for the past half-hour. Good afternoon, my bold Sergeant," he said, as the officer came within hearing. "Been to a weddin'?"

"No, sir, I only just heard that there was trouble here."

"Did you just?" asked Sooper sardonically. "Was that why you were runnin' like mad?"

"I didn't think it was necessary to run, Sooper," said the other coolly. "One of the servants up at the house told me what had happened, and I thought I'd come round the cut road in the hope of picking up a trail. It is obvious he must have broken this side of the wilderness."

Sooper did not reply.

"Can I pick up anything here, sir?"

The old man pointed to the road.

"There's a whole lot of dust, if you're makin' a collection," he said. "Go up to Mr Cardew's house an' tell him what's happened, an' stay by him till I relieve you. He's not to be let out of your sight, and the house must be patrolled at night. Got that?"

"Yes, sir. Am I to tell Mr Cardew that he's under police protection?"

"Tell him anythin' you like," said Sooper. "But when he sees you sittin' on the doorstep, maybe he'll guess. And, Sergeant, if he wants to go to the wilderness to take measurements, humour him, but let him go when there's plenty of people in the grounds. I'm holdin' you responsible for his life, an' if he's found dead in his room I'll take no excuses from you."

"Very good, sir," said Lattimer, and turned back the way he had come.

Jim stood watching him till he disappeared on the main road.

"Lattimer's a good feller," said Sooper, "but he's got no instincts. All animals have got instincts, including detective-sergeants, if they only like to cultivate 'em."

"You trust Lattimer rather much, don't you, Sooper?" asked Jim quietly.

"Don't trust anybody," was the surprising reply. "I may seem to trust him, but that's my artfulness an' cunnin'. To be a good policeman you've got to be artful an' trust nobody, not even your own wife. That's why policemen ought never to marry. Lattimer will make a good detective sooner or later if he doesn't go crook. That's a temptation that comes to every young detective. He mixes with such bad company."

They made their slow way back to Hill Brow, Sooper devoting himself to a search of the dead man's room. He found little of importance except a steamship ticket, a letter of credit for an extraordinarily large sum, and a quantity of English money. There were practically no documents in the drawers of Elson's writing-table, except tradesmen's bills and the deed conveying Hill Brow. His secretary, an anaemic-looking female of middle-age, told Sooper that he had no correspondence.

"I don't think he read or wrote very well, poor man!" she whimpered. "And he's never taken me into his confidence about his private affairs."

"Perhaps he didn't have any private affairs," said Sooper.

In the basement, where the furnace was, there was evidence confirming Mr Cardew's suspicions. The furnace was filled with the ashes of burnt paper. There were traces of two books, but what had been their nature, it was impossible to say.

"He certainly had papers of some kind, whether he wrote them himself, or whether they were written for him; most certainly he burnt 'em. In fact, he was preparing to do a quiet flit."

Before returning to town, Jim went up to see the lawyer. It seemed to Ferraby that Mr Cardew was much less confident about his own immunity from danger than he had, from Sooper's description, apparently been in the morning. He sat in his library, a pallid man, ready to jump at every sound, inexpressibly agitated by the news which Lattimer had brought.

"Tragedy on tragedy!" he said hollowly, as Jim was shown in. "This is awful, Ferraby. Whoever would have thought that poor Elson…" he choked. "You know, of course, that he was warned? Sergeant Lattimer told me the story. A piece of paper was pasted on his door the other night."

Obviously the warning worried Cardew as much as, if not more than, the murder, for he constantly came back to the subject. His passion for criminal investigation was momentarily in eclipse. Jim saw the covered model, well knowing what it was, but Mr Cardew seemed to have lost interest in it. Jim was entirely ignorant about the sheet of paper that had been gummed to Elson's door, and he wondered why the superintendent had not thought it worth his while to tell him of this remarkable occurrence. Probably, had Elson been arrested, that fact would have come out. He mentioned this circumstance and Cardew stared at him.

"Elson was to have been arrested? Why?" he gasped. "What had he been doing?"

"He had stolen something, or at least had stolen property in his possession. I was not particularly keen on signing the warrant: it is the first time I have ever put my name to that type of document: but Sooper was so insistent that I fell. He had come up to effect the arrest when he discovered the murder."

"But Elson to be arrested?" repeated Cardew incredulously. "I can't understand it. My mind is all muddle and confusion! I hope they will not require my evidence at the adjourned inquest. I am completely knocked out by this new horror."

And yet the ruling passion must have been very strong, for he went on: "Is it possible that Hannah and Elson were really married, and that some unknown rival destroyed them both? There have been such cases." He made a gesture of despair. "I am a fool to bother my head about these things. Men like the superintendent are so much better equipped, for all my learning and my studies. I am beginning to feel a sense of my own inferiority," he said with a faint smile.

Lattimer was sitting in the garden when Jim went out. He had brought a chair to the shade of the mulberry tree, and was apparently half asleep, for he started when Jim called him by name.

"Thank heaven you're not Sooper!" he said. "This is a drowsy kind of place."

From where he sat, Jim saw that he commanded a view both of the front entrance of Barley Stack and the windows of Mr Cardew's study.

"Do you share Sooper's view that Mr Cardew is in danger?"

Jim thought he detected a hint of irony in the reply.

"Were you with Sooper when the body was found, Mr Ferraby? How was he killed – shot?"

"Yes," said Jim quietly, "and we were lucky that we were not found with him."

Lattimer opened his eyes.

"Really?" he said politely. "Did he, they, or whoever it was, shoot at you too? That fellow has some nerve! I thought Sooper was a little peeved. That accounts for it. You didn't see the shooter, I suppose, Mr Ferraby?"

"No," said Jim. He thought the question was a little superfluous.

"Sooper didn't see him, or think he saw him? Sooper has very good eyesight, though he pretends he hasn't. Two years ago he pretended he'd gone stone deaf, and half the station were deceived. Shot at you, eh?" he mused, looking at Jim with a speculative eye. "That's why they're giving Mr Cardew protection! This Big Foot is certainly some bird." He stifled a yawn. "I was up late last night," he said, and took out a handkerchief and wiped his lips. As he did so, Jim was conscious of a faint fragrance.

"That is a vanity I should never imagine you would indulge in, Sergeant," he said good-humouredly.

"The perfume?" Lattimer sniffed at the cambric. "My landlady put a satchet amongst my handkerchiefs. I don't think she will do it again."

And then, with a cold sensation at his heart, Jim's mind flashed back to the scene of the murder, to Sooper snuffling about the bush. Controlling his voice with an effort, he was about to ask a question when Lattimer supplied the answer.

"Sooper would raise hell if he smelt that. He's got as keen a scent as a fox-hound. That man is superhuman." He yawned again. "I should like to think I was getting to bed early tonight," he said.

It was late when Jim Ferraby returned to Whitehall, but his chief was still at the office and sent for him the moment he heard he had arrived.

"You seem to be tumbling into murder cases lately, Ferraby," said old Sir Richard. "What is the inside story of this?"

Jim told him all he knew, which was not very satisfying.

"Sooper's in charge," said the chief thoughtfully. "There couldn't be a better man. Is he very mysterious?"

"Painfully so."

The Public Prosecutor laughed.

"Then you may be sure that he's very near to an arrest," he said. "It is when Sooper is open and frank that the situation is most hopeless."

Jim finished his work, which Sooper's summons had left in arrears, and hurried off to call on Elfa. She was still at the nursing home when he reached Cubitt Street. There had been a consultation between the surgeons, at which certain decisions had to be taken, and her consent was necessary. She was looking fagged and weary when he met her at the corner of Cubitt Street.

"They are not operating until next week," she told him, "and Mr Cardew has sent me a most urgent message asking me if I will come down to Barley Stack. He has some work that he wants done at once, and he says he cannot leave his house."

"You will certainly not go to Cardew's," said Jim peremptorily. "He himself is under police protection, and I can't allow you to run a risk."

He was saved the trial of telling her of Elson's death: she had read it in the evening newspapers, but her anxiety about her father's health had been so overwhelming that she had been almost too absorbed to realize what had happened.

"I scarcely knew him," she said, "but in any circumstances that would not keep me away from Barley Stack. Only I'm so tired, Jim, so utterly, utterly tired!"

"Cardew can wait," he said resolutely.

But evidently Mr Cardew could not wait. When he followed the girl into her sitting-room, the telephone bell was ringing furiously, and it was the lawyer who spoke. As soon as he realized who it was, Jim took the instrument from her hands.

"It's Ferraby speaking," he said. "I've just come in with Miss Leigh, and she's far too knocked out to come down to Barley Stack tonight."

"Persuade her to come," urged Cardew's voice. "Come down with her if you wish. I should certainly feel safer if there were somebody I knew in the house."

"But won't this wait?"

"No, no! The business is vital!"

The trouble in the lawyer's voice carried across the wire.

"It is absolutely necessary that I should settle my affairs immediately."

"But surely you do not think there is any great danger?"

"I am certain of it," came the vigorous reply. "I want to get the thing finished and the girl out of the house before any trouble comes. Sooper has forbidden me to leave the grounds. Could you not come with her?"

He was so insistent that, covering the mouth of the receiver with his hand, Jim explained the situation to the girl.

"Is he really in that state of mind?" she asked in surprise. "I never dreamt Mr Cardew could be so panic-stricken." She hesitated. "Perhaps I'd better go," she said. "Will you take me?"

The prospect of spending a night under the same roof, of the drive through the cool of the evening, had entirely changed Jim's attitude on the subject. And yet he could not regard his own selfish wishes as paramount, and he tried to persuade her not to go, but there was a certain half-heartedness in his argument which she, womanlike, detected.

"Tell him I will come down," she said. "The change will be good for me, and perhaps for him too."

Jim delivered the message and hung up the receiver.

"I've been keying myself up to meet the strain of the operation," she said. "I suppose that is why I feel so flat. If you will go down to the car, I will pack my bags and join you."

She had had no dinner, but would not wait.

"Mr Cardew dines very late," she said, "and he will probably be waiting for us."

In this surmise she was justified. They found Cardew pacing his library, his hands clasped behind him, and the girl was shocked at the change which had come over him since she had seen him last. In the presence of his danger he seemed to have aged ten years; and he was conscious of her concern at his appearance.

"It was very good of you to come," he said, grasping her hand warmly. "I waited dinner. I hope you have not dined? I may be a little more normal when I have eaten something – I can't remember my last meal!"

He did not as a rule indulge in wine, but on this occasion there was a golden-necked bottle on the ice, and under some of the stimulant Mr Cardew's spirits rose, and he approached nearer to normality.

"It is partly this awful happening to Elson and partly the knowledge that I am what the superintendent calls 'under police protection', which has so thoroughly upset my nerves. And yet" – he paused, his glass in hand – "this infernal passion for investigation has become so ingrained in my system that I find myself engaged in what Minter calls 'the'ries an' deductions'."

Later, he explained why he had sent for the girl.

"In my saner moments I do not imagine that there is the slightest danger to me personally," he said. "And yet my training as a lawyer tells me that I must be prepared for any eventuality. It came as a shock to me this afternoon to realize that I have made no will, that I have done nothing to put my papers in order – in fact, that I am as unprepared for dissolution as any layman whose muddled affairs occupy the time of our courts. My will I have drafted. When Miss Leigh has made two copies, I will ask you, Ferraby, to glance over it and witness my signature; one of the servants can be the second witness." And then, as the girl was about to speak, he smiled. "Unfortunately, you cannot be a witness, because I have taken the liberty of making you a large beneficiary."

He stopped her protest with a gesture.

"I am an old man – I never felt so old in my life as I do tonight – without any relations whatever, with very few friends, and very few people towards whom I have a sense of gratitude." He smiled. "I have at least made the *amende honorable* to Superintendent Minter, for I have left him my criminological library."

He laughed for the first time, and Jim could enjoy the joke.

"I may add," Cardew went on, his eyes twinkling, "that I have also bequeathed him a sum of money which will enable him either to buy a house in which the library can be displayed, or to purchase a motor-cycle which does not make his fellow citizens leap out of their shoes every time he brings it on to the road."

After dinner, he and the girl went to the library together, and Jim, left to his own resources, strolled out to smoke a cigar in the garden. He had not taken two steps before the inevitable watcher appeared. It was not Sergeant Lattimer, Jim noted, but a detective whom he had met in Sooper's office. They talked about the weather, and the fineness of the night, and the prospects of the candidates in the forthcoming Derby – everything, in fact, except the object of the inspector's vigil. As they paced up and down the walk, the blinds of Cardew's study were raised, and he could see the lawyer sitting at one side of the desk, Elfa at the other, and she was writing rapidly at his dictation.

"Isn't that a little dangerous?" asked Jim nervously. "Those people must be plainly visible from the plantation."

"Perhaps you'd ask them to pull down the blinds, sir?" said the man.

Not wishing to interrupt the lawyer himself, Jim sent a message in by one of the servants, and had the satisfaction of seeing the shades drawn down.

"I wonder that Mr Cardew didn't think of that himself," said the officer. "I understand he makes a hobby of police work."

At that moment, from the plantation came the first few liquid notes of a nightingale, and then silence.

"Perhaps you'll go inside now, sir?" said the officer respectfully.

Jim stared at him in wonder.

"My relief is coming," explained the man, "and Sooper might not like to see me talking with you."

Jim went into the house puzzled. He strolled up to his bedroom and unpacked his suitcase, which he had picked up at the club. After he had given the relief time to come and go, he walked out into the garden again, and was surprised to find the same officer on duty, more surprised to discover that the blinds which had been pulled down were raised, and that Cardew and his secretary were visible.

"Sooper thought we ought to be able to see into the room. He said anything might happen behind closed blinds."

"Was Mr Minter here?"

"Only for a minute, sir," said the other, and was not inclined to continue the conversation.

Accepting one of Jim's cigars, he plunged immediately into a complicated complaint about the iniquity of the police pension system. It was a quarter to one when the girl came out and invited Jim into the library.

"I think we've finished everything. It's rather a gruesome business, and made my blood run cold," she said in a low voice. "And Jim, he's left me an enormous sum! He really ought not, but he refuses to alter the will."

Cardew had rung for his sleepy-eyed servant, his signature was affixed to the document and witnessed.

"I wish you'd keep this," he said, to Jim's surprise, "at least, keep it until tomorrow morning, when I will send it to a place of safety. This has been a very good night's work, and I am glad it is through."

He was calmer, more his old self, brought out, with some pride, the model cottage, and would have launched forth into a restatement of his theories but for the presence of the girl.

"Now, young lady," he said, "you had better go to bed. The maid will show you to your room: it is the old one you occupied when you were here last."

She was glad to escape, and, turning the key in the lock with a feeling of relief, began quickly to undress, and in ten minutes was in bed and had fallen into a heavy, dreamless sleep.

From the plantation, Lattimer saw her light go out and drew closer in towards the house.

THE NOOSE

Tap, tap, tap!'

Elfa heard the sounds in her dream, and stirred uneasily.

Tap, tap, tap!

It was the sound of a blind tassel on the window, she decided, half-asleep and half-awake. Then, just as she was sinking again into a doze:

Tap, tap, tap!

She was wide awake now, and raised herself on her elbow. The sound had come from the window; its regularity removed all doubt that it was caused by accident. The night was very still; not a breath of wind moved. She drew aside the heavy curtains. Her casement window was wide open, as she had left it. There was no sign of a dangling blind tassel that could have caused the noise. Outside, the world was wrapped in inky darkness.

As she looked, she heard the soft crunch of gravel and her heart leapt, before she remembered that the house was being patrolled.

"Is that you, Miss Leigh?" a voice whispered.

"Yes," she answered in the same tone. "Did you knock at the window?"

"No, miss," was the staggering reply. "Did you hear somebody knock? You must have been dreaming."

She went back to bed, lay down, but sleep had finished for the night. And then:

Tap, tap, tap!

She got out of bed, pulled the curtains aside gently and listened in the intense silence. And then she went softly to the window and leant out, straining her eyes into the gloom below.

She could see nobody, but far away, towards the trees, she saw the dull glow of fire and guessed that the watcher was smoking a cigarette. Who had tapped at the window? She leant out a little farther and then something hard and supple dropped on her head from above.

Before she could recover herself, the noose about her throat had tightened. She threw up a hand and clutched wildly at the strangling cord. It was dragging at her, pulling her off her feet. She gripped frantically at the window-box, and in her struggles thrust it away from her. It fell with a crash. Then, from somewhere in the garden, a white beam of light flashed out and caught her, and at that instant the silken rope relaxed and Elfa staggered back into the room and fell half-conscious by the side of her bed, the rope still about her neck.

The man in the garden took one leap, caught the top of the window coping below and in a few seconds had swung himself into the room and had switched on the lights.

She looked up into the face of a middle-aged man who was a stranger to her. He had drawn the rope from her neck and laid her on the bed before he went to the window and whistled shrilly.

Jim heard the sound and was out of his room in an instant, guessing from the direction that it had come from Elfa's room. He opened the door to find the detective with whom he had been speaking on the night before, bathing the girl's face with a sponge.

"Look after this lady," said the man curtly and, handing the sponge to Jim, darted out of the room and up the stairs which were immediately opposite the door.

Jim heard the sound of his heavy feet in the room above and then a voice hailed him from the garden.

"What's wrong there?"

It was Sooper.

Elfa had recovered consciousness, and Jim passed to the window and in a few words told all he guessed from the rope on the floor and the red marks about her throat.

"Leap down and let me in," said Sooper.

Jim flew down the stairs as Mr Cardew came out of his room, a revolver in one hand, a lighted candle in the other. Ferraby did not wait to explain, but unbarring the door admitted the old man.

By the time they reached the girl's room, she was sitting up on the edge of the bed, pulling her dressing-gown about her slim shoulders. Her throat was sore, she was dizzy, her head was swimming, and every limb seemed to be shaking of its own accord, but she succeeded in telling her story.

At the moment she had finished, the detective who had gone upstairs returned, carrying a long bamboo.

"It is a store-room," he said. "There is a trap-door to the roof. This is all I found – he must have tapped at the window with this."

Sooper did not trouble to take the bamboo in his hand.

"He taps at the window, she looks out and he nooses her," he muttered. "And there's the trap-door open for him to escape. I tell you, that feller forgets nothin'! Up on the roof after him! You've got a gun? If you see him, shoot…don't break your neck, it's not worthwhile, because I think he'll have gone before you can start your search."

Cardew was at the door, clamouring for admission, and with a wearied expression, Sooper went out to tell him the cause of the commotion.

"The room above is a store-room and is never used," he explained superfluously.

Sooper grudgingly opened the door and allowed him to come in.

"Know this?" he said. He picked up the rope. It was made of dark red silk and nearly three yards in length. The end had been neatly spliced into a running noose.

Mr Cardew shook his head.

"I've never seen that before," he said. "It is an old-fashioned bell-pull, isn't it? We have nothing but electric bells in the house."

He examined the rope carefully.

"This is very old – " he said.

"I guessed that," interrupted Sooper. "You can buy that sort of thing at almost any junk shop. Feelin' better, young lady?"

She nodded and made a brave attempt to smile.

"We'll get out an' give you a chance to dress. I think you'd better come downstairs. It's nearly three an' early risin' does nobody any harm."

At that second the detective came back to report his fruitless search of the roof.

"Where's Lattimer?"

"He's at the side of the house, on the plantation, sir," said the man.

Sooper made no comment. When the girl had hurriedly dressed and had gone downstairs, he walked out on to the lawn. Suddenly Jim heard those three liquid notes of melody that had come from the plantation on the previous night.

"I'm a regular nightingale," admitted Sooper modestly. "Always had a gift for bird-calls, but nightingales are my speciality...nightingales an' chickens."

And, to Jim's amazement, he gave a remarkable imitation of a brooding hen that at any other time would have moved him to helpless laughter.

"That you, Lattimer?" called Sooper, as the sergeant came running quickly towards them.

"Yes, sir."

Lattimer came into the light. His clothes were dusty and the knee of one trouser torn away. Jim particularly noticed that his hands were covered with grime.

"What's happened to you, Lattimer?"

"I fell down... I was in such a hurry," was the cool reply.

"Seen anybody or anythin'?" asked Sooper.

"No, I heard a commotion at the house, but I knew you were somewhere around. I thought I'd better wait in case anybody tried to break through the wood."

If Jim expected the superintendent to continue his cross-examination, he was to be disappointed. Sooper growled an order and turned again into the study, where the girl was putting a light under a spirit kettle.

The young man was not satisfied, and, seizing his opportunity, slipped out of the house, taking one of the two torches which Mr Cardew kept on the hall table, and made an inspection of the house from outside. He had not far to go before he made an astounding discovery. At the back of the house a long ladder had been reared, and, flashing his lamp upwards, he saw that it extended to the roof. And then, a little above his own height, he saw something hanging from the ladder's side, and, mounting two rungs, he found it was a piece of cloth of irregular shape that had caught on a nail projecting from the side of the ladder. He had particularly noticed that Lattimer was wearing a dark-grey suit with a faint check, which was more obvious by artificial light than it would have been by day, and this piece of cloth was not only of the same pattern, but the piece corresponded in size with the hole in the knee of Lattimer's trousers.

Putting the cloth in his pocket, he went back to the house and, calling Sooper outside, told him what he had found. Sooper listened without interruption, and accompanied him to where the ladder was standing.

"That's certainly queer," said Sooper at last. "But Lattimer may have seen the ladder and gone up to investigate."

"He didn't say so."

"No, I admit he didn't say so," said Sooper. "I'll look into this, Mr Ferraby. And if you don't mind, I'd be glad if you would say nothin' whatever to the other people. It is certainly strange and almost suspicious, but it is quite likely that what I said is right. It'd be his duty to investigate that ladder."

"But he didn't come from the direction of the ladder when you called him, he came from the plantation," insisted Jim.

Sooper rubbed his chin irritably.

"That's surely queer," he agreed, and again uttered his warning. "It's likely I'm gettin' past my work," he said. "Things are happenin' that I don't ever expect to happen, and I can't understand *why* they happen.

When a man gets that way, he's goin' bad. In half an hour we'll get some sort of light, and then I think the danger's over for the night."

He lounged into the library, took some coffee from the girl's hand, and sat down on a low settee.

"I'm goin' to tell you sump'n' that'll make the roses come to your cheeks, young lady."

"Tell me?" she said in surprise. "Why, whatever do you mean, Sooper?"

"That operation on your father was a great success."

She sprang to her feet, her colour coming and going.

"Operation? But it is not until next week."

"Last night," said Sooper. "I arranged with the doctors that you shouldn't know till it was all over. But I thought you must have guessed when the matron told me about the letter you left for him to read, as soon as he could read anythin'."

"But I left no letter!" she gasped. "I had no idea that the operation would be last night."

Sooper's eyes narrowed.

"Is that so?" he said softly.

He grabbed the telephone and gave a number.

"She's in bed, is she? Well, wake her up and tell her Superintendent Minter wants to speak to her right now!"

He waited with the receiver at his ear, glaring into vacancy, and then the girl saw his expression change.

"Is that you, Miss Moody? About that letter…yes, the one that Miss Leigh left for her father to read. Do you mind openin' it an' readin' it to me? No, that'll be all right, I've got her permission."

He waited, Elfa saw him nod.

"Yuh! Thank you," he said at last. "Yes, keep it for me, please."

He hung up the receiver.

"What was in the letter?" asked Ella.

"Somebody playin' a joke, I think. Tryin' to do you a good turn. It just said 'Love from Elfa to Daddy'…that's all."

Sooper was not speaking the truth. What the letter had contained was one line of writing, which ran:

Your daughter was strangled last night.

"Thinks of everythin'," said Sooper, with a cluck of admiration.

MR WELLS

Mr Cardew had taken a decision. He would close up the house, dismiss the servants, and either take a house in town or spend the remaining days of the summer abroad.

"That seems a good idea to me, and you can't go too soon," said Sooper, when he was told. "I'd like you to leave tonight."

Cardew shook his head in a hesitant way.

"No, I don't think I could get away tonight. I have to pack – "

"A couple of my men will help you to pack," said Sooper.

"I'll stay the night," decided the lawyer, after consideration. "Perhaps you will come up and dine?"

Sooper shook his head.

"Can't do it," he said. "Got a friend of mine comin'."

"Bring him along."

It was Sooper's turn to hesitate.

"Means takin' advantage of you. This feller's not what you might call a swell, and yet he's a man I admire. He never argues with me, an' he's not clever. An' when a man doesn't argue with me an' he's not clever, he's a man after my own heart."

"Superintendent," said Mr Cardew, "I've never asked you if you have any very definite views about these outrages which have been committed in our neighbourhood, or to people we know. I am going to ask you tonight. Bring your friend along by all means. Mr Ferraby has also promised to come."

"Young lady, too?" asked Sooper.

"No, she's staying with her father. We have arranged a room at the nursing home, so that she will be on hand."

Sooper nodded.

"You ask me whether I've got any definite views. Well, I have and I haven't. I've got views but no proof. And I can't get proof without motive, because it stands to reason this fellow Big Foot ain't going round the country killin' people to keep his hand in. That sort of thing doesn't happen except in books, and I should say not in the best books. An' he's not tryin' to strangle young ladies so as the shock shall send their fathers mad again, just for the fun of murderin'. There's a bit of poetry about 'the tangled web we weave, when first we practise telling lies'."

" 'To deceive'," corrected Mr Cardew with a faint smile.

"It's the same thing," said Sooper petulantly. "Deceiving is lying, and lying's deceiving. And that's just what happened to this feller, Big Foot. He started deceivin' an' had to go on deceivin', an' every time it looked as though Somebody was going to give him away, out came his little gun an' that was the end of Somebody. There are no what I might term 'sporty murderers' in this world outside of lunatic asylums. A man commits murder for the same reason as a boy washes his neck – because there's no other way of being allowed to go to the party. And behind all these certain crimes there's a party of some kind, or what's as good as a party. A nice home, motorcars, champagne suppers with chorus girls, an' everythin' else that makes life worth livin'. I know a man who poisoned his wife because she wouldn't let him smoke in the house – that's a fact. You look up the Armstrong trial an' read the evidence. An' I know another man who killed his brother because he wanted money to play the races. Murder is the only crime that people never commit for itself alone. That's where you catch 'em. It's easy to hide up a murder, but it's hard to put away the little crimes that led to the murder. Is Ferraby coming down?"

"Yes," nodded Cardew.

"That's fine," said Sooper.

"There's one thing I wanted to ask you, Superintendent," Cardew broke in suddenly. "My gardener says that you found the marks of a ladder at the back of the house, so deeply embedded in the grass that they could not be mistaken."

"There was a ladder there," said Sooper carefully. "I had it shifted before daylight, because I didn't want to alarm anybody. I don't know where that ladder came from either, because you haven't got one as long. I'll make enquiries. And about this friend of mine, Mr Cardew – he's like me, he won't know one knife from another, and he's sure to get all hot and bothered over the glasses. He's not much of a talker either."

"You're certainly doing your best to discourage me from inviting him," laughed the lawyer. "But you can bring him along; I shall be glad to meet him."

"Man named Wells," said Sooper absently. He seemed to invite further inquiry, but evidently Mr Cardew was not curious.

Suddenly the superintendent slapped his thigh with an exclamation of annoyance.

"Knew I'd forgotten something! I asked that sergeant of mine, Lattimer, to come in and meet him!"

"Bring Lattimer too," said the other cheerfully. "Lattimer at least will know what knives to use. He always struck me as being a man of education, a little too good..." he hesitated.

"Say it," groaned Sooper. "But he's really not too good for the police, Mr Cardew. In fact, he's one of the comin' men. He's got a line on anthr'pology that certainly gets me baffled, How many toes has a horse got? Lattimer knows. An' he can tell the difference between the stains produced by high eggs and the stains produced by a premachure explosion of dynamite."

"Superintendent, you're pulling my leg, and I won't allow it," said the good-humoured Cardew.

He insisted on going to town that afternoon, and reluctantly agreed to Sooper's suggestion that he should be accompanied by a police officer, who took up his station outside King's Bench Walk, while, single-handed, Mr Cardew conducted his business.

He had a number of letters to write, yet found time to phone through an inquiry to the nursing home. When she learnt who it was, Elfa came to the instrument.

"How are you feeling yourself?"

"Desperately tired," she said. "I was just lying down when I heard you had called. Are you in town, Mr Cardew?"

"Yes, I'm here for an hour; I am returning to Barley Stack tonight. Tomorrow I am shutting up the house, and shall be in London for a day or two. This means, I fear, that our pleasant association is about to finish," he added, "and I have taken the liberty of posting you a cheque in lieu of notice. You remember the burglary at this office? Seems years ago, doesn't it?"

"It was last week," said the girl.

"I've just been going through my papers, and I pretty well know now what was stolen and why it was stolen. Even Sooper will not deny me the credit for my discovery."

"What was the reason?" she asked curiously, but he would not satisfy her. It was evident, she thought, as she went back to her little room, that Mr Cardew's revelation was of so stupendous a nature that he would not take the risk of being forestalled.

He came down into King's Bench Walk, posted his letters, and, beckoning to his protector, re-entered the car. He did not see Lattimer, because Lattimer took particular care to keep out of view. But the sergeant had been a spectator both of his coming and going, and followed him back to Barley Stack in a small car, so close upon his heels that, had Mr Cardew turned his head, he could not have failed to see his pursuer.

Lattimer did not go up to the house: he shot his car beyond the narrow roadway which led to Barley Stack and turned the machine into a cornfield, driving it along by the side of the hedge till it was safe from observation. Only then did he descend and turn up the road on the trail of Cardew.

He strolled carelessly to the lawn, and the officer who had accompanied the lawyer to town hailed him with pleasure.

"Sooper's been asking for you, Sergeant."

"I've been around," said the other. "You can go."

He found a chair and, carrying it to the shade of the mulberry tree, sat down. Mr Cardew, glancing through the study window, saw him on duty and sent him out a box of cigars. Sergeant Lattimer smiled his thanks through the window. He seemed to be amused about something.

THE FAREWELL FEAST

"Meet Mr Wells," said Sooper grandly.

The little man who was sitting uncomfortably on the edge of a chair in Sooper's office, rose awkwardly and put out his large hand. He was a mild and inoffensive man, with red hair going grey, carefully parted at the side and brought in a large curl over his forehead. It seemed to Jim that he was unused to wearing the stiff new collar that encircled his neck, and from time to time he moved his head uncomfortably. He wore a silver albert, from which depended two large athletic medals.

"Who is he?" asked Jim when he got Sooper by himself for a few minutes.

"He's a reprimand," said Sooper. "He's a blot on my sheet, he's trouble, an' maybe three months' correspondence with the Deputy. But I couldn't resist it: I just had to ask him down."

"Is he a detective?" Remembering the physique of the man, it seemed impossible that it should be so.

"No, he's not a detective, he's a friend of mine. I told Cardew the kind of bird he was – "

"You're not taking him up to dinner, are you?" asked Jim aghast.

"I am," said the calm Sooper, "and I'll tell you why. I didn't know it when I invited him up, but I've got it since: Cardew's goin' to give us a new theory – by the way, you'll be wanted for that second inquest the day after tomorrow – and I respect Cardew's theories, but at the same time I want to show him where he's wrong. This feller is what I might term the missin' link in the case."

With this explanation, Jim had to be content.

He had not come from town with any great pleasure; it was only the thought that he might afford moral support to Cardew that had made him agree to spend another night under that fatal roof. He did not even know Sooper was dining there until that gentleman told him, and the prospect of sitting *vis-à-vis* this very commonplace and nervous man added little to his happiness.

"It's Cardew's farewell dinner. Tomorrow, if he's alive…"

"You expect something to happen tonight?"

Sooper nodded.

"If he's alive tomorrow, he's going to town, and from London he's going abroad. Mr Leigh's operation was successful."

He turned the subject in his quaint way.

"Recognized his daughter this afternoon, an' that's good. But he's still too weak to make a statement. What's worryin' me to death, Lattimer will be there."

"At dinner?"

Sooper nodded solemnly.

"You'll like Lattimer: he can eat with both hands, and has never been known to drink water out of a finger-bowl. Lattimer's got swell manners, an' he's a whale on psychology. We ought to have a pleasant evenin' when him an' Mr Cardew get on to Lombosso, the well-known the'rist."

Jim went up to the house before the others, and the lawyer asked him not to dress for dinner.

"I've told Sooper to come up, and he's bringing Lattimer, his sergeant, and a friend…have you met his friend?"

Jim smiled.

"I hope you're not going to be very shocked, but he looks rather like an odd man to me."

"He must be pretty odd if he's a friend of Sooper's," said Cardew dryly. "I'm getting into the habit of calling him by that absurd name myself. Ferraby, I shall miss this place. I'm only now beginning to realize how much I am attached to Barley Stack. I've had a very happy time here," he said in a low voice.

"You expect to come back?"

Cardew shook his head.

"No. I shall sell this place: I've already written to an agent asking him to negotiate the sale. In all probability I shall take up my residence in Switzerland, and endeavour, in my humble way, to add my contribution to the literature of criminology. I shall certainly earn the undying scorn of Superintendent Minter" – his lips curled – "but for that I must be prepared."

"You really don't think that you're in danger, do you, Mr Cardew?"

To his surprise, Cardew nodded.

"Yes, I think I'm in the gravest danger. For the next few years at any rate, I intend residing abroad. And the superintendent agrees with me."

Glancing out of the window, he saw Lattimer at his post.

"I couldn't endure very much of this protection," he said; "it would drive me mad! Now tell me about the superintendent's odd friend."

Jim described him with greater faith than kindness.

"It doesn't seem that he will add greatly to the gaiety of the evening," said Cardew, "but I really had to invite them both. Sooper had asked him down for the evening, and I particularly wanted our old friend at what is virtually my farewell dinner. I wish," he said with a sigh, "it could have been given in happier circumstances, and that dear girl could have been here. But the outrage which was attempted last night was the last straw... I could not risk another shock like that."

It was ten minutes after the time fixed for the dinner when Sooper came, with the red-haired man riding pillion behind him, and anything funnier than the spectacle of the gaunt superintendent and his nervous little guest clutching him by the waist Jim did not remember.

"Meet my friend Mr Wells."

Cardew shook hands.

"Lattimer, meet Mr Wells."

The sergeant came forward and joined the two.

"Now," said Cardew, "I think we had better start dinner. The soup is already on the table."

They followed the lawyer into the dining-room; Cardew indicated their places, and they sat down. It was not true that the soup had been served, but the maid was ladling it out on the sideboard, and presently the plates were set. The red-haired man looked appealingly at Sooper, and Sooper lifted the one big spoon.

"That one!" he said in a hoarse whisper, and then, in his natural voice: "Before we start this farewell dinner, I'm surprised that nobody wants to know who my friend Mr Wells is."

"I confess I am one of the curious," said Mr Cardew.

"Stand up, Mr Wells. Meet Mr Cardew, the lawyer. Mr Cardew, meet Mr Topper Wells" – he paused – "public executioner of England!"

Cardew shrank back, his face puckered up into an expression of distrust, and even Jim, staring horrified at the nervous little man, had a feeling of sickness.

"Meet him, Lattimer. Maybe you've met him? And you'll meet him again."

Sooper's eyes were fixed upon the sergeant.

"And don't touch that soup, Lattimer. Nor any of you, because – "

"What do you mean – " began Mr Cardew.

"Because it's doped," said Sooper.

Cardew sat back from the table, the same look of surprise and distrust on his face that Jim had seen before.

"Poisoned?"

"Poisoned," said Sooper. And again: "Meet Wells, the hangman. And…"

It happened before he could realize the man's intention. With one stride, Cardew was at the door; in a second he was through and the lock snapped.

"Window, quick!" said Sooper. "Take a chair to it. He's fastened the window, you can bet."

A heavy chair wielded by Lattimer crashed through the window. In another second the sergeant had followed.

"Round to the back of the house," grunted Sooper. "Ought to have had another squad on duty up here!"

Jim was running, he did not know where or why. His mind was in a whirl. Cardew? Impossible!

They came into the stable-yard panting. Cardew was nowhere in sight. Sooper pulled open a door that was unfastened. Beyond was a path which sloped down to a side road. It was the tradesmen's entrance to the kitchen.

For a second they saw him, just his head moving with extraordinary speed level with the top of the hedge. And then he was gone.

"Motor-bicycle," said Sooper, "the same as he had in his flivver when he killed Hannah Shaw. That's how he got away without going through Pawsey. Across the field path, lifting his bicycle over the stile. Get your car, Ferraby...get it quick!"

Sooper flew back to the library, and he had only to lift the hook to know that the line had been cut.

"Thinks of everything," he said under his breath, "Cut before dinner, too. He was mighty sure he would put us all to sleep."

As he came back to the drive, Lattimer was climbing into the car.

"Don't stop!" yelled Sooper, and swung himself to the running-board as the machine gathered speed.

There was a patrol at the crossroads, but no motor-cyclist had been seen.

"He doubled back," said Sooper, looking at the sky anxiously. "It'll be dark in half an hour."

There were three roads which the fugitive might have taken. The first, the direct route through Isleworth; the second, a longer way round through Kingston into Richmond Park; the third, one of the many field paths in the neighbourhood. Sooper drove back to the station to give his instructions.

"Cardew's ordered a private machine tonight to fly him from Croydon to Paris," he said. "He'll guess we'll stop that, so we'll rule that out. His only hope is to get to London, and that he'll do. I tell you, this feller's a pretty quick thinker, and he sees a long way ahead."

He came out of the station and stood, gloomily surveying the car.

"Yes, he'll go to London, but not to his flat and not to his office. Bound to have a bolt hole somewhere. He'll be easy to recognize" – he was speaking to himself – "so he won't try the rail, and certainly won't try a car, and I'm bettin' against him goin' by air."

When they arrived in town, Sooper's first step was to double the guard at the nursing home, his next to pay a visit to Cardew's town apartments. The lawyer had not been there, he learnt, nor had he been seen in King's Bench Walk. Joining Jim in the street, he accepted his invitation to join him in a hasty meal.

"Yes, Cardew killed Hannah Shaw. She had a pull on him and wanted to marry him. He hated her worse than poison. And she held over his head a letter he'd written years and years ago, an' threatened to expose him till he agreed. They were married the day she was murdered, at Newbury Registry Office, in the name of Lynes. She didn't mind the name so long as she got him. But she was determined that he should acknowledge her, so she wired Miss Leigh to go down to the cottage that she should be a witness. He got the letter – that was the price of her marriage – and then he shot her. He arranged to meet her after the marriage – that bluff Cardew put on you, that he wanted somebody to go with him to the theatre, was easy stuff because he knew you were engaged for the night. But he didn't know how.

"He used to be a motor-cyclist, and there was a machine in one of the rooms at the house. I saw the marks of the handlebars when I was giving the place a look over. He'd arranged to meet his wife late that night; they were to drive down to the cottage together, but on some excuse he persuaded her to let him ride in the back part of the car, and crouched down so that nobody could see him. He thought of everything, I tell you! He planned the hat she should wear and the coat. And when he shot her he put it on, because she'd told him about the girl coming, and he was afraid he might meet her on the way."

"But why...in heaven's name why? He was a rich man."

"Rich nothin'," said Sooper. "He'd got money...yes, but how did he get it? I'll tell you the whole story, and though I'm guessin' some of it, Leigh won't contradict me. I'll bet money on that!

"Mr Leigh was a Treas'ry official; came from America in the last days of the war, bringing over in his personal charge four large boxes of currency. They were numbered 1, 2, 3, and 4. You remember he talked a lot about '3' and '4'? The ship was torpedoed in a storm off the south coast of Ireland, but rescued by a destroyer. They only had time to get two of the boxes on board before the vessel sank, and the little destroyer, with all her wireless blown to blazes, made the best of her way across the Irish Channel and up the English coast. The storm lasted for three days. She could neither make harbour nor communicate with the shore, until she came into Pawsey Bay, and that was her bad luck. She was blown out of the water by a German submarine.

"Now at that time," Sooper went on, "Cardew was broke, and worse than broke. He had a lot of money entrusted to him by his clients, and he had lost it in every kind of foolish speculation. One of his clients started makin' a fuss – a man named Brixton, a City alderman – and he even wrote to the Yard, and said he had a statement to make to the police. I was sent down to interview him, havin' got a line as to the trouble, an' knowin' pretty well from things I'd heard that Cardew was in Queer Street. Instead of hearin' the story, I got a message from Brixton saying that he had nothin' to communicate. And for a good reason…he'd been paid. And why had he been paid? I'll tell you."

Sooper drank a large glass of beer.

"This fellow Cardew was in his cottage on the night of the shipwreck. He'd made up his mind what he was going to do. He was going to row out to sea and drown himself. But before he went, bein' a lawyer an' somewhat precise, he wrote a long letter to the coroner, givin' a full confession of the amount of money he'd stolen from his clients. An' then he heard the explosion. His skiff was on the beach, and for a few minutes he must have been a human man. He drove into the sea, and found two men clinging to a raft. You'll hear some day that boxes 3 and 4 were lashed to a raft, which was carried on the main deck of the destroyer. He got them off and towed them ashore. One of the men was Leigh, nearly dead. The other was Elson, a cattleman who had shipped as a stoker to get out of the hands of the police. Elson knew about the money and told Cardew. They got the boxes high an' dry, an' then Leigh recovered. Elson knew that the money was in his charge, and that the only hope of getting it was to put him out. He may or may not have consulted friend Cardew, but he certainly hit John Leigh over the head with an axe and flung him into the sea.

"How he escaped, God knows! All trace of him was lost for twelve months, but there is a possibility that he crawled into Pawsey, where there was a marine hospital, and that he was there for the greater part of the first year. I've seen a record at the Admiralty of an unknown man who was treated for a scalp wound, and the report is marked 'Mentally deficient. Discharged to infirmary.' I don't know whether Cardew was in it...maybe he was. But they got the boxes into the cottage, and Hannah had to know. She was staying there at the time, looking after Cardew. The boxes were opened, the money taken out, and the wood destroyed. They had to share with Hannah, and it's likely that she knew for the first time the terrible position that Cardew was in. My the'ry is that the letter was written and signed when the explosion took Cardew out of doors. She had a chance of readin' the letter, which he'd hid and which he probably forgot all about."

"But you guess this?"

"I know...the envelope written to the coroner told me a lot. I've dealt with suicides.

"Cardew had a house at Barley Stack, on which there were heavy mortgages. He paid off the mortgages, met all the demands of his creditors, and got out of his business, as he could well afford to do. He might have gone on for ever and ever, only Hannah had her ambitions. She wanted to take the place of the woman who had befriended her, and she never gave Cardew a minute's peace. Once she put the initials of the lost ship on the grass under his window to remind him of the pull she had on him – you remember that?"

"But have you known all this long?"

Sooper nodded.

"You bet I've known a lot of it!" he said. "The thing I was scared about was what would happen to Elson, once he got it into his thick head that Cardew had killed the woman. I had planted Lattimer on him months before. Lattimer went up and borrowed money from him, so as to make Elson feel that he had him under his thumb. I was hopin' that one night, when he was drunk, Elson would blow the whole story. Lattimer had to play crook, and I must say he did it alarmingly well. He carried out all my instructions – all except one, when he followed me up to town, because the darned fool thought that Cardew was waitin' for me."

"Then it was Cardew who tried to strangle Miss Leigh?"

"Yes, sir. Lattimer was on the roof – that was his station. We'd planted the ladder there as soon as it got dark. He heard the tapping, but couldn't see what was happenin' till the trap door came open with a crash. Then Lattimer waited, expectin' somebody to come out, and when they didn't, he guessed the man who thought of everythin' was puttin' up a blind, and slid down the ladder as quick as he could."

Jim was overwhelmed by what he had heard.

"What did you mean when you asked Cardew if his hands were scratched that morning he was found chloroformed?"

"And why he was found chloroformed?" asked Sooper, with an absurd smirk of satisfaction. "He tried a very elementr'y trick. Picked up a man on the Embankment and sent him to the messenger office with poisoned food. By good luck we found the tramp and put him inside. I came up to Cardew with a fairy-tale about wantin' him to cross-examine this feller, and I had to use you as a goat, an' I'm truly sorry, Mr Ferraby. Cardew fell for it at once, until I mentioned casual that the man was the guy he picked up on the Embankment, and then he knew that, the moment he spoke to this Sullivan, Sullivan would recognize his voice. That's why I asked him to come down and cross-examine him. There was only one way to get out of it, and that was for Cardew to fake a story of being chloroformed. He kept a whole lot of drugs on the premises. He soaked a wad of lint, threw the bottle out of the window, lay on the bed, and very nearly went out. In fact, it was a narrow escape for Cardew – he's got a weak heart. When I was examinin' his fingers, I was smellin' 'em, and they smelt of chloroform. I've got a nose for scents. The day he shot at us in the bush I could still smell it. There's a lot of clever fellers who'll tell you that the smell of chloroform will disappear in half a minute. You can send 'em to Patrick Minter and he'll tell 'em different.

"Mr Ferraby, I'm not goin' to speak against amateur investigators any more. That Cardew learnt a lot of things quick. I'm gettin' a high respect for anthr'pology, an' psychology has gone into the first class.

'That burglary at the office, when he burnt all Hannah's papers. It *must* have been him, because he didn't pull down the blind and put the light on – he could find his way in the dark! There was a month-old memo caught up in the blind."

He put down his tankard with a gasp and clasped his forehead.

"I left that little hangman with nowhere to go," he said hollowly.

"Why on earth did you bring him at all?"

"It was the last straw. We tried to frighten Elson into talkin'. Lattimer put a warnin' on his door, and never dreamt what the result would be. Thought Elson would come across with the whole story. But he didn't. Like a fool, after he'd heard Leigh singin' in the wood, he got on the phone and told Cardew. I know because I'd got the telephone exchange straightened. That's where the trouble began. Cardew came down to put my light out that same night. I'll tell you the truth, Mr Ferraby: I got Cardew wrong. Thought I'd got his nerves so jangled up that he'd drop the whole story. That feller's clever!"

He shook his head.

"That Big Foot – "

"Big Foot?"

"Surely, Big Foot. I've got 'em in my room under the bed. Pair of prop boots that he bought from a theatrical man, a feller in Cath'rine Street. He never forgot anythin', prepared for everythin'! He had those trick feet ready to leave his mark on the sand and throw all the clever police officers off the track. Only he left 'em under the seat of the car and I found 'em. That story about Hannah Shaw gettin' a threatenin' letter was a stall. She never had a Big Foot letter – Cardew was makin' preparations."

Jim Ferraby sat back and gazed in open-mouthed admiration at Sooper.

"You're a genius!" he breathed.

"Deduction an' the'rizin'," said Sooper modestly. "And I've just had a brainwave! There's another way out of London!"

It was half-past one o'clock in the morning, and the great waterway of London was silent and deserted. Far away to the north the reflected glare of the arc-lamps of dockland glowed in the sky. A big sea-going motor-boat came silently down the falling tide, its green and red lamps reflected in the still water. It moved steadily, as though its owner were in no great hurry to leave behind him the lights of the romantic river.

Opposite Gravesend the speed increased a little, as it turned to the left to avoid a moored steamer. It had nearly passed the vessel when, from the shadow of the big boat, came a fussy little launch that swung broadside over the bows of the motor-boat.

"Who are you?" boomed a voice from the darkness.

"Motor-boat *Cecily* – owner the Count de Freslac. Bound for Bruges," came the answer.

The boats drifted nearer and nearer until the launch had swung alongside. And then the owner of the motor-boat seemed to realize his danger. There was a splutter and roar of engines, and the boat almost leapt forward. But by now the launch was grappled, and Sooper was the first on board.

"Bit of luck for me, Cardew. Never thought I'd catch you first pop."

"Even your theories and deductions must be right sometimes," said Cardew pleasantly, as the handcuffs snapped over his wrists.

Edgar Wallace

Bones In London

The new Managing Director of Schemes Ltd has an elegant London office and a theatrically dressed assistant – however Bones, as he is better known, is bored. Luckily there is a slump in the shipping market and it is not long before Joe and Fred Pole pay Bones a visit. They are totally unprepared for Bones' unnerving style of doing business, unprepared for his unique style of innocent and endearing mischief.

Bones of the River

'Taking the little paper from the pigeon's leg, Hamilton saw it was from Sanders and marked URGENT. *Send Bones instantly to Lujamalababa... Arrest and bring to head-quarters the witch doctor.*'

It is a time when the world's most powerful nations are vying for colonial honour, a time of trading steamers and tribal chiefs. In the mysterious African territories administered by Commissioner Sanders, Bones persistently manages to create his own unique style of innocent and endearing mischief.

EDGAR WALLACE

THE DAFFODIL MYSTERY

When Mr Thomas Lyne, poet, poseur and owner of Lyne's Emporium insults a cashier, Odette Rider, she resigns. Having summoned detective Jack Tarling to investigate another employee, Mr Milburgh, Lyne now changes his plans. Tarling and his Chinese companion refuse to become involved. They pay a visit to Odette's flat. In the hall Tarling meets Sam, convicted felon and protégé of Lyne. Next morning Tarling discovers a body. The hands are crossed on the breast, adorned with a handful of daffodils.

THE JOKER

While the millionaire Stratford Harlow is in Princetown, not only does he meet with his lawyer Mr Ellenbury but he gets his first glimpse of the beautiful Aileen Rivers, niece of the actor and convicted felon Arthur Ingle. When Aileen is involved in a car accident on the Thames Embankment, the driver is James Carlton of Scotland Yard. Later that evening Carlton gets a call. It is Aileen. She needs help.

EDGAR WALLACE

THE SQUARE EMERALD

'Suicide on the left,' says Chief Inspector Coldwell pleasantly, as he and Leslie Maughan stride along the Thames Embankment during a brutally cold night. A gaunt figure is sprawled across the parapet. But Coldwell soon discovers that Peter Dawlish, fresh out of prison for forgery, is not considering suicide but murder. Coldwell suspects Druze as the intended victim. Maughan disagrees. If Druze dies, she says, 'It will be because he does not love children!'

THE THREE OAK MYSTERY

While brothers Lexington and Socrates Smith, authority on fingerprints and blood stains, are guests of Peter Mandle and his stepdaughter, they observe a light flashing from the direction of Mr Jethroe's house. COME THREE OAKS, it spells in Morse. A ghostly figure is seen hurrying across the moonlit lawn. Early next morning the brothers take a stroll, and there, tied to an oak branch, is a body – a purple mark where the bullet struck.

OTHER TITLES BY EDGAR WALLACE AVAILABLE DIRECT
FROM HOUSE OF STRATUS

Quantity		£	$(US)	$(CAN)	€
	THE ADMIRABLE CARFEW	6.99	11.50	15.99	11.50
	THE ANGEL OF TERROR	6.99	11.50	15.99	11.50
	THE AVENGER	6.99	11.50	15.99	11.50
	BARBARA ON HER OWN	6.99	11.50	15.99	11.50
	THE BLACK ABBOT	6.99	11.50	15.99	11.50
	BONES	6.99	11.50	15.99	11.50
	BONES IN LONDON	6.99	11.50	15.99	11.50
	BONES OF THE RIVER	6.99	11.50	15.99	11.50
	THE CLUE OF THE NEW PIN	6.99	11.50	15.99	11.50
	THE CLUE OF THE SILVER KEY	6.99	11.50	15.99	11.50
	THE CLUE OF THE TWISTED CANDLE	6.99	11.50	15.99	11.50
	THE COAT OF ARMS	6.99	11.50	15.99	11.50
	THE COUNCIL OF JUSTICE	6.99	11.50	15.99	11.50
	THE CRIMSON CIRCLE	6.99	11.50	15.99	11.50
	THE DAFFODIL MYSTERY	6.99	11.50	15.99	11.50
	THE DARK EYES OF LONDON	6.99	11.50	15.99	11.50
	THE DAUGHTERS OF THE NIGHT	6.99	11.50	15.99	11.50
	A DEBT DISCHARGED	6.99	11.50	15.99	11.50
	THE DEVIL MAN	6.99	11.50	15.99	11.50
	THE DOOR WITH SEVEN LOCKS	6.99	11.50	15.99	11.50
	THE DUKE IN THE SUBURBS	6.99	11.50	15.99	11.50
	THE FACE IN THE NIGHT	6.99	11.50	15.99	11.50
	THE FEATHERED SERPENT	6.99	11.50	15.99	11.50
	THE FLYING SQUAD	6.99	11.50	15.99	11.50
	THE FORGER	6.99	11.50	15.99	11.50
	THE FOUR JUST MEN	6.99	11.50	15.99	11.50
	FOUR SQUARE JANE	6.99	11.50	15.99	11.50
	THE FOURTH PLAGUE	6.99	11.50	15.99	11.50

ALL HOUSE OF STRATUS BOOKS ARE AVAILABLE FROM GOOD BOOKSHOPS
OR DIRECT FROM THE PUBLISHER:

Internet: www.houseofstratus.com including author interviews, reviews, features.

Email: sales@houseofstratus.com please quote author, title and credit card details.

OTHER TITLES BY EDGAR WALLACE AVAILABLE DIRECT FROM HOUSE OF STRATUS

Quantity		£	$(US)	$(CAN)	€
	THE FRIGHTENED LADY	6.99	11.50	15.99	11.50
	GOOD EVANS	6.99	11.50	15.99	11.50
	THE HAND OF POWER	6.99	11.50	15.99	11.50
	THE IRON GRIP	6.99	11.50	15.99	11.50
	THE JOKER	6.99	11.50	15.99	11.50
	THE JUST MEN OF CORDOVA	6.99	11.50	15.99	11.50
	THE KEEPERS OF THE KING'S PEACE	6.99	11.50	15.99	11.50
	THE LAW OF THE FOUR JUST MEN	6.99	11.50	15.99	11.50
	THE LONE HOUSE MYSTERY	6.99	11.50	15.99	11.50
	THE MAN WHO BOUGHT LONDON	6.99	11.50	15.99	11.50
	THE MAN WHO KNEW	6.99	11.50	15.99	11.50
	THE MAN WHO WAS NOBODY	6.99	11.50	15.99	11.50
	THE MIND OF MR J G REEDER	6.99	11.50	15.99	11.50
	MORE EDUCATED EVANS	6.99	11.50	15.99	11.50
	MR J G REEDER RETURNS	6.99	11.50	15.99	11.50
	MR JUSTICE MAXWELL	6.99	11.50	15.99	11.50
	RED ACES	6.99	11.50	15.99	11.50
	ROOM 13	6.99	11.50	15.99	11.50
	SANDERS	6.99	11.50	15.99	11.50
	SANDERS OF THE RIVER	6.99	11.50	15.99	11.50
	THE SINISTER MAN	6.99	11.50	15.99	11.50
	THE SQUARE EMERALD	6.99	11.50	15.99	11.50
	THE THREE JUST MEN	6.99	11.50	15.99	11.50
	THE THREE OAK MYSTERY	6.99	11.50	15.99	11.50
	THE TRAITOR'S GATE	6.99	11.50	15.99	11.50
	WHEN THE GANGS CAME TO LONDON	6.99	11.50	15.99	11.50
	WHEN THE WORLD STOPPED	6.99	11.50	15.99	11.50

Hotline: UK ONLY: 0800 169 1780, please quote author, title and credit card details.
INTERNATIONAL: +44 (0) 20 7494 6400, please quote author, title and credit card details.

Send to: House of Stratus Sales Department
24c Old Burlington Street
London
W1X 1RL
UK

Please allow for postage costs charged per order plus an amount per book as set out in the tables below:

	£(Sterling)	$(US)	$(CAN)	€(Euros)
Cost per order				
UK	2.00	3.00	4.50	3.30
Europe	3.00	4.50	6.75	5.00
North America	3.00	4.50	6.75	5.00
Rest of World	3.00	4.50	6.75	5.00
Additional cost per book				
UK	0.50	0.75	1.15	0.85
Europe	1.00	1.50	2.30	1.70
North America	2.00	3.00	4.60	3.40
Rest of World	2.50	3.75	5.75	4.25

PLEASE SEND CHEQUE, POSTAL ORDER (STERLING ONLY), EUROCHEQUE, OR INTERNATIONAL MONEY ORDER (PLEASE CIRCLE METHOD OF PAYMENT YOU WISH TO USE)
MAKE PAYABLE TO: STRATUS HOLDINGS plc

Cost of book(s): —————————— Example: 3 x books at £6.99 each: £20.97

Cost of order: —————————— Example: £2.00 (Delivery to UK address)

Additional cost per book: ————— Example: 3 x £0.50: £1.50

Order total including postage: ——— Example: £24.47

Please tick currency you wish to use and add total amount of order:

☐ £ (Sterling)   ☐ $ (US)   ☐ $ (CAN)   ☐ € (EUROS)

VISA, MASTERCARD, SWITCH, AMEX, SOLO, JCB:

☐ ☐ ☐ ☐ ☐ ☐ ☐ ☐ ☐ ☐ ☐ ☐ ☐ ☐ ☐ ☐ ☐ ☐ ☐ ☐

Issue number (Switch only):

☐ ☐ ☐

Start Date: **Expiry Date:**

☐ ☐ / ☐ ☐   ☐ ☐ / ☐ ☐

Signature: _____

NAME: _____

ADDRESS: _____

_____

POSTCODE: _____

Please allow 28 days for delivery.

Prices subject to change without notice.
Please tick box if you do not wish to receive any additional information. ☐

House of Stratus publishes many other titles in this genre; please check our website (**www.houseofstratus.com**) for more details.